THE OCEAN IN THE FIRE

RENEE N. MELAND

Cover Art by Deranged Doctor Designs
Formatting by Polgarus Studio

The Ocean in the Fire

ISBN: 978-0-9960029-1-2 (Epub)
ISBN: 978-0-9960029-5-0 (Mobi)
ISBN: 978-0-9960029-9-8 (Print)

For Madelyn Renee

CHAPTER ONE

CONNOR

The ripples on the surface of the water slowed to a stop, and Connor Holloway wasn't afraid.

"Are you sure they will come, Dad?" his daughter, Poe, asked softly, hopefully.

"Of course they will. Children always do."

As his daughter sat down next to him, he looked out across the pond that had helped draw him to the property when they were first shopping for land. He glanced over at Poe and saw her face was vacant, devoid of a smile, but that was nothing new for the withdrawn sixteen-year-old. She had always been one to worry about whether the flowers would freeze in the winter, instead of experiencing the joy that came from their colorful blossoms in the spring.

Connor knew he had done that to her.

They let themselves sink into the soft earth as they stared out at the vastness of their land, covered with thick willow trees and thicker promises of change and new beginnings. He watched as the wooden swing, held together by a fat brown rope turned green with age, swung in the slight evening breeze. "Will we be ready?" Poe asked.

"There are plenty of fish in the pond, both young and old, and your mother has been curing meat for safe keeping." He threw a rock at the pond's surface, and the water danced once more. Each time he threw a rock, it seemed to land in the exact same spot. He pictured the rocks piling up at the bottom of the pond, a pyramid of grey and brown stones. He took comfort in the fact that in a thousand years, when he and his children were long gone, that pile of rocks would still be there, a reminder of his own existence standing tall long after the pond itself had long dried up. "We have plenty of blankets, and firewood for the colder months."

Poe's deep dark eyes, the ones that matched his own so perfectly, radiated concern. "I don't mean with that kind of stuff. We've been doing that forever. I mean how do we know we can trust them?"

He placed a comforting hand on his daughter's shoulder and responded simply, "We don't. Never forget that."

***

"Kate, how's the meat coming?" Connor asked his wife as he entered the kitchen with Poe close behind him. Their metal pots and pans sparkled as they hung from the ceiling rack. He kissed Kate on the forehead as she jokingly pretended to smear a streak of flour down the side of his face. Magazines were scattered mindlessly on the far end of the dinner table.

"Very well." As her mother talked, Poe carefully pushed them back together into a neat, even stack as she listened to her parents' conversation. Kate had left the jars of paprika, chili powder, and chives she had used to season the chicken that would be their dinner sitting directly under the cabinet where the spice rack was. Quietly, Poe set them back in their alphabetically-ordered slots, the same as Connor would have done if no one was watching.

Though he was speaking to Kate, he looked at Poe. "We don't know how many we will take yet." Connor sighed. "Also, once people get desperate, there's a chance we won't be able to go out for a while. Those who don't have what we have may try to take it from us. There may be a period of time where it's unsafe to step beyond our walls. We have to be ready." Poe gave him a slight nod.

Kate smiled as she kneaded a ball of dough that would soon see their oven. "We will be ready, I promise. Harper and I killed another deer this morning. She's preparing it downstairs as we speak." Carefully, she sprinkled rosemary, tarragon, and sage into the dough as she flattened it with her fists over and over, only to flip it and do it again. This time after she was finished she put the spices back in their slots.

"That's three this week. You and Harper make quite the hunting team." He was always impressed, and thankful, that his wife and daughter somehow wound up being expert markswomen. He preferred to busy himself in the vegetable patches, growing carrots and broccoli for his family. Equally as important, it gave him time to continue studying which herbs and compounds could combine to make a lethal concoction. Between tending their orchard and gathering the berries that grew on the outskirts of their property, he discovered that arsenic looked a lot like powdered sugar.

Connor glanced up as he heard the front door open. His son Gabriel shut the heavy door behind him. His jeans were covered in grease, and his hair had specks of black sludge peeking out from his dark locks. A t-shirt that used to be white hugged his muscular arms, which had grown so from twisting heavy bolts and latching engine parts together. His breath was heavy. "It's getting worse out there. I was listening to the radio. The announcer said it's getting closer."

"How's the truck coming?" Kate asked.

"Should be done soon. I just have to replace one more part and she should be ready." He went over to the fruit basket that was sitting on the kitchen island and grabbed an apple. The flour that Kate had been using on her dough had wafted over the kitchen, and he had to wipe his apple on his shirt to clean off the dusting. "I'm going back to it—just needed a snack." He put the apple to his lips, and took a big bite. Between chews, he said, "Dad, maybe we can make one run to town before it gets really bad? It wouldn't hurt to get some more supplies before people realize they will need them. And there's no time to order anything either. They said on the news that there's a month's wait for most packages, and that's probably a low estimate if I had to guess."

Connor sighed. "Gabe, you know if they're finally admitting on the news that it's bad out there, that means it's even worse than their saying. I think we're going to have to stay here."

He heard footsteps from the stairwell that came up from the basement, and looked to see Harper eying him predatorily, evidently hearing their conversation as she was

4

coming up. "But, Dad, I just wanted to go one time," she said, her voice raising an octave or two from where it usually was. She was Poe's twin sister, and neither girl was used to hearing the word 'no.' Connor knew that was his fault too. "We need some more fabric if there's going to be more people here. And besides, going into town won't make much difference now. I bet hardly anyone will be out and about."

"Let's wait for one more news report then we'll talk about it."

Harper ran up to him and threw her arms around him, careful not to touch his shirt with her blood-soaked hands. There were little bits of fur stuck under her fingernails. The juxtaposition of her yellow-flowered dress and the bright red blood wasn't lost on him. "Thanks, Dad!"

Kate sighed. "Connor, you know that's not a good idea. I'm sure the new people will have clothes of their own. Most will come with at least some form of their own supplies."

Gabriel came over and poked his sister in the ribs, making her wince in imaginary pain. "What do you need more fabric for? Your closet is overstuffed as it is."

"I was thinking for the other people."

He rolled his eyes. "Uh huh…Harper, you don't need a dress in every color of the rainbow."

"Don't you have a piece of metal to screw into an engine or something?"

"Close enough," he said with a grin. "Maybe all your dresses can tell you."

The sun was starting to set on the farm, and Poe asked if Harper could help her put the cows back in the barn. The door had sliding hinges that had rusted with time, so it took two people to push it open. Connor watched as they ran over to the back door, threw it open, and raced each other down the steps. Poe's long black hair was tied into a tight ponytail and stayed against her back as they ran, while Harper's long waves flowed behind her freely as both girls increased their speed. Small holes in Poe's jeans had ripped open to the size of a baby's fist, exposing the pale flesh on the back of her calves. It was unnatural how much time she spent in her room, reading herself into eye-strain and the occasional migraine. Always on the other end of the spectrum, Harper had taken on a bronzed summer glow, same as her mother, and couldn't seem to take enough pictures of herself floating face up in the pond as she found shapes in the clouds that floated over her head.

As Gabriel started to head toward the door, Connor put his arm around his wife. "Son, take your keys with you. You know I don't like having the door unlocked after dark."

"Dad, this place is a fortress. I—"

"Do it."

Gabriel sighed. "Fine. Whatever." He grabbed another apple before returning to the garage, slamming the door a little louder than usual. A few seconds later, they heard the radio as it blared some overly-screaming heavy metal band that Connor didn't think he'd heard before, but wouldn't recognize anyway.

Connor felt his wife looking at him. "What?"

She smiled warmly. "He's just trying to be independent. That's all. It's kind of difficult in our situation. They missed all that teenager-spreading-your-wings-my-parents-know-nothing stuff."

"You want to be somewhere else?"

"Of course not. I'm just saying that our children are older now and they aren't going to have the normal chances to become individuals and have their own opinions like other people. That's just the nature of our situation."

Connor scoffed. "Well, getting to skip curfew or go to prom won't teach them to stay alive. We know who lives in town, and our children are definitely not missing out." He looked at his wife and realized his tone was harsher than he'd meant it to be. Her jovial expression had been replaced by one more serious, more willing to be complacent to avoid continuing the discussion. He hated himself when he caused that look on her face. "I'm sorry. I know you're right." He pulled her into an embrace. That was something he prided himself on; at least with her, he was always willing to say *I'm sorry*.

Ever since they had met when they were teenagers, Kate smelled like laundry soap and walnuts. He inhaled the fresh, familiar scent, and let her blonde hair tickle his nose. With her in his arms, and his kids home and safe, he had everything he could ever want. No matter who potentially joined them, it would always be their house, their family home that, if he had his way, his children would always call their own. Strangers would always be strangers. They would serve their own purpose, and that was all—just tools that were useful in their own ways, tools that could be thrown out if necessary. "Just right now...this is what we've been

7

preparing for their whole lives. And very soon, it's going to be knocking on our doorstep. We can't ruin everything we've worked for because he lets his guard down."

He heard Kate's voice, mildly muffled against his chest. "I know. It's just hard on them sometimes."

Poe and Harper returned from outside, shutting the door behind them. There was an elaborate series of thick metal locks, and they shut each one carefully. At times, Connor wished the view he had through the windows downstairs could be left uninterrupted by the iron bars that ran on the outside of them. But he knew better. So instead he would have to settle for always enjoying their surroundings from his and Kate's bedroom window. Since it was on the highest floor with no roof access points, Connor had left the view free. "The cows are tucked in tight," Poe said. "Abby, Bailey, and Crete are at the far end, furthest from the door."

"Why do you name them? You know you'll have to eat them eventually," Harper said, looking at her sister with a mix of pity and annoyance.

"Yeah, but until then, doesn't everybody deserve a name?" With a shrug, Poe started to go upstairs, head hanging low at the thought of eating her friends. Harper followed close behind.

"Hold on a minute, girls." Connor pulled out two leather-covered stools that rested against the kitchen island. "Sit."

"What is it, Dad?" Harper asked. Kate looked at him too, as if she had the same question.

"I just wanted to go over some things with you." The

three women in his life looked at him with confusion. He took a moment to ponder the fact that though his and Poe's eyes were the same color, where Kate's and Harper's matched, all three of his girls' eyes had the same shape: big and doe-like, innocent. It was his job to protect them from being hunted.

Kate spoke first. "Honey, we've gone over this several times. The girls know the rules."

"Yes, but we've never had to put them into practice before." He turned to his daughters. "I know it's been a long time since we've been around them. It may seem tempting to make them all your new friends, to trust them. After all, you were so young when we stopped going into town. Time heals wounds but sometimes that isn't a good thing. It makes you soft. Remember who they are, and why we stayed here in the first place." He gently reached out and brushed both their cheeks. "This is our home. What we do with anyone on the outside must be in line with our only goal: protecting our family."

Harper sighed. "We know, Dad." A smile spread across her face. "Besides, all I need is Brian and I'll be happy." She didn't seem to realize that her relationship with him wouldn't last past the power going out.

Brian was a boy that Harper had met on the internet. Connor didn't like her getting too attached to people from the outside, especially someone none of them had ever met, but Kate had convinced him that the girls needed some form of social interaction, even if it was just in front of a computer screen. "Eventually, the girls will need to know how to talk to a boy other than their brother," she had said. "How are they ever supposed to get married?"

Connor knew he would be perfectly happy if they never did. His family would remain intact, all under one roof, free from all the evils of the world. They would never experience what they saw on the news every day: a drunk driver taking the life of an innocent, a loved one catching an incurable illness while trying to help someone else. Harper would never fall victim to the honey-coated words that boys her age said to get beautiful girls like her into bed. Poe would never suffer through the venom that teenagers can spew when they encounter someone different and smarter than them. She'd been on the receiving end of enough nastiness when she was younger, the kind made worse by youth and inexperience.

They would never suffer, and they would never be betrayed.

"Just make sure you don't tell him about us, about what we have here. No one who doesn't already know needs to hear about it. Especially now."

Harper gave Connor a kiss on the cheek, her long eyelashes fluttering. "Okay, Dad." She looked over at her sister. "Poe and I are going to go up to our room. I'm teaching her how to play poker."

"Where did you learn that from?"

Harper just grinned, running upstairs with her twin. Connor and Kate shuddered as they heard the door slam shut. "She's got to stop that," Kate said.

Connor grabbed her hand. "Come with me, I have something to show you."

He guided Kate to the outside edge of their property. Next to a section of their fence of impenetrable plant life that served as backup for their walls—bushes with thorns as long as thimbles—he had planted a flower garden several years back. Since everything else on their land had a functional purpose, he thought it would be nice to have something whose only job was to bring more beauty into the world.

And of course, keep the pollinators on their land.

He led her to the middle of the garden. They strolled in amongst greens, yellows, pinks, and reds, flowers as fat as a baby's cheeks. As he held her hand, he noticed her fingers were smooth, and he liked the feeling of them against his own. Evening fog floated around them, and broke apart as they walked inside it, sending the transparent mist scattering.

The flower in the middle was his favorite, his prize. It was a temperamental plant, and he had never gotten it to bloom before.

Until now.

"Oh, Connor! It's lovely." She gently rubbed one of its bright yellow and orange petals between her fingers. "How did you get it to bloom?"

"A magician never reveals his secrets." He winked at her. "But it was a new combination of ingredients in the fertilizer."

"A-ha!" They stared at it for a moment as they wrapped themselves in each other's arms. Kate started to speak again but paused, though she eventually giving into the question resting on her tongue. "We have enough weapons, right?" Kate sighed, and Connor could feel her wanting to glance back at the house, as if their lives could change at any moment, and probably would.

"Yes. And when it's time, I will make sure they know who is in control here."

Kate bit her lip. "It's so close. I just hope we're ready."

Connor looked down lovingly at his wife. Despite the fading light, her smile shone brightly. "This has been our life for years. Nobody knows how to do what we do better than us. Remember, we're the ones in charge." He kissed the top of her head. "Don't worry. Everything will work out fine."

She snuggled against him. "You're right, you're always right."

"Of course I am." He smiled at her. He shivered at the thought that if he hadn't gone on that vacation at the last moment, so many years ago, the stunningly beautiful, funny, and smart woman before him would have surely been snatched up by some other man. Gratefulness that he had come to his senses overwhelmed him as he thought about suffering in the backseat of his boarding school roommate's minivan for those excruciating hours.

She was worth it.

When they got back inside, Gabriel was sitting at the kitchen island, right where his sisters had been minutes before. "She's running good now. Should be fine if we have to split."

His mother looked at him. "We won't. We are going to be extremely careful about who we let in. And the only people who will be let in will be the ones who arrive right away. Otherwise, there's too much risk."

"What if they all wait too long?"

Connor joined in. "Then they will have to go back to where they came from." He put his hand on his son's shoulder. "We can't risk being exposed to this thing, not after working so hard."

"I understand." He stared down toward a spot in the floor across the room, the place where he knew they kept the extra gun safe: a secret compartment, hidden by boards in the floor. A couch sat on top of their hiding place, but it was fairly light weight. And even if it had been heavy, they knew how strong a person could become when something important was at stake. "How will we choose?"

"We will choose whoever will be the most useful to us."

"That seems pretty inhumane, Dad."

Kate cut in. "We can't keep everyone here who will need help. We just can't. Unfortunately, that means making some tough decisions." She ran her fingers through her son's hair. "If the situation were reversed, they would do the same to us."

"How do you know that? We haven't seen them in years."

Connor held his hand just next to the wall as he considered slamming it down. But after a moment's hesitation, he rested it softly against it. "People are creatures of habit, Gabriel, and people's habits don't change."

Gabriel took a deep breath. "I'm going to go listen to some music." He kissed his mother on the cheek. "Goodnight, Mom. Dad."

Despite wearing the thick-soled combat boots that protected him when he worked on cars, his steps were much quieter than his sisters'. They could hear the gentle shut of his door against its hinges, and the quiet snap of the lock. They expected to hear music, but they were met with silence. They both knew from experience that Gabriel only put his headphones in his ears when he wanted the whole world to leave him alone.

When Connor and Kate went to bed that night, Kate immediately picked up the Steinbeck novel that was on her nightstand and began reading. She used her pillow to prop herself up, and rested the book on top of the sheets. She wore the perfect expression of concentration, but they had been married too long for him to not know that something in her manner, something in her being, was off. He stared at her until she noticed him. "What is it?" she asked.

"I know you're thinking something." He reached out and placed his hand on top of hers. He took note of her wedding ring: passed down from his grandmother, to his mother, and now to her. It was simple, with one stone in the very center, attached to a solid gold band. She had told him she loved it, but he always wondered if she really did. He realized that thought said much more about him than her.

"I'm fine, I'm just reading."

Kate saying she was fine just meant he would have to pry a little harder. "Tell me."

Kate shut the book and let out a deep sigh. "I just wonder if we're going to have time to do the simple things, like reading in bed, after everything changes. I know it's about survival, but survival doesn't have to mean no more books or games with the kids or chocolate brownie Tuesdays does it?" She tossed her book back on the nightstand and it landed with a loud thud. "I mean what's the point of surviving if we can't live?"

"Of course we will. It will be hard for a while, but we'll establish a routine. You'll see. Where is this coming from?"

Kate wouldn't make eye contact with him, instead staring out their bedroom window. "I wanted to eventually take a road trip with the kids, maybe to the ocean. They've never even seen it other than online. I wanted them to be able to go to college if they wanted to. Go to a museum, see something. I always said we'd do one of those things…all of those things someday." She laughed. "So much for eventually. Eventually's come and gone." She hesitated. "I'm a little bit mad at you."

"Why?"

She whispered, "Because we never did any of them, and now it's too late."

Connor didn't know what to say. "I didn't realize those things were so important to you."

"You never asked."

She turned away and switched her reading lamp off. "I love you, Connor. I don't regret our lives one bit. We've done more as a family in the last ten years than most people do in their whole lifetimes. We built something special together." She threw the covers over her head. "But sometimes you can't see past your own nose."

He continued to stare at her, overcome by the all-encompassing darkness.

That night, creaking sounds from atop their roof woke Connor up. By the time he realized it was just branches hitting the house, his heart was pounding and sweat covered his skin. He looked over at Kate, who was still sleeping soundly. Her eyes fluttered, and her face took on a conflicted expression while she slept, as if going through a dream full of movement and hard decisions.

He got up and walked to the window, where he could almost see the entirety of his property laid out before him, glowing eerily in the moonlight. The pond glistened, reflecting a mirror image of a sky full of stars. They were the same as they had always been, but without Poe looking at them by his side as she did when she was a little girl, their magic was gone. He looked at the perimeter, and remembered how long it took him to find a plant with thorns big enough to rip apart any intruder before they could get inside. Anyone who did make it past the walls would be so mangled they wouldn't be much of a threat any longer. The gate was the only thing on that side of the property that he couldn't see, resting just beyond his line of sight. The cameras and motion sensor alarm he installed there would protect them while they still had power, and he and Gabriel would stand guard when that was shut off for good. Of course, they had a generator, but their fuel supplies were finite, and he had always trusted the human eye more than technology.

Glancing toward the other side of their property, he admired another part of his handiwork: his vegetable garden. It lay safely tucked behind a cage of chicken wire, enough to keep the deer and rabbits from taking their crops. His lettuce, zucchini, spinach, and carrots, along with several other vegetables, would be devoured by woodland creatures in a matter of minutes if they were not protected. He hoped that garden would be enough to sustain him, Kate, and the children, along with as many strangers as they deemed worthy. He smiled to himself. They certainly hadn't deemed him worthy so many years before. And now, they would pay for it.

At that moment, Connor Holloway was sure that the universe had a way of righting itself.

As he stared out at what they had built, he felt arms wrap around his waist. "You can't hold what happened against everyone. Sometimes I think you hold it against the world itself. That'll eat you alive." He felt her cheek resting against his back, and listened to the smooth, soothing tone of her voice. "Depending on what they can provide, we may need them as much as they need us."

Connor thought about opening his mouth, but decided against it. Kate could let it go. Kate could always let it go.

He could not, especially now.

He pulled her face toward his own and kissed her softly on the lips. "If they can help us, then I will behave." A mischievous grin spread across his face. "Sometimes…"

Kate smiled. "I love you. Come to bed." She kissed him again, this time more passionately. As they wrapped their arms around each other and fell on top of their sheets, Connor vowed that no one would ever take her from him.

God help anyone who tried.

CHAPTER TWO

DREW

By the time Dr. Drew Matthews came home, the night had become black. Usually he was home before most of his neighbors' lights went out, but that night his own porchlights were the only thing illuminating the way from his car to his door. His wife Vera was sitting at the dinner table waiting for him, reading a book to distract herself from the fact that her husband wasn't home yet. It looked to be one of those romance novels she was so fond of. A shirtless, well-sculpted man graced the cover, and a woman with long hair falling past her shoulders lay breathlessly in his arms. The roast that had been simmering all day had developed the softness of baby food, so she elected to put the meat into some taco shells instead of attempting to slice it, knowing it would just disintegrate against the blade. She had told him that morning she was making him her special pot roast for dinner, the one with the perfectly crusted red potatoes, something that usually he would have made sure he was home in time for—but not that night.

Drew looked at her as he entered the kitchen area, giving

her a warm smile—always a smile, no matter how his day had been, no matter who he had healed—and who he hadn't.

He would have to work extra hard to produce one that night.

"You didn't have to wait for me." He walked over to her and kissed her on the forehead. "But I'm very glad you did." His jacket was still crisp, white, and wrinkle free, the same as it had been that morning when he had left. If someone who didn't know what he'd just been through had judged his day by his coat, they would have assumed it was uneventful. He hoped that was exactly what Vera would believe. No need to alarm her, not yet.

As she placed their plates on the table in front of their respective chairs, she asked the question he knew was coming. He had considered driving around town for a while, perhaps stopping at the dock to look at all the boats gently floating on the water, but knew that absorbing himself in the before would only make the after more painful. He hoped she didn't notice him wincing as she opened her mouth.

"It's bad there, isn't it?" She looked at him with a kind, sympathetic expression, as if she didn't know how scared she should be. If it were up to him, she would never know. Drew had gone to the closest major hospital that day. He wanted to see for himself how fast the disease was spreading.

He didn't tell his wife what he'd found.

"It's not as good as we would like it to be, but that's to be expected." He took a sip of the wine she had poured him: a deep red color, with thick legs of alcohol dripping down the inside of the glass. Tannins, he thought to himself as he watched them slowly crawl. "As long as we're careful and don't do anything stupid, we'll be fine." Lying to his wife made a heavy feeling erupt in his stomach, but he ignored it.

He didn't want to let her know that the town with the closest hospital was almost deserted, aside from the hospital itself. The smart ones had left, while the naïve ones had stayed behind, and paid the price for their brash ignorance. Saying out loud that as he passed through the town, people were dragging themselves down the street, looking at him with sunken eyes and sharp cheekbones was too much to bare. He couldn't bring himself to tell her that as he approached the hospital, he saw a man in a medical facemask standing in front of the door, pointing behind him at the road which Drew was driving down. It was only when he started to get out of his vehicle that he realized it was his friend, Michael, the college buddy that he had been planning to visit that day, hoping he could somehow help with the pandemic that had reached Michael's city. Michael had helped him get through a particularly tough loss of a patient several years earlier, and he had finally seen an opportunity to return the favor.

He thought he'd get the chance.

Drew took a moment to scan the building, and realized that all he could see through the windows were clusters of people, some in doctors' and nurses' uniforms, but most in hospital gowns. There were so many beds in each room that he couldn't imagine how the doctors reached the patients in the back without leaning over the patients in the front—a recipe for a quick spread. The patients' gaunt bodies seemed unnaturally pale in the hospital's fluorescent light, but after passing so many sick people on the street, he guessed that their coloring had nothing to do with the bulbs. As he started to walk toward the steps, his friend yelled in a tone muffled by the mask, "Drew, don't come any closer! Get back in your car and go!"

"But why? What's going on? I can help!" He took one last step forward, only to have Michael wave him away.

"The hospital's overrun. Hospitals east of here are bursting at the seams, so they started sending people here." He reached up and wiped the sweat from his brow. "We can't contain it anymore. We're doing the best we can but people just keep getting sicker. At this point, we are just trying to make them comfortable." He removed his mask and took an extra deep breath of air that Drew hoped wouldn't end up killing him. They had said on the news that they were fairly certain the disease was not airborne, but he was skeptical. They had also said it wouldn't make it past the east coast, and it had traveled all the way west in a few short weeks. The revelation that Michael removed his mask to make sure Drew could hear him clearly hit him like a steel beam. If he was willing to forego any possible protection the mask may have provided, he knew he was already gone. "I can't let you come in here. Everyone inside…you need to go home. Take care of Vera. There's nothing to do here now."

Drew didn't want to tell his wife about the nausea that enveloped him as he turned around and drove away, leaving behind the friend who had turned down a potentially helpful hand in order to keep him and his family safe. So instead, he smiled.

"Totally good." He knew he would have to tell her eventually, but he figured there was no reason to take away her peace of mind any sooner than he had to. It reminded him of the fact that, though he hadn't had to often, he would always go get a cup of coffee before he had to speak to a terminally ill patient's family. Those three extra minutes of not knowing was the only gift he could bestow on them, and he gave it gladly.

As they ate their makeshift tacos, Blake Turner and her four-year-old son Jackson walked through the front door, and sat down at the two remaining chairs at the kitchen table. Blake had known the Matthews since she was born, and didn't bother to knock anymore.

Drew and Vera didn't mind one bit.

"Hi, sweetie!" Vera said as Jackson ran up and threw his arms around her. She turned to Blake. "Hi, baby, have you eaten yet?" She nodded toward the extra roast sitting on the counter. "You want some?"

"Naw, we ate already. Just wanted to come say hi."

Jackson crawled into Vera's lap, and she adjusted masterfully to eating her tacos with one hand. "Mom and I had nuggets. With BBQ!"

"Oohh…sounds yummy." Vera smiled at him. "McDonald's?"

"Nope, Mommy said those have weird stuff in them. We had veggie nuggets."

Drew sighed. "Blake, you know the chemicals in those

things are just as bad as whatever random meat parts they put in the chicken nuggets."

"Eww! Meat parts! Gross!" Jackson stared at Drew in wide-eyed horror. He clutched the teddy bear that he carried with him a little harder, and buried his face in Vera's shoulder.

"Believe it or not, Drew, he actually likes the veggie ones better." She pretended to shake her head at her son. "My strange child, I tell ya." Ruffling his hair with her hand, she said, "Hey, why don't you go upstairs to the office? I bet Miss Vera still has some coloring books up there for you." Jackson nodded enthusiastically and ran up the stairs.

As soon as he was out of hearing distance, Blake asked Drew what Vera had already. "So? How'd it go? Was it bad?"

"Not as bad as it could be. We will be vigilant though."

Blake leaned back in her chair. "Well if the shit hits the fan, come get us would you?"

Vera reached over and grabbed Blake's hand. "Of course we will. And watch your language."

Blake was Drew's best friend's daughter. The men had been next door neighbors since they were kids, both living in the same houses where they grew up. Vera and Drew never had children, but they raised Blake right alongside her parents. Her mother had died in a car accident when she was twelve, so Vera was the one that held her hand through Jackson's birth. Before Blake's father died of cancer six months ago, he left her the house, and told Drew to look after her and his grandson when he had gone. Drew said he never had to ask.

"So exactly how likely is it that the shit will, in fact, hit the fan?"

Drew swallowed hard. Lying to his wife was hard enough. Lying to someone he considered his daughter was next to impossible. The only other time he had lied to her was when he told her there was no such thing as monsters. Monsters did exist; sometimes in nature, sometimes in people. Both were terrifying. "We will be okay."

"Oh good. Because I have a job interview tomorrow at that new salon! It's about an hour from here. Horrible commute but I need the money and I can't stay in my house any longer. I'm going stir crazy. I need to get my hands on some scissors and hair!" Blake smiled brightly. She had been out of work for months since her father had passed, and once she had decided she was ready to go back, no one wanted to hire her. She had been combing the newspaper ads for so long Vera had started teasing her that her fingers would turn black from the ink. "Vera, I was hoping you could watch Jackson for me tomorrow."

"You can't go," Drew said, louder and sterner than he meant to. If he could help it, they would never travel outside of their town until the pandemic was over.

Both women stared at him. "What do you mean she can't go? You said everything was fine."

"Drew, what aren't you telling us?" Blake looked at him with the same expression her father used to: the kind that said tell me the truth now, or tell me the truth later. Either way, you're talking eventually. Her father had often told him to stop carrying life's burdens alone. Family and friends were supposed to help each other.

He had never seen a load quite this heavy.

Drew took a deep breath, looking at the faces of the two most important women in his life. It seemed he needed to drop a bomb in the middle of a snowstorm that would scatter icy shrapnel at its victims, leaving only bloody surprises behind. As much as he wanted to keep the truth from them just a little longer, he knew Blake. He would have to do nothing short of tie her to a chair to make her miss that interview if he didn't tell her what was going on. The bomb would have to go off. He got up and yelled up the stairs. "Jackson, close the door, would you?"

A small voice yelled back at him, "How come?"

He was so much like his mother.

"Because I told you to." He waited until he heard the door shut before he sat back down at the table.

Vera and Blake leaned in, lowering their voices despite the door being safely closed so Jackson couldn't hear. "Please, tell us," Blake said.

"I didn't want to say anything until I had to, but since you're planning to leave town tomorrow, I guess I have to…" He sighed and looked at his wife. "I never made it inside the hospital."

Vera's hands stiffened against the surface of the table. "What? Why?"

"The hospital is stuffed with patients. Michael wouldn't even let me get near the entrance." He grabbed his wife's hands. "He told me to stay home and take care of you."

Vera sucked in a breath. Used to being a doctor's wife

and hearing about life and death every day, she seemed to realize what Drew already had—that his friend was lost forever. "So what does this mean, Drew? What do we do?"

"Well I think it's best to just stay here for now. We don't know how bad it is anyplace else, but we do know we're okay right here." He looked at Blake. "I need you to stay home tomorrow. Promise?"

"Of course. No job is worth that."

"Good girl."

Blake hesitated. "So, what do we do if…when it reaches us?"

Drew looked down at the table. He didn't know the answer. He hadn't thought the disease would ever reach them, and didn't have so much as an extra can opener. The only emergency item they had in the house ready to go was a first aid kit, but ointment wasn't going to help them. He cursed himself for thinking there would never be such an all-encompassing emergency. They were in the United States after all. Their country knew how to handle a crisis.

He bit his cheek hard to keep from crying out when he realized how wrong he was, and how right someone else had been. He knew there was one person, somewhere close by, who saw it coming. While everyone else was in fear for their lives, that person was sitting in his home comfortably…and laughing.

Drew cursed him most of all.

He got up and busied himself straightening pictures on the wall. His father and grandfather looked back at him, as if to tell him he better come up with something quick. He heard them in his ears. Suck it up, crybaby, and get on with it. They're counting on you. Usually, they were referring to work that had to be done around the house, some undesirable chore that he would hide from in his tree house, or hope that he could escape from by swinging just high enough on the swing set to fly away from there.

Drew doubted that in their time, they could have ever fathomed the importance of the work he knew he would have to do, what they would all have to do if they wanted to live. He wasn't sure he had grasped it yet himself.

He came up with an answer as fast as he could. "This cul-de-sac. Everybody's good people. If we need to leave, we should go as a group. People do crazy things when they're scared, and we will have a better chance if we all work together to protect ourselves. When we decide to go, we'll tell everyone to grab what they can, and we will all caravan out together." He didn't even know some people in the neighborhood, but it seemed to make sense. They were probably all good people anyway. He liked to think that most people were.

Vera got up and hugged her husband. "How much time do you think we have?"

"I don't know. All I know is we should stay here as long as we can. The devil you know is better than the devil you don't."

"I'd prefer to not have to deal with any devils," Blake said.

"You and me both, but we don't seem to have a choice now." Drew opened the door and gestured for Blake to go upstairs. "Grab Jackson and go get some sleep. As soon as I know anything else, we will come get you."

Vera came up to Blake and wrapped her arms around her. "Be safe, baby. And keep that boy of yours safe too. Don't even go to the grocery store until we know more, okay?"

"I'll be good."

Drew watched Blake and Jackson from their porch as they walked back to their house. She waved at him as they turned away. He didn't go back into his own house until he could see them safely inside.

When he came in, Vera smiled. "Still watching over her. Her daddy is smiling down on both of you, I know it."

The mention of Blake's father stirred something inside Drew that made him swallow hard. "I sure hope so."

He didn't sleep that night. So when their phone rang at 2:00 a.m. he picked it up on the first ring, with a clear voice that wasn't marred with sleep and confusion. "Yes?"

"Drew, it's Michael. I'm so sorry man, but you've got to get your family out of there now."

"What happened?"

"Everybody got desperate. People here are now looking up the names of doctors who have practices within driving distance and telling people to go there instead."

Drew didn't like where the conversation was heading.

"They gave people your name."

His heart started to throb in his chest, so much that he wondered if Vera could feel it next to him. He turned to look at her, wondering how he was going to tell her the time had come already, but found that she was already awake. Softly, she whispered, "It's happening, isn't it…"

"Thank you, Michael. Thank you for everything."

Drew could hear the smile in Michael's voice, and it tore him up just a little bit more. "Thank me by getting out of there. Live long and prosper so to speak." He shuddered as he heard a deep cough coming from the other end of the phone.

As he hung up, he realized that was the last time he would hear his friend's voice. He pushed the hurt down deep. There would be time to grieve, but that moment was not it. That moment was for honoring the sacrifice his friend had made by doing his job, and helping everyone he could. He vowed to remember it every day, every precious minute that he still had with his family, every second he got that Michael didn't. "Vera, wake up Blake and tell her and Jackson to get ready fast. I'm going to go tell everyone else what's going on and have them do the same. Then come back here and grab whatever you can. Food, blankets, medicine—whatever we might need."

"And photo albums."

The look on his wife's face when she realized they might never come home broke him in two. "And photo albums."

By the time Vera and Drew had locked their house and loaded their car, the cul-de-sac was lit up as if it was daytime. There were several houses in their circle, and each one illustrated its own brand of panic: the one right across from theirs had suitcases flailed across the grass in the front. The one right next to Blake's had canned goods stacked high on the surface of its wraparound porch next to two gray plastic containers. The owner shouted to anyone who would listen: "I need more bins! Does anyone have more bins?"

Someone shouted at the owner: "Just start using suitcases. There's no need for organization right now. Just move!" Drew looked over to see it was Cassius Melone, the youngest Melone brother. Darius and Cassius lived in the house two doors down from Blake. Cassius was a police officer and probably fairly used to telling people what to do. Drew had only talked to him briefly, but thought he might be an asset later. Most policemen knew how to shoot guns.

Drew made a mental note to move from acquaintances to friends.

The last house at the very end of the cul-de-sac belonged to a pharmacist and an engineer. Tonia and George Carson had moved in around the time Blake was born, but the two couples had not become any more than acquaintances. Vera said she'd spoken to Tonia on several occasions, exchanging recipes and listening to what her new building project was. Tonia reminded Vera of people she knew from high school: the kind that call you a friend later but won't give you the time of day while you're there. "Not her fault though," she'd said.

George ran over to Drew with a large black medical bag. "I thought I should bring this. I've been stockpiling ever since this whole thing started." He opened the bag to reveal a collection of pill bottles that filled to the top. "You never know what we might need."

Drew looked at the man's face. His expression reminded him of a small child showing his parents a picture he drew at school that he was extra proud of. It seemed to ask, "Did I do good?"

He put a hand on George's shoulder. "Great idea. Good job." George ran back to his house looking rather pleased with himself.

Vera, Blake, and Jackson came up. "It's getting late. People are going to start showing up as soon as it's daylight. Shouldn't we get going?"

He didn't want to tell them where exactly they were heading to, but he knew there was no other choice. Once he had the group gathered, they would all want to know.

He cupped his hands to his mouth to give him more volume. "Everyone! Gather over here. Let's go." He stood still as the people in his neighborhood put down whatever they were working on and circled around him. Looking around at all of them, hopeful and panicked all at the same time, he realized that this was going to be another time, like countless before, that he had people's lives in his hands.

The idea made him shiver.

He focused his eye contact on his wife, and only his wife. Speaking in front of a crowd in normal circumstances made his skin itch, let alone in an emergency situation: "Friends, we are about to face a crisis, and we have a better chance if we face it together."

A voice asked, "Where will we go? We have to get out of town. Maybe Arborville is okay."

Another, "Didn't you hear Drew? It's spreading too fast.

Even if Arborville is okay now it's not going to be for long. This thing is going to push us right into the ocean. There's nowhere to go to."

Cassius waved his arms, silencing the crowd. "Let Drew talk, he said he had a plan."

Drew took a brief moment to give him a grateful nod before he turned his attention back to Vera. "You're right. It is going to push us toward the water."

"Then what do we do?"

He took a deep breath. "We go up."

Even Vera's eyes widened.

Darius, the second Melone brother, spoke: "You don't mean—"

"Yes. He's our best shot."

"But the guy up the mountain's crazy," Tonia said. "I've heard he keeps his family locked away up there. The whole town talks about how nuts he is."

Her husband added, "He'll never help us."

The group fell silent. For a moment, Drew tried to concentrate on the sounds of the night—the chirping of the crickets, the breeze blowing through the trees, anything to help him contain the panic that was growing in his gut. There was a real possibility that they were right: Connor was their best shot, but Drew could very well see them begging for his help and Connor turning them away, laughing all the while, telling them that their fate would be payback for the way he was treated so many years ago. That scenario was just as likely, probably more so, than what he'd hoped would happen.

There was another possibility too. Perhaps Connor would let them in. But, at least the last time Drew saw him, Connor seemed unbalanced, and he doubted that ten years in isolation would have done much to help his mental state. Connor's compound could be the ocean in the fire: something that at first glance looks like salvation, but could be just as deadly as what they were running from.

But his audience didn't need to know that.

"He will. No matter what kind of compound he thinks he's created up there, there's things we can offer that he can't possibly have."

"Like what?" the pharmacist asked.

"Well, for one thing…" Drew paused then grabbed the medical bag out of the George's hand, opening it up for the neighborhood to see. "I doubt he has a lot of this laying around." He turned to the pharmacist's wife. "And he can't possibly know how to build everything he may need. You could offer him a way to build a better water system or something. Something he hasn't thought of." He marched over to Cassius and Darius. "You, a cop, and you, a pilot? I'm sure he could use some extra security around there, right?"

Cassius grinned. "And these perhaps?" He opened the back of his pickup truck to reveal what was sitting all across the back seat.

Sprawled across the leather were rifles and handguns from all different eras. There were some that looked like they could have been used in mafia hits in the 1930s, while others looked like cowboys may have carried them on their hips;

then there were the .45s and the Glocks.

Darius and Cassius then lifted their shirts to reveal the revolvers on their right hips, and the switchblades sticking out of their pockets. "We're weapons enthusiasts," Darius said.

Drew had never been comfortable with guns, never had a taste for them, but the realization hit him hard that he would have to develop one. "Very good, guys." He turned to the group as a whole, now confident enough to raise his eyes to each and every one of them. "We all have something to offer. Don't forget that. If you do, he will too."

The rest of the people in the neighborhood all had something to offer Connor and his family. There was a firefighter among them, a lawyer that was exceptionally fast, and a salesperson who could negotiate their way into a peaceful resolution if a rival group was ever in the picture. Drew hoped Connor could see everyone's value the way he did. Every life was precious, especially when healthy people were apparently going to be harder and harder to come by.

Despite Drew's confidence, some people in group elected to go their own way. George, Tonia, Cassius, and Darius stayed, perhaps more confident in Drew's plan than any they had come up with on their own. Three other couples stayed, the lawyer and her husband among them, and Drew didn't want to admit to himself that he couldn't remember their names.

Everyone deserved to be remembered.

After loading the vehicles, they lined up in a caravan, with Drew's SUV in the lead. Vera started to get in the front seat, when Drew stopped her. "No, you get in back with Blake and Jackson." He pulled her close to whisper in her ear, so that the others wouldn't hear. "If something happens, I want you to be able to duck."

"Not a chance."

"Vera, I—"

She shook her head. "We have a better chance of seeing something coming with two sets of eyes looking for it."

Drew considered arguing with her, but as she lifted herself into the passenger seat, he realized she was right. "Okay, but if I say duck—"

"I'll duck."

Before they left, Drew went to each car behind him, starting with Cassius and Darius at the back. As Cassius rolled down the window, he said, "Darius is going to be lookout in the back as I drive. That way we're covered if someone tries to sneak up on us." Drew started to say he can't imagine someone would, but he realized he would have never imagined them abandoning their homes in the middle of the night either. "Good idea. Thank you."

Tonia and George's car was the second in line, directly behind Drew. He tapped on the window and George rolled it down. "Everything's going to be fine, you'll see. We're going to make it through this."

George extended his hand. "Thanks to you."

He swallowed hard, thinking to himself to save the thank-yous until they were inside the property at the top of the mountain. Until then, he couldn't allow himself the luxury of hope. He resolved that on their way up, he would focus all his concentration on coming up with a Plan B.

Except he already knew there wasn't one.

CHAPTER THREE

CONNOR (before)

Connor remembered the exact day their faces started to change. It seemed to happen to all of them at once, like a mist sweeping across the tiny northwest town. He admitted to himself that a small part deep within him wanted to blame Kate: a face filled with sorrow could always have her spilling her soul within minutes, and that morning was no exception. This time, the pleading face belonged to their daughter. "Of course you can have a birthday party, Harper. Why wouldn't you be able to?"

"I thought Daddy would be mad."

He watched from around the corner as Kate held their daughter's face in her hands. A six-year-old Harper was a force, a hurricane with fluttering lashes and a dimple in her chin. More so than her sister, Harper knew from an early age how to bat her eyelashes and pout her lips in the exact way that got her what she wanted, despite the catastrophic consequences. "Daddy would never be mad at you for having a birthday party. There's no better reason to celebrate after all!"

"Can I invite all the girls in my class?"

"I wouldn't have it any other way. We don't want anyone to feel left out."

"Yeah that's the worst."

"We can have it in the park downtown. Nothing better than a summer birthday party outside." Kate kissed Harper on the forehead. "Now we will also make sure to have enough cake and punch for the mothers too. They'll want to be here also since their kids are so young."

Harper sighed. "Awww, do we have to? Moms always make things less fun."

Kate gave her a playful shove. "Oh really?"

"You know what I mean, Mom."

"Well would picking out which flavor cupcakes you and Poe get make you feel better?"

Harper clapped her hands together excitedly. "Yes! I'll go get her."

When Harper left, Connor revealed himself. "Why did you let her do that?"

"Come on, Connor…the girls should be able to have a birthday party. I want them to experience things, you know?"

"They do experience things. They're with other children all day at school. Isn't that enough?" He felt the familiar fluttering in his stomach, and a tingling sensation spread across his limbs.

"I want them to experience normal things. Normal kid things, like having a birthday party. I want them to build forts with their friends. I want them to go to sleepovers."

"You would let them go overnight somewhere? We hardly know any of the other parents in this town."

As soon as he said it, Connor realized his mistake. He had given Kate an opening, and of course, she took it. "Well then maybe it's time. We can get to know them at the party."

After Harper came back downstairs, Poe trailing behind her, Connor watched his girls hovering over the cookbook with wide smiles on their faces. He wished he didn't have a sinking feeling in the pit of his stomach, but he did. And every time he got one of those pangs deep in his gut, he knew something was about to go terribly wrong.

**

Connor watched every guest at the party from his post at the grill they had brought for hotdogs and hamburgers. He peered over the top of it but kept his head down so as to not invite anyone to initiate a conversation. Experience had taught him that: eye contact breeds interaction. He knew he had to be careful, so as he did a visual sweep of the party, he kept his eyes aimed at neck level of all their guests—close enough to the eyes to not be noticed, but far enough away to not initiate contact.

All the mothers were whispering with each other as their daughters ran through the grass in their bare feet. None of the women were recognizable to him. He and his family kept to themselves, usually only going places that were necessary, like the post office or—at least to them—the bookstore, and for the children, school. He would also go to the grocery store, but he didn't make a habit of small talk with any of the townsfolk. So he was surprised when he felt a hand on his shoulder. "Connor?"

"Yes?"

"Hello. It's Dr. Matthews."

Dr. Drew Matthews had a friendly face, but Connor knew not to be fooled by friendly faces. "Oh, hello. How are you?" He attempted conversation as a formality. Dr. Matthews was pleasant enough, but of course, he had to be.

"I'm great. My wife Vera and I just thought it would be a nice day to take a stroll in the park, and I saw you over here. You haven't been in in quite a while. Everything going okay?"

Connor forced a smile. "Oh yes. You're right; we have been busy. I'll get Kate to give you a call and set up physicals for all of us next week."

"Excellent. Are you enjoying your summer?"

He had thought agreeing to the physical would be the end of the conversation, but he was mistaken. "Yes absolutely." His mind went blank, and the awkward silence that followed made him feel like he was suffocating. Just as he thought he was about to spit out any sentence at all just to make the quiet stop, Connor saw a woman around Kate's age with hair in perfect ringlets waving and smiling at the doctor. "Looks like you're being beckoned."

Drew smiled. "Yes, it looks like I am." He gave a wave as he walked toward his wife. "I'll see you next week. We just got a fresh bin of stickers for the kids. Have a good day!"

As Dr. Matthews headed back toward Vera, Connor noticed several people at the park wave at him. He returned the gestures with smiles and pleasantries, and it seemed to take him more than a few minutes to get back to his wife. The rest of the town seemed to revere the doctor. Connor knew from moving around when he was young that though doctors seemed to be held in high praise everywhere, it was even more so in their small town. There seemed to be nothing like the ability to save a life to give you prestige among the mob. He felt an ember from the grill leap onto his forearm, and he fought the urge to curse.

Maybe he should have been a doctor, he thought. His father had always said he could be anything he wanted to be, and after he saw all his report cards from school, he had said it with a passionate enthusiasm. Connor had barely hit puberty when his father died, but that was plenty of time for him to confidently tell Connor that everything he wanted out of life was his for the taking.

Too bad Connor never believed it himself. He never quite knew what he wanted, except that he wanted to belong. So when on the first day of elementary school, a couple of the bigger kids asked, "Are you rich?" he didn't know what to say. Saying yes could, and would, get him ostracized forever, but saying no would be an easily-exposable lie. So instead of saying anything, he said nothing at all.

His mother had written a self-help book that had taught America how to reach deep within themselves to find their inner peace, something that a million books had done before hers, but it gave her enough money to soak up the guilt she may or may not have felt when she walked out on his father.

She paid them a huge stipend every month, and probably thought that was enough to heal the pain in his father's heart that he used nature walks and sweat lodges to try and mend. Sometimes, she would even send Connor a postcard from her travels, a picture of the Las Vegas strip signed Take care, the same thing a classmate signs in the yearbook of someone who they can barely remember the name of. Every postcard made going back to the social world just a little more complicated, yet made him ache for it just a little bit more. The longer he lived in solitude, the harder it became to come back, like when you forget the name of an acquaintance, and the time passes where it would have been acceptable to ask them. Eventually you just pray someone addresses the person in front of you so you can get that all-important answer to the question you can no longer ask.

As he got older, he didn't think about it much anymore, until he had to be around a group of people, and the same glistening sweat spontaneously covered his body—the same way it had on the first day of elementary school so many years before.

After the doctor left, Connor continued to watch the party guests as little pods of people formed, clustering together in conversational groups. He could swear a couple of the pods were looking at him, but he couldn't be sure. The whole ordeal made him anxious. The little pink banners and ribbons and fluffy cupcakes did nothing to make him feel less on edge.

They lived up the mountain so he could avoid situations like the one he found himself in at that very moment. He let the children go to school instead of being homeschooled because Kate insisted, and everything seemed to have worked out until that point. Harper and Gabriel seemed to enjoy it, and even Poe did on occasion. But Connor always worried that if other people found out how they lived, they wouldn't understand. They were all-too-happy to just keep existing, going from one PTA meeting to the next, washing their cars on Sunday afternoons and baking cookies, and ignoring the very real danger that showed itself time and time again. Every night on the news there was some disease, mass shooting, or other phantom that could come knocking on their door at any time. He wondered if it was ignorance or stupidity that made the vast majority of people assume they could never be a victim: it was other people that got torn apart by bullets. It was other people who went on vacation somewhere and came back with a bacterium that ate their flesh. The life of a prepper shone a beacon on the reality of their naiveté, and no one likes to be made a fool of. If they knew, he and his family could no longer stay pleasantly hidden in the background. The truth did not always set you free…sometimes it made the earth cave in at your feet. Just like before, his family would only know the magnitude of their mistakes when it was too late to correct them.

***

During rainstorms, he saw him. When he saw his own hands submerged in a sink of soapy water, he saw him. And even on that day in the park, staring into the grill flames, he saw him.

His father said they could wait out the storm. Their small house was across the street from an office building that had been there for two hundred years… "a strong one," he had said.

"But everyone else is leaving, Dad," a young Connor had pleaded. "We need to leave too. Please. I'm scared."

"Don't worry, Son. Worst-case scenario, the government will send the Coast Guard in and rescue us. We've got a couple backpacks full of food and water. We'll be fine." His father smiled as he stroked his beard, something he always did when he was absolutely sure of himself. Connor made it a point not to pick up that habit.

The first night in the office building, Connor clung to his father, listening to the walls bend and shake against the wind. A part of him thought he was too old to need his father's reassurance, and another part of him didn't care and squeezed him tighter. "It's going to collapse," he said.

"It'll hold. Trust me, Son." His father wrapped his arms around him, and he felt his beard tickle the top of his forehead. He felt he was being cradled like a baby, but he let it happen anyway, chasing the adolescent boy in his head away and giving in to the scared child who wanted to be told it would be over soon. "Let's sing that song you like. The one about the river and the tent." Connor obeyed, and they sang, their voices probably echoing through the empty halls, but the storm whipped their notes right out of the air.

He'd never sung that song since.

When the helicopters finally came, Connor's heart raced as the ladder fell from the sky. "I hate heights, Dad. You go first," he said.

His father nodded, and was about to take the first rung, when one of the Coast Guard members spoke. "We're only taking women and children, sir. You're going to have to wait for the second helicopter."

Connor's heart raced. "No! Dad they can't! I'm not leaving you."

"It's okay, Connor. I'll be right behind you. Just get on the helicopter with the man, and I'll be there soon. And look…" he pointed up into the helicopter where there were already several faces staring back at them. "There's a bunch of people up there already. A bunch of new friends, okay?"

His father did an admirable job of pretending the situation was going to turn out okay, but when he reached out and hugged his son, Connor felt the panic in his embrace. He clung to his father with all his strength, but the rescue worker was able to pull him free. As the worker pushed him up the ladder, he looked down to see his father smiling and waving. "Everything is going to be fine, you'll see."

That was the last time Connor ever saw him. Months later, he saw a photo of the devastation the storm left behind it. In that photo was the office building they had cowered in. The roof had imploded on itself, and all that was left were four walls with a hole in the center. If Connor had to guess, his father was buried under that pile, surrounded by water and debris and the lies that he told himself and his son.

Anyone who had been through what he had would have understood why Connor's family lived the way they did. He couldn't be sure how long he waited before his mother was able to pick him up from the place where displaced people were housed after the storm. He spent the time curled up on a cot, trying not to be noticed by anyone. A couple times, grown men came up to him and asked him to come over to stay with them, promising protection, but he could tell in their faces that protection was the last thing they had planned for him.

His mother tried, in her own way. She cared for him for about six months before he always saw her looking over her shoulder wherever they went. It wasn't long after that when she told him she was sending him off to a very prestigious, very expensive boarding school. "You'll love it there," she had told him. "They have basketball, and tennis, and a bunch of the other sports you like so much."

He'd never played a sport in his life.

As his mother drove away from the front steps of the boarding school, he vowed that when he had a family, he would never have to depend on anyone else to protect them. When she died, she had left him all her money, which he had been surprised she hadn't burned through. Maybe she thought it would make up for leaving him on the front steps that day. If he had believed in an afterlife, he would have shouted at her about how wrong she was.

When he had a family, they would rely on themselves alone, making their own means of food, shelter, and anything else they needed to survive, and to Hell with anyone who thought that was strange. To Connor, anyone who didn't do whatever they needed to do to care for the people they loved were the strange ones.

There would never be any reason, emotional or otherwise, for him to leave his own children on the front steps to fend for themselves. His children would always know that even when the world stopped spinning, they would be fed, and they would be loved.

***

A week after the party, he went to the hardware store to pick up some parts for their vegetable gardens. A tiny speck of a bird, fast with a little sharp beak, had been picking at them through a hole in the netting that normally protected them, and he knew if he didn't get it covered soon, the cucumber harvest would be lost, and there would be none to can for the winter. As he walked down the lane, he noticed each person he passed seemed to be staring at him for just a second too long. He passed the coffee shop, and glanced back subtly enough that he could see several people follow him with their eyes as he moved past the window. Even the people in the bookshop that he had frequented for years sneakily glanced up from their books to look at him. The one place in town where he felt safe didn't feel that way any longer.

Something had changed.

He had planned on puttering around the hardware store for a while. Since it was a Sunday during church hours, he knew it would be virtually empty. It was the only time during the week when he would make a point to go there, a time where he knew he wouldn't be bothered. He enjoyed going aisle by aisle and seeing which new gadget caught his eye. All the shiny metal tools lining the shelves made him think of wandering Santa's workshop at the North Pole: new toys ripe for the picking. The idea always gave him a sense of giddy anticipation, sometimes settling over him as early as the night before his trip out. But instead, he grabbed exactly what he needed, and paid with cash, crisp new one dollar bills to be exact. "How's it going?" he asked the pimple-faced cashier who he had seen dozens of times before. Usually, the question would be followed by a quick running of his fingers through his hair, and some comments about his wife never cleaning up the house, or his baby daughter keeping him up at all hours.

But that's not what happened. Instead, Connor got a short, quick, 'Fine' in response. He even tried to follow the question up with one more, which he thought for sure would leave the cashier unable to give him a one-word answer. "I heard the shop has been open now for ten years. That's wonderful. Charlie must be excited. What do you think he will do to celebrate?"

"Yeah. I don't know." Three additional words, Connor thought.

He decided to walk back to the bookstore and go inside. If there was anywhere in town that would make him feel comfortable, it was there. He would just ignore the customers inside and go sit in the big brown leather chair at the back of the store like he usually did anyway. He could feel safe there again; he would just have to work at it a little harder. But on the way in, a woman was coming out, and in his overzealous desire to get inside, he bumped into her. He glanced quickly at her, muttered an apology and thought that would settle it, until he felt the hard snap of her palm against his cheek. "Stay away from me, you pervert! We've heard all about you and your people up there. You can't just do whatever you want. Not here!"

"What are you talking about, lady? It was an accident."

"You touched my breast! That was no accident."

Connor took a couple deep breaths and tried to remain calm. "If I did, I didn't mean to. I'm sorry."

As he was apologizing for a second time, a man with over-gelled hair and a tattered leather jacket joined the woman, standing at her side like a guard dog. As the man looked around at the other patrons, he said, "He just said he was sorry. He did do it." He pushed Connor in the chest. "Get away from my sister, asshole."

Of course, Connor pushed him back. But before things could escalate, one of the employees came out of the back room and stepped between them. "You both need to leave now. Figure this out on your own time." He ushered Connor and the other man out the door and closed it loudly behind them.

Connor glared at the man and his sister, and assumed the fight would continue. But instead, the man said loudly, "Come on, Holly. Let's get away from this guy. Obviously he's not right in the head."

Somehow, even after the incident, Connor thought since they had walked away without throwing punches, that would be the end of it. He would be able to go back inside the bookstore and his life would continue on as normal.

He was sorely mistaken.

When he walked back through the door, after the little bell on the doorknob stopped shaking, he heard a voice from behind the counter. "I'm sorry, you can't shop here anymore." The clerk was staring at him with her arms folded. Her blonde hair hung in her face, and Connor recognized her by her distinctive chomping on her gum. If he remembered correctly, her parents owned the store.

"Why not? I come here all the time."

"You know why."

"But that was an accident. Why would I have done what she said I did? Especially right in front of people?"

The clerk sighed. "Because…" she took another breath. "Whatever the hell you people do up there, you make our customers uncomfortable, and we can't have that. This is a family business."

"But I didn't…"

"Go."

Connor looked around at the other patrons. Surely, one of them, maybe one who had been closer to the door when he had ran into that awful woman, would stand up for him. One of them certainly saw what didn't happen. He looked at each face, desperately searching for someone to have an ounce of sympathy, someone who would come to his defense.

They all looked away.

Every. Single. One.

As he left the bookstore for the last time, he hoped that the hostility he had just felt was relegated to just the bookstore, and once he was outside, he would figure out how to make everything okay again. It was one thing to be stared at, it was quite another to be accused of a crime. But he held out to the hope that perhaps it could all be fixed, and once it was he could comfortably fade into the background as before.

After he made his way back to the truck, he sat in the driver's seat for a while, listening to the vinyl squeak as he settled in. He turned his radio down and watched as the world carried on around him. From his parking spot, he could see down both sides of the street. He had the perfect view of every passerby, and as much as he wanted to, he couldn't deny that something was wrong, and whatever it was had reached beyond one single business. Perhaps there was a misunderstanding, something that could be corrected with a quick explanation.

Then he remembered the birthday party.

***

When he walked into his house, he stuck his bag of newly purchased items on the kitchen counter. The wire had poked a hole in the bag, and sat menacingly in the air, waiting to scratch the first passerby who was not paying attention to his or her surroundings. "Poe? Are you home?"

His daughter came running to him from around the corner, shoes clomping loudly on the stairs with each step. "Daddy!" She threw her arms around him. He felt the tug of her little fingers squeeze the fabric of his shirt. The difference between a hug from Poe and a hug from Harper was that Poe didn't want anything in return. Then there was his son,

Gabriel, who preferred a stiff pat on the back above anything else. "Did you have fun in town? What did you do?"

He patted the top of her head, gently messing up her hair. If it had been Harper instead, she would have thrown a fit. Poe didn't care, and left her hair in disarray. "Come sit out on the porch with me for a moment."

"Sure." Poe happily followed her dad outside, pigtails bouncing as she walked. He sat down on the top step, and motioned for her to sit down beside him. "What's going on, Daddy?"

Even at six, Poe was extremely perceptive. Sometimes Connor had an easier time hiding things from Kate than he did Poe. "When you had your birthday party a couple weeks ago, did you have fun?"

"Oh yeah. It was great." Poe smiled, but glanced at the ground as she said it. That was always her tell.

"Poe?"

The little girl sighed and bit her lip, as if she was worried that what she was about to say may hurt her father's feelings. Connor couldn't imagine Poe ever hurting him, especially not on purpose. Harper was the calculating one. With Poe, he could always be sure he would get the truth, and he hoped that would remain the case as she aged. "I had a great time; really I did. But the kids kept asking me and Harper about our farm, and why we live so far away. We didn't know what they were talking about. We don't make any of our stuff to sell like farmers do, and Harper told them so."

A lump formed in Connor's throat. "What did you girls say we did?"

"Well, Violet Reynolds kept saying we had to make money somehow, and asked what you and Mommy do for a living. I said you were a prepper. Then Annie Masterson asked me what that was. I told her we're preparing for the end of the world."

"What did they say?"

"Well, first Violet said you don't make money doing that."

Connor put his arm around Poe. "She's right. We're very fortunate that your grandmother left us with enough money that we can live off of it and still afford to do what we do."

"Oh." Poe's eyes averted back toward the ground.

"What else happened honey?"

That's when Connor saw the tears in her eyes. The boards of the porch squeaked as she shifted her weight to lean into him. "Violet kept saying things. Like her daddy told her once that we live all the way up here because you're a murderer and probably kidnapped us and that we're a cult. I didn't know what a cult was."

"What did you say?"

"Well she said that a cult's a group of people who live together, like a family. So I said yeah, I guess we are. We're just a family. Then she said cults are bad. We aren't bad are we? You never killed anyone right? And you're my real mommy and daddy too?"

"No, of course I never killed anyone. And yes of course we're your real parents. We did not kidnap you." He paused. "And we aren't a cult either, honey. A cult is something much different than a family. Sometimes people make up things to find explanations for what they don't understand." He felt her squeeze his wedding ring and spin it as it sat around his finger. "And sometimes other people will take those made-up things as fact."

Poe nodded. When he looked in her eyes, he could see the corner of their compound looking back at him in their reflection, an odd juxtaposition of flowers and tall grass with iron and steel. He could tell that even at such a young age, she was able to understand such a complicated concept as rumor and insecurity. It was almost worrisome how much of an adult was hiding in the tiny girl before him, jeans dirty with mud and a small leaf hanging from one of her pigtails. The pink ribbons in her hair did nothing to mask how deep her thoughts travelled. He was proud she was so much like him, yet he wished she wasn't.

She continued. "All the other kids told her to stop it, but then as they left, they kept asking us about the end of the world." She hesitated. "They looked really scared. I didn't know what to say, so I told them their moms and dads probably knew."

Connor swallowed hard, and the lump in his throat settled down in his insides. He had always meant the end of society as they knew it when he referred to what they were preparing for as the end of the world. It sounded far less dramatic when he said it privately at home than when he pictured his young daughter saying it to her classmates, then those same children telling their parents about it. Oh the stories that they must have come up with in their own, creatively sinister minds. Poe looked at him. "Was that bad, Daddy? I'm sorry…"

He forced a smile. "No, of course not. You should be proud of who you are. It wasn't a bad thing to say, not at all." Or at least it shouldn't have been. How they lived their lives shouldn't have mattered to anyone else. They should have been able to live as they saw fit, without so much as a blink from the community around them. Their way of life should have been respected, the same way a religion or someone's culture was respected, something not to be touched or ridiculed by a supposedly progressive society. They should have been able to continue on without trouble. But all Connor needed to do was look at history to know that the masses never quite behaved like they were supposed to. Usually, the people that called themselves progressive were the first to pass judgement, and were all too eager to light the torches. It just took a little spark, a little static in the dark to set the world on fire.

And burn it would.

CHAPTER FOUR

POE

The clearest picture Poe Holloway had of her sixth year on earth was one of the sky being blocked by thick metal bleachers. The blue and gray stripes had a dusting of green at the outer edge, where the grass of the playground peeked through the base of the giant structure. Everything could be categorized as "giant" when she was six years old. At the time, she couldn't imagine anything larger, thinking that any skyscraper or towers that she had seen in magazines were just tricks of the eye, towering monsters that were only real in someone's vivid imagination.

She spent her recesses hiding beneath them, sometimes with a book, probably filled with poetry from another time where life wasn't so complicated, or in some ways, was more so. But most days, she would just sit there, with her knees held tightly against her chest, trying to concentrate on the soft grass between her toes instead of the hard words in her head.

It wasn't always so.

Her fifth year on earth was much more pleasant, filled

with days in the classroom where she safely disappeared into the landscape, and used that time to read the stories that her mother had introduced her to.

Poe tried to think of that year, the year filled with the bliss that comes from not knowing any better, instead of what followed, as she sat up in her camouflaged guard tower. It was her turn to keep watch, and as she looked around she chuckled to herself, realizing what her father liked to refer to as the guard tower was more like a tree house piled on all sides with branches. Her dad knew that they would be getting visitors soon, and they had to all take turns watching for cars coming up the mountain in order to conserve the fuel they would need for the generator. Besides that, Poe and her father viewed it as one more opportunity to establish in a very visceral way that they had the upper hand. Once she saw them, it was her job to tell her mother or father over the radio that they had arrived, and to greet the newcomers. She would guide them up the mountain and into the one visible entry point to their property. Of course there was another, but the strangers never needed to be told that information.

New people were dangerous. Poe knew that. Her father had told her that from the beginning, and no one had ever done anything to prove otherwise, except perhaps one person. Everyone else she had ever met had stayed true to her father's word, so though she appreciated the exception to the rule, she knew her as just that: the exception.

Her mother had made the mistake of signing her up for a playgroup at one point during her aforementioned sixth year. She had begged her mother not to; it was Harper's idea of course. But no amount of pleading would sway her. "Harper can do it by herself," she'd said.

"Nonsense, Poe, it'll be good for you. You'll enjoy it, you'll see. Once you get there everything will be fine." Their mother: the eternal optimist. Poe considered herself more of a realist, and she really knew it was not going to be the fairy tale her mother had hoped for. She also wondered why it seemed to never occur to her mother that their definition of enjoyment could be two different things. To her, it was enjoyable to spend time in her room and to talk to the farm animals that they raised on their land. Of course sometimes she got lonely...very lonely. But maybe everyone on earth was just a little bit lonely anyway, a crowded planet filled with solitude.

The day they (everyone is a "they" when you have no friends) almost got her was the day that her playgroup supervisor decided to take them to a park. Harper had caught the flu, so Poe was forced to go all by herself. "You'll have fun," her mother declared.

How wrong she was.

The swings were wide plastic yellow rectangles, and she remembered her pants getting caught in the small gap between the chain and the seat. Luckily, she managed to free herself before the tear became something more than a small hole. The whole scene that she avoided played out in her head nonetheless—her pants ripping wide open, and everyone, including her supervisor, pointing and laughing: because laughing at the misfortune of others is what people do.

As always, the other children had dispersed like a flock of birds, flying away to all different corners of the playground. There was a small shed toward the far end of it, covered with a thin layer of moss and brown film, and Poe had thought she could hide out there until the supervisor called them back to go home. The woman was very easily distractible, sitting on a bench, legs crossed, with her nose deep in a celebrity magazine during every playgroup activity, so Poe slipped past her with no issue. Glancing backward, she noticed the woman kept her feet slightly elevated off the ground as she sat there, and Poe guessed she was trying to make sure her heels didn't dip into the mud.

Poe had just sat down in the grass behind the shed when she heard a voice from the other side of the chain-link fence that surrounded the park.

"Freak," it said.

Poe glanced up from the blades of grass that she had been weaving into a tiny braid. "What?"

A group of kids from the other side of the fence seemed to emerge from the pavement, multiplying before her eyes: girls that seemed to be carbon copies of one another, each with almost the same scowling face, just with different outfits. They looked like a pastel-laced hit squad, and Poe knew she was their next target. The leader stood closest to her. "Tell me, freak, does your father keep dead bodies up there? Is that why you live in the mountains?"

She looked down toward the ground. After the birthday party, she had learned that sometimes it's best not to tell the truth to strangers: actually, it was probably best all the time.

"No. We just live up there. We farm and stuff." Her explanation wasn't entirely a lie: they did farm, they did garden, and they did live off the land.

And when she was old enough, her dad would teach her how to shoot a rifle.

Another voice: "All alone? Must be a reason. I bet your dad's a murderer. That's what everyone says. I heard he went all crazy in the middle of the bookstore too. Scared some poor lady to death."

And another: "Yeah, no other reason for somebody to be all the way up there. That's where murderers go. They hide in the woods. Someday the cops'll get him. They'll take him away and you'll never see him again. Ever."

Something inside Poe twisted and bubbled, and for an all-important moment she lost all reasoning. "What do you know anyway? Maybe your dad's the one who's a murderer." As soon as the words slipped from her mouth, she winced. A voice in her head told her she should have just stayed silent. They would tire of tormenting her eventually; they always did.

But she had spoken up. And because of that, there were now four girls twice her size starting to climb over the fence, and her supervisor was nowhere to be seen. As their hands clawed the wires, she could see the dirt under their fingernails. Or was it blood?

They shouted at her as they rose, growing, hovering over her as they climbed. "I'll teach you! Don't talk about my dad!" and "Yeah, Victoria! Get her!" Her brain told her to run, to get away from this angry mob disguised as preteen girls, but her feet wouldn't move. Their eyes were wide, and they were gritting their teeth so hard that spit was flying out of their mouths like the ravenous werewolves she had read about in countless books. And now they wanted to do what all wolves do: hunt their prey, and tear it apart.

As they reached the top of the fence, Poe shut her eyes tightly. Even if the supervisor saw her, she'd never get there in time. She could cry out, but her voice was stuck in her throat, and doing so would have made her look like a coward anyway. So instead, she shut her eyes. She would not give them the satisfaction of cowering before them. Maybe not knowing when the blows would come would make them less painful.

Maybe not.

But instead of the beating she was expecting, she heard several "thuds." And the thuds were not coming from fists pummeling into her. They were coming from the other side of the fence. She cautiously opened her eyes just in time to see the last girl be grabbed by the collar of her pink polka-dotted dress and pushed down hard onto the pavement. Poe looked up to see another girl, much older than her or her potential attackers, hovering over them. She looked about thirteen, and her blonde hair was pulled tightly back in a ponytail. She was in a soccer uniform, and Poe guessed that the girl had stumbled upon her situation on her way to practice in the park. She watched as the girl grabbed each person in the group one by one and turned them toward herself. They were still grabbing at themselves, clutching whatever area of their bodies the girl had elected to pummel.

"You leave her alone, do you hear me? What gives you the right to treat someone that way?"

"But she…" one of the girls started.

"But she nothing. You're going to have plenty of crap coming at you in your life just because you're a girl. The last thing you should be doing is being mean to each other." Poe couldn't tell which one, but one or several of them started crying. "Now go home and get it together. I don't want to see you doing anything like this again, got it?"

They all nodded like little bobble heads as they ran down the sidewalk and back to wherever they had come from. As Poe watched the cloud of Easter egg colors disappear down the street, she pictured them running home and telling their mothers their version of what happened: that a big mean girl pushed them down and yelled at them through no fault of their own.

But at that moment, it didn't matter.

"Thanks," she said.

The blonde girl smiled. "No problem." She shrugged good-naturedly. "What did those girls want with you anyway?"

Poe shrugged. "I don't know. They called me a freak and said my dad killed somebody." She took a deep breath, afraid that her guardian angel might think her impolite. "So I said 'what do you know,' and that her dad was the one who probably did that. She got really mad." She managed a nervous chuckle. "Not the best comeback ever, but I tried. I'm not used to talking much."

The blonde girl nodded knowingly. "Got it. I know that girl. The chubby one."

Poe giggled.

"I heard her dad's in jail for something or another." The blond girl snickered. "Maybe you hit a nerve." She wiped her calloused hands on her pants, perhaps to wipe the bully-germs off her skin. "Good for you for defending your dad like that. You take care of yourself, okay?"

"Okay." Poe managed a smile as she waved and ran back toward her playgroup supervisor, who had finally decided to pay attention to where the children under her care had ended up. As she approached, she saw the woman wagging her finger at her, and considered telling her that perhaps elementary school kids shouldn't be trusted to look after themselves..

As she hopped in the back of the woman's van to go home, she glanced out the window behind her, and watched as her savior ran down the field and kicked the soccer ball straight into the goal. Poe hoped maybe that was a sign that sometimes, good does win in the end, even if that win is just a point on a scoreboard.

***

Poe took her baseball cap off and wiped her brow. The guard tower became stuffy in the afternoon, as though she were trying to breath under a thick blanket, the way she did when she lay in her bed, hiding from the shadows that danced on her bedroom wall. One would think the structure would let the air flow freely through the cracks in the wood, but not something built by her father. In his effort to make it strong, he had built an oven. The walls were sealed shut for protection, and sealed even further by the massive branches that camouflaged it. There was only a small window that let air through, and acted as the vantage point. Poe stuck her face through it as far as she could; sucking in the cool air and pushing away any stray branches that attempted to scratch her. She gazed out over the hill to the only visible road that led to their property, which ended abruptly at the beginning of a forested area. It wasn't paved; more of a path that was barely better than driving straight through the woods.

She heard the cars before she saw them.

They came around the corner in a line: an SUV followed by several sedans, all being trailed by a large truck. When she squinted, she could see the top of a man's head cautiously sticking out the back window. If she shaded her eyes with her hand, she could make out the end of a gun barrel.

It was time.

She notified her mother and father on her handheld radio, then attached it back onto her belt, right next to her gun. Like she had done a thousand times before, she expertly crawled her way out of the lookout tower and shimmied down to the ground, landing with a thud and a cloud of dust. Brushing the dirt from her face, she stepped out into the open, placing her feet in the stance of someone who was ready for whatever was coming, and putting on her aviator sunglasses. She had to practically step in front of the first car before they saw her.

She waved her arms as they slowed to a stop. Inside the car, she could see the man turning to the woman in the front seat. She could see their lips moving, but could not decipher what they were saying. Both of them looked like they had just rolled out of bed, which given the status of the pandemic, Poe guessed was exactly what happened. She remembered when she and her family had frequented the town that all the women looked as if they would rather be pecked to death by birds than be caught without their makeup on. She giggled to herself, thinking how the apocalypse could make even the most grooming-obsessed person change their ways. No point in putting on rouge when there was no one left to impress.

The woman in the SUV carried a worried expression, and Poe couldn't blame her one bit: she didn't even know what was coming, not yet. There were two faces visible in the seats behind them, one belonging to a young woman, the other to a child.

The man driving the first car got out cautiously, at first keeping the car door between him and her. Smart, she thought. "Do you need help young lady?"

She laughed. "No, but I'm sure you do." The man looked at her quizzically. Poe straightened her baseball cap, pulling it tightly onto her head and making sure that her ponytail was centered. She was in her element, relishing in what her family had accomplished, and the fact that now the same people who had shunned them so long ago were asking for their help. She was bred to live their way of life, molded by her father from the beginning, feeling most like herself when she had a knife in her hand, and a forest around her. Now, instead of her having to adjust to the world, the world would have to adjust to her. Her family had been seen as the little boy who cried wolf: warning of impending tragedy long before it arrived. But when the wolf did show its teeth, the boy was prepared while others were not, because he saw it coming. "You're on your way to the Holloway's to seek refuge from the plague, right?"

The man nodded in agreement. He looked as though he was about to ask a question, right as he realized who she was. "You're Poe Holloway."

"Last time I checked."

"I'm Drew Matthews. That's my wife Vera and goddaughter Blake with her son in the car. I was your doctor when you were a little girl. Maybe you remember…" He smiled and extended his hand. She didn't take it.

"You're going to have to follow me if you want to find our place." She gestured to the caravan. "Dump your cars in the woods. From here we go on foot. And be sure to tell the rest of your group that if they're thinking about trying anything, I'm not the only one out here." That was another reason Poe was supposed to notify her parents: Connor wanted the opportunity to not only have the rest of the family be able to protect Poe from the strangers, but to observe the new group from a distance, to see them brave and scared and lost.

Drew looked backward toward the other cars. "We have a lot of supplies. There's no other way through?"

"Well, only grab what you absolutely need right away. If you want in, you have to leave your cars. We can't have you ramming our perimeter and stealing from us, can we?"

Drew stared blankly.

"Those of you who make it in will have to make a couple trips."

"Those of us who make it? What do you mean by that?"

Poe smiled the smile of a person with a secret, one that would be revealed when the time was right. "Follow me."

After Drew informed the group what the new plan was, they followed Poe's instructions, rearranging bins and dumping out anything that wasn't an absolute priority. She noticed what these strangers considered essential, and an annoyed sigh escaped her lips. Yes, they did get some of it right: bringing their warm clothes and canned goods…some even brought surgical masks in an attempt to protect themselves against the spread of the disease. But they also took photo albums, shoved into all-too-small containers, while they left knives behind. Though a picture of a beloved grandmother might bring a small amount of comfort, being able to fend off an attacker should have brought more…though Poe would have guessed they wouldn't know how to use them properly anyway. She considered taking a second to point out the error of their ways, but knew that experience was the best teacher of all. Most of the people in front of her struck her as the kind that had to learn things the hard way.

No matter, they will adjust soon enough.

Those who brought bags and backpacks filled them to the brim, while the rest of the group was stuck hauling large plastic bins up the hill toward the property. Some could lift them, while others were stuck dragging them along the ground, hoping they didn't fall apart in the effort. They looked like tourists trying to play some sort of survival game, clinging to their cans of food with no openers, and clutching their favorite pillows like they were filled with gold.

Poe guessed that Drew didn't share the last part of their conversation.

Drew and someone she learned was named Cassius lead the new group. They followed directly behind her as they trudged toward the house. Listening to them struggle with the hike, Poe imagined she could hear the sweat seeping down their brows. Sure, they were in shape; they probably worked out several times a week. But they weren't trained for a hill that size, in woods that dense. Every step that seems easy on a hard surface was ten times more difficult on soft earth. Poe glided up it with ease, wondering if they were cursing their treadmills and weight rooms for failing them when they needed them most. They certainly hadn't prepared them for her father's land, and her father's mountain. She watched, enjoying the fact that for them, every step was a struggle. She almost wanted them to complain about it: then she could tell them that fighting for every inch of ground was nothing compared to fighting to live your life the way you saw fit, with every single person you'd ever met working against you, pushing you back down the path from where you came.

The women of the group were struggling even more than the men. Poe scoffed to herself as she watched them hurl themselves up the hill. Could none of them be bothered to go jogging between their day jobs and laundry? Or did they just assume that their men folk would always be there to protect them? Her father had taught her many things, but the one that he said was most important was this: never rely on someone else to save you. Be prepared to save yourself.

Poe guessed that the women in front of her were taught something different, and between lifting supplies and a quick pace, whatever it was had failed them miserably.

Fighting their exhausted breath and burning muscles, the two men in front were not whispering as softly as they intended. Between heavy inhales, she heard Drew hiss, "Put that gun away, Cassius. She'll see it. Do you want to get us thrown out before we even get in?"

"Not a chance in Hell I'm putting it away. For all we know we're walking into an ambush and they're just going to take all our stuff and leave us to fend for ourselves."

Cassius didn't see Poe give the signal.

A bullet whirred over Cassius's head and into a nearby tree, sending sharp bits of bark flying. She recognized the perfect aim, and knew exactly who had fired. The group stopped cold, except for Poe, who calmly turned around to face them. "Go ahead, Cassius, keep your gun. If you try anything my sister will take your head off before it leaves your holster."

She turned to Drew. "Evidently, your warning didn't sink in."

Cassius' head whipped around, trying to find the location of his assailant. He started to step toward Poe then thought the better of it, fighting the urge to yell at her by talking through clenched teeth. "Where is she? Your sister?"

Poe winked at him as she turned back, continuing to

head up the mountain. She couldn't answer his question, even if she wanted to. Harper was a master at blending in—a hunter at heart, probably even better than her mother. The only time either of them would find her is if Harper wanted to be found.

And at least right then, she certainly didn't.

As they got closer to the gated area of the property, Poe turned around and looked at them, smoothly walking backwards as she talked. Her feet seemed to know the terrain by themselves, not needing the aid of her eyes. "Dad said you would come, you know. Children always do."

"We're not children," Cassius said. Drew elbowed him in the side.

Poe smirked. "Are you about to ask an adult to clothe you, house you, and feed you because you don't think you can make it on your own in this world?"

Cassius didn't have an answer.

But Poe did. "Then you're children."

They walked in silence after that for quite a long time. The only thing letting Poe know that they were still behind her was the soft crunch of their footsteps on the frozen grass and their labored breathing. Typical of Washington, one minute the weather was beautiful, the next, the Earth seemed intent on freezing out its occupants. In their case though, the extra cold evening seemed to fit the mood of the situation. She thought about them as individuals, wondering what their stories were, and who they were before this day came upon them. How did they all know each other? Were they family? Were they neighbors? Or had they just stumbled upon each other as they were driving toward the Holloway's home? She took a moment to glance back at the group, sizing them up one by one.

That's when she saw her.

She barely recognized her at first. Ten years adds a thousand changes to a face, and it took her a minute to find the teenage girl that had saved her so many years ago. The blonde girl from the first car, who held on tightly to who she could then tell was a small boy with hair as yellow as his mother's, was the one from the park that day, the one who had saved her from being beaten up, and worse, humiliated. Poe assumed that she didn't recognize her. She had stayed behind Drew since they had arrived, probably at Drew's instruction, and her attention was, understandably, on the boy.

Poe wasn't sure why, but she decided to keep the information to herself. She would reveal it at the right time, and that was not it. She would need it later, of that she was sure. It seemed important somehow, too important to reveal on a hike full of out-of-shape, exhausted strangers.

As she watched the sun disappear behind a row of gray clouds, she realized that moment was more significant than any other. That moment was the time to get ready, because she saw the top of her house revealing itself just over the horizon.

CHAPTER FIVE

DREW

As the house came into view, a tight, tangled knot formed in Drew's stomach. He felt a spontaneous burst of sweat all over his body, and he was sure it wasn't from the long hike they just finished. He hadn't seen Connor in ten years, not since the day he and another man carried him out of his office as he fought and flailed, humiliated as Drew's other patients looked on, all looking down to avoid his eyes, all doing nothing to stop it. He could still hear the shrill panic in his voice, and feel the walls vibrate as the door slammed shut. There was no telling how Connor would react when they arrived: he could invite them in, or he could tell him to go back down the path where he came from. He swallowed hard when he realized that he would be less surprised by the second outcome than the first. And if Connor's past with Drew cost Vera, Blake, and Jackson their lives…that was a truth that Drew knew he would be unable to carry.

The compound seemed to have grown from the earth itself. It seemed to Drew to be a mix of metal and wood, and from the shapes, Drew guessed that the basic structure was made of shipping container material. Some of the plants looked as if they were trying to take back the land, snaking up the walls and clawing at them with their green tendrils. Other shrubs with large needles surrounded the perimeter, and Drew winced at the thought of being stuck by one.

There was a barn on one side of the compound that looked as though it was plucked straight from the cover of a grocery store puzzle—red with white trim, with huge double doors on the front. It struck Drew as odd, seeing something so tranquil in the same place as steel and thorns. There was a fenced area near the barn, where horses, cows, and pigs roamed peacefully, munching on grass without a clue that the world was crumbling around them.

Poe held up her hand and gestured for the group to come to a stop. He noticed a ring on her thumb that looked as if it should be found on the hand of a man. The white gold looked darker than it should against her pale skin, and he wondered how she had come to have such a ring. He forced himself to slow down his imagination, trying not to create a number of undesirable scenarios that, if they were true, would mean they were in even more trouble than he had previously thought. A deadly father with a deadly daughter? He knew he would soon find out.

Her words crackled against the air around them. "Everyone, please pay attention. You're going to want to." At the sound of her voice, several people emerged from the house. Drew watched as they all formed a line in front of the door. Gabriel, the son, had become a tanned, muscular young man with the visible self-assurance of his mother and the bitter expression of his father. A girl in a sunflower dress, whom he assumed was Harper by process of elimination, stood next to him with a French braid in her hair, looking more like a doll from a toy shop than the trained killer they had encountered in the woods. Kate stood with them, and Drew noticed her take a brief second to squeeze each of her children's hands and smile reassuringly.

The last person to come out was Connor. Time appeared to have taken its toll on him more than it should have: wrinkles had aged his face not ten years, but twenty. The whites of his eyes had seemed to grow less bright, like a shirt that had been washed too many times, but they still had the gleam of self-proclaimed superiority that Drew remembered so clearly.

Poe smiled and nodded toward her father, then took her place on his right, while her mother stood on his left. He was at least happy to see Kate looking healthy in a pale pink dress and sandals, her freshly painted toes shining: the color had returned to her face since last he'd seen her.

Connor smiled and it sent a chill down Drew's spine. "Welcome, welcome all of you." He paused, studying the face of each person. Drew looked at those same faces, wondering if they felt the same discomfort that resided in his own bones. "Most of you know me already, but for the new ones, I am Connor Holloway. This is my home where, I gather, you are hoping to stay given your current circumstances. We have resources here that, as you know, your town is sorely lacking. And though I realize my property resides, technically, within your boundaries, I am by no means mistaken when I say, your town. You all made it perfectly clear that we were not welcome ten years ago." He looked at Poe before he continued. "You were right about one thing though. We didn't belong there. No planning for tomorrow where you all came from. Lucky for you that ignorance is something that my family and I do not have in common with you." He gestured toward them. "I recognize most of you, but I'll still include introductions because, if the past is any indicator, you thought us unimportant enough that you would forget about us as soon as we disappeared." A cryptic smile appeared again. "Today…you will remember us forever."

He paused for a moment, studying the faces around him once again. Drew realized that their whole group had, in fact, been living in town back when Connor and his family disappeared. Some were barely around back then, like Blake who was in school, and Cassius, who commuted to work at a precinct a few towns over. But Drew could tell that made no difference to Connor. All were guilty, and all would potentially pay the price.

"This is my wife Kate, daughters Poe and Harper, and my son Gabriel." His family each waved awkwardly, and though Kate's smile seemed kind, it didn't extinguish the uneasy feeling in Drew's heart. "Now that you've met my family, it's time for us to meet yours. Please form into family groups."

Everyone in Drew's group looked at each other. Vera whispered in his ear. "Why does he want to divide us?"

He wished he could extinguish the concern in his wife's

eyes, but he knew Vera: nothing but the truth would do. So, like so many times before, he elected to avoid the question. "Just do what he says for right now."

Vera nodded and stood arm and arm with Drew. She was rigid, and Drew tried to hold her tighter for reassurance, but he was unsure if it was for her sake or his own. As Blake and her son stood on the other side, Connor's voice rang through the crowd. "Oh no dear, you and your son stand alone."

"They're our family," Drew said. "They're with us."

Connor grinned. "Drew Matthews, do you really think I've forgotten everything about you? I definitely haven't been gone long enough for you to have a child as old as this beautiful girl here. You two never did have children... such as shame." Drew's face flushed, knowing that Connor drew pleasure from something that caused both he and Vera a deep, unending pain. He walked toward Blake. Standing barely a foot in front of her, he brushed her cheek. "You're John Turner's daughter, dear, not his. I remember many of you quite clearly." He turned to Drew. "I can appreciate the sentimentality and all, but for our purposes today, we will be divided by blood and blood only."

"No." Drew stepped between him and Blake.

Connor inhaled to speak, but Blake pushed between them. She looked Drew in the eyes. "It's okay, really. We'll stand over there." She took Jackson's hand and separated into her own unit, standing between the Matthews and the Melone brothers. Drew tried to ignore the visible shaking in Blake's limbs.

"See now, that wasn't so hard. Your dear friend's daughter

is apparently much more cooperative than you ever were. A much better listener too." Connor sauntered into the middle of the clusters of people, who had inadvertently formed a circle. He folded his hands behind his back casually, far too casually for the announcement he was about to make. "Now, I'm sure you all realize we only have limited resources here. As much as we would love to adopt you all, we simply can't. It's just not feasible...basic mathematics and such." He paused, letting his words sink in.

Drew and Vera looked at each other.

"So sorry."

Drew watched as Connor silently stared at each face in the crowd once again, taking the time to watch the realization seep into all their minds that not everyone was going to get to stay, and those who didn't were going to be sent back out into a diseased world, probably facing certain death. Anger bubbled inside him when he realized that Connor was enjoying it: the fear, the panic. Each trembling hand made him stand just a little bit taller.

It made Drew sick.

"It's true," Kate said. "Taking you all...condemns everyone. We just can't support a group this large. Our food supplies would dwindle down to nothing before we could grow more." Her eyes were wet. "Truly, we're so sorry. But our children have to come first...we're sorry." Though she said we, it was obvious to Drew that her husband did not share her pain in his heart over what had to be done.

"How will we ever decide though?" Connor's head whipped around, as if he honestly expected someone to answer his disgusting question. "Anyone?"

Kate spoke again, her expression hardening as she watched her husband. "Connor, stop this." She turned to the crowd again, pleading for the understanding that she had to know would never come. "We're only doing what we must to survive. No more, no less."

Drew shuddered. If even his wife could see he was enjoying what he was putting them through, there's no telling what they were in for once they got inside the house: if they were even chosen. His heart raced, and there was a strange tingling in his fingertips.

"All right, all right. I already know the way," Connor said.

Drew glanced over at Poe. She was watching her father, a smile of pride stretched across her face. It appeared she had inherited his sadistic side as well as his propensity for survival. He turned his gaze to Connor's other children. Harper's expression was vacant, impossible to read whether she didn't understand the horror that she was witnessing or just didn't care. Gabriel, however, seemed to be looking past all of them and into the woods at their backs, unable to look anyone in the eye. The pride in Poe's eyes was completely absent in those of his son. Drew remembered them when they were young, the little ones who used to love picking out stickers from the prize bin at his office. Those innocent faces had long since gone.

"Everyone here contributes to the household: my son's the mechanic, my wife and daughter hunt, and Poe and I grow our food, among other things." His eyes fell on Drew's.

"How will you all contribute? I want each group to tell me why they should be let in. Of course we won't separate families, but be sure to tell us why yours would be an asset. All come in, or all don't." He paused, smiling. "This is where you get points for being useful human beings."

He started at the opposite end of the group from where Drew was, which happened to be Tonya and George. Though George stood in front of his wife, he seemed to be cowering under the weight of Connor's stare. His eyes stayed level with the ground as he spoke. "I'm a pharmacist. I brought lots of medicine with us. Everything I could find." Tonya handed him the bag that he had shown Drew earlier. He threw it open and thrust it toward Connor. It crossed Drew's mind that he may just snatch the bag and kick them out immediately, but that didn't seem to be Connor's style. He wanted to drag out the decision, make people squirm for as long as he could. "Right here. Lots of it." Connor stepped toward him and started digging through the bag, picking up one bottle at a time, examining the names as if he knew what each of them meant.

Perhaps he did.

"Interesting…go on."

George stuttered and gestured toward his wife, who remained behind him. "She's an architect. She can build anything. Could help you fortify your place against intruders. And I know my medicine. I can help take care of everybody. I know what you can mix with what." Tonya attempted to nod pleasantly, but her chin trembled.

Connor looked him over from head to toe, forcing him to meet his eyes. "Very good."

78

He started to walk away, when George burst out, "Do we get to stay?"

His head whipped back toward George. "We will see."

The next groups that Connor approached stuttered their way through their sales pitches. Drew hated to think of it that way, but that was exactly what it was: they were selling themselves to the man with the power, trying to prove that their lives were worth saving more than those of their peers. Connor was attempting to do God's job, and trying to do God's work always ended badly for the person trying to do it. Unfortunately, it usually ended badly for other people too.

The firefighter seemed to sell himself very well, citing his years in the field, and mentioning some of his hardest won battles. Drew couldn't see any reason why Connor wouldn't pick him to stay, thinking that a firefighter would be perhaps one of the most useful people to have around in a post-apocalyptic situation. They couldn't exactly call 911 if something happened, and Drew guessed Connor, despite his skills, would be no match for a flame-covered building. To handle a situation like that required years of experience, something that Connor couldn't pick up by reading a book.

Though the firefighter did well, the salesman seemed to become a quivering mess of the person he was before they arrived. His voice shook; even his wife looked horrified as she listened, knowing that her husband may be signing their death warrant with his stuttering mouth and quaking stance. Drew almost stepped in to try and save him. Except when he opened his mouth, he looked at Vera and Blake, and found himself closing it again.

When Connor got to the Melone brothers, they unzipped their duffel bags full of weapons: knives of every size and shape, guns found in every decade from the 1920s and beyond. Some looked as though they belonged in a mob movie, others on alien space ships. He took one out and examined it, twirling it around in his hands. "You know how to use these?" Both brothers nodded. "Harper, come here." The girl who had fired at them from the safety of the trees sauntered toward her father, confidence dripping off of her like too much perfume. He handed her the gun. "What do you think?"

She conducted her own examination, ending with her pointing it directly at the older Melone brother's head. Drew watched as Darius tried to appear unshaken, though Drew knew it had to be impossible for him to be as calm as he appeared. She squinted with one eye as she gazed down the barrel, as if she was about to fire. Darius's eyes grew wide, but she handed it back to her father. "Looks good, Dad."

"Do you have ammo with these?" Connor asked.

The brothers nodded.

"Excellent."

Next came Blake and Jackson. Drew's mouth went dry as Connor knelt down to face Jackson at eye-level. "What's your name?"

The little boy smiled, having no idea what was at stake, and how drastically their lives could change in the next few minutes. Drew was glad he didn't understand. Even before the pandemic, Blake had done an excellent job of keeping Jackson innocent in a society that seemed all-too-eager to take childhood away and replace it with ugly acts and uglier people. Every time he saw Jackson playing with his trucks and building castles in his sandbox, hope filled his heart that maybe, just maybe, he would make it until he was at least a double-digit age before he became tainted by the world. As he looked at Connor's face, he saw that dream float away with the breeze. "Jackson. I'm four." He held out four fingers.

Connor smiled back. "Impressive! You're practically a man now."

Drew watched as Blake gently pushed Jackson behind her and away from Connor. Connor noticed and quickly rose to stare in Blake's eyes, a sneer across his face. "And what can you contribute?"

"I—"

"She's an EMT! She can help me." Drew quickly interrupted her. He could feel Vera staring at him, but refused to meet her eyes. Blake's degree in cosmetology would have eliminated her from getting to go inside the compound in an instant. For a moment, Connor continued to stare at her, studying her. Drew held his breath. He looked around at the other groups. Only a couple people knew that he was lying, and he prayed that they would keep their mouths shut.

They did. Drew couldn't help but wonder if it was because their hearts were truly that big, or if the rest of them still didn't understand that they were fighting for their place inside the house. Perhaps it hadn't hit them yet that if Blake made it in, someone else didn't. Or maybe it meant that even in a survival situation, people could hold on to their humanity enough to do whatever they could to make sure a child lived, even if it meant possibly giving up on themselves.

The seconds stretched long, but finally Connor came over to Drew and Vera, the last candidates. He came so close that Drew could feel his breath on his face. "I know what you are. Great to see you again, especially under these circumstances." Connor briefly broke eye contact. "Word is you still call yourself a doctor. Even after…" He turned to Vera. "And what are you?"

"Psychiatrist," she whispered.

A maniacal laugh burst from Connor's mouth. "Of course you are! He screws people up physically while you play around in their heads." He looked back at Drew, his lips pursed as he hissed through clenched teeth. The calm façade had slipped away and the maniac had stepped into its place. "I should eliminate you right now. You're a miserable excuse for a man."

Panic swept through Drew in a wave. If Connor's grudge against him got his family killed he would never forgive himself. He had to stay strong, and act quickly. His eyes hardened; he was sure Connor could see fear, and Drew was not about to give him the satisfaction. He pushed it down deep inside himself, so all Connor could see was a man who knew his abilities, and who knew that the compound needed him as much as he needed the compound. "Tell me, do you know what to do if someone has a seizure out here?" Connor stood silently. "I do. What if one of your daughters gets a high fever? Don't tell me you just plan on setting a cold washcloth on her forehead and hoping it goes away." He stepped forward, forcing Connor to back up. "I may be a joke to you, but I'm going to be the one to save someone's life up here, not you. All your guns and fences and carrots won't help you if you stop breathing."

To Drew's surprise, Connor started clapping. His face changed from a crazy person to a child who had just opened a birthday present. "Well done! Sold! I tell you, sir, I'm impressed. You had me convinced that your cowardice knew no bounds, but some fighting spirit has appeared before my eyes!" As sudden as Connor's outburst was, he grew silent just as quickly. He crept toward him and whispered, "Sold." As he backed up toward the center of the circle, he repeated himself so the rest of the group could hear. "Sold! Please stand over there next to Poe." Drew quickly took Vera's hand and pulled her toward the spot that Connor directed them toward. As they approached, Poe glared at them. He blocked Vera's view so that she couldn't see. Drew had always wondered if Connor had shared what had happened between them to his children. Apparently he had his answer.

"All right all, I've come to a decision. Are you ready?"

Drew watched as Kate draped her arms around Harper and Gabriel, like she also had something to lose. As he watched her husband basking in the misery of others, soaking up the agony in their faces, he wondered if maybe she did.

"Melone brothers, take your weapons and go join the good doctor. Only a couple more spots. Hmmm…"

He looked around, dragging out his decision as long as

possible, even though Drew had a suspicion that he had known from the second he saw them who he would pick and who he wouldn't. "George and Tonya, go join them. So sorry for the rest of you. Be safe now."

Blake's face went white as she looked at Drew, both realizing at the same time that her name was not called. Drew looked away from her for a second to see Kate with her hands over her mouth. He hoped she would speak, but the shock of her husband's decision seemed to have overtaken her. "No, please! My son! You can't do this!"

Connor feigned a pained expression. His eyes were empty. "Sorry sweetheart, there's no room. Now please get going."

Drew ran toward him. "I need her! I need help! I can't keep your family safe by myself." Connor rolled his eyes and started back inside. Drew grabbed him and turned him around. "Please! She needs to stay! What about her child?"

"She didn't make the cut. All or nothing. Sorry."

The rest of those who didn't get picked lingered at the edges of the entry, hoping that Connor would change his mind. The fireman seemed to be looking for the right words, the ones that would save his life after his sales pitch had failed him, while the salesman stood there sobbing so hard he seemed barely able to catch his breath, leaning into his wife to keep from collapsing toward the ground. As Connor drew a gun from the back of his jeans, Drew started toward him, Vera close behind. He blocked her from a potential bullet as he stood in front of Connor. "You are now all officially trespassing! Get out of here before I shoot you where you stand." He watched as everyone who was not picked frantically hurried down the hill, dragging the packs filled with all they had from their homes close behind.

Keeping his wife behind him, Drew demanded, "Take Blake and Jackson instead of me. Let them take my place."

Connor laughed, louder than the buzz of the frantic crowd before him. "Suddenly concerned about a child, Drew? How odd…"

Vera frantically grabbed Drew's arm, gripping it with all her strength. "No! Please no!"

Blake was close behind her, trying desperately to keep her voice steady and calm, but failing. Jackson cried at her feet. "No let him stay please. Just take my son. Just him. Let him stay with Vera and Drew."

Jackson wrapped his arms around his mother's leg. "No mommy! I want to stay with you! Please don't leave me here! I want to stay with you!"

Kate finally came back into herself and approached her husband. "Connor, really, let the child and his mother stay. You can't send him out there. Please, he won't make it. She's a waif of a girl; neither will require much food at all. It will be fine if they stay." There was a desperation in her voice, the kind that Drew hoped would convince a husband who loved his wife to do the right thing. But from the smirk on Connor's face, he knew he was too far gone.

"Did our children matter to them? Any of them?" He gestured to the entire group, both the condemned and the saved. "All of them knew what happened. People talk. Yet they all stood by and did nothing. No one helped us make things right. No one. Those who stand by and do nothing are just as guilty as the ones who hurt them, the ones who beat them down over and over again until there was nothing left. Now I'm supposed to care about their children?"

Kate stood silently. It appeared she knew she had lost, or maybe, just maybe, a part of her thought Connor was right after all. Regardless, she didn't utter another word.

For some reason that Drew didn't understand, Poe had left her place in line and was heading toward her father too, joining the swarm of people pleading their case. She kept looking over at Blake. "Dad please—"

Collecting himself, he cut her off, continuing his conversation with Drew. "Sorry, Doc, you did too good of a job convincing me that we need you. You stay."

Drew felt sick, but he knew what he had to do. He would hate himself forever, but he knew. For Blake to stay, someone else had to go. He felt his own soul slipping away, but, unlike what Connor claimed everyone had done to his family, he would not stand by and do nothing. Connor had whittled people's lives down to basic math: more people than spots at the house. And if he couldn't volunteer himself to go, he had to make sure it was someone else. He used the only piece of information he had to make up the perfect lie, a lie that he knew would potentially make him a murderer. He knew you don't always have to fire a gun to kill another human being: sometimes your words are enough. "George has a drug problem. That's why he has all those. He had been keeping a stockpile long before the pandemic hit. You can't afford to have someone like that here." George was almost inside when Gabriel grabbed him and dragged him toward his father. He pushed him forward, standing between George and the safety of the house.

His face went white, along with Tonya's, who had been grabbed on one side by Kate and the other Harper. The women dragged her outside and held her next to her husband. "He's lying! I swear! He's just trying to save the girl! He's lying! I swiped those from the pharmacy yes, but it's my pharmacy! I was trying to protect my family. Please! You need me." He flailed in Gabriel's grasp. "She's not an EMT! He is lying about all of it!"

Tonya sobbed, staring at her husband. "She can't contribute anything! He's lying! My husband hasn't ever touched drugs in his whole life."

Connor stared into Drew's eyes. Drew knew if he let on at all, Blake and Jackson would both die, out in the forest alone. "You telling the truth?"

He kept his face steady. "Yes."

Tonya glared at Drew, eyes filled with rage. "You're killing us, you bastard!" Kate and Harper continued to hold her as she struggled. "No! You can't do this!"

Connor nodded at his son, who seemed to know exactly what that meant. Drew had won. Gabriel grabbed George and Tonya's stuff and threw it toward them. His face was sullen, and there wasn't an ounce of hope within it. "I'm so sorry, but you have to leave. Go now while you still can. Please…he will shoot you."

During the commotion, Drew grabbed Blake while Vera quickly picked up Jackson and carried him inside. He felt

Poe behind him, and he couldn't figure out why she seemed to be helping them make it in the house before Connor changed his mind, ushering them in quickly and quietly. He heard her whisper to Blake: "Keep your head down, and he won't regret this."

George's voice rang in Drew's ears as he and his wife were escorted away from the house, back towards the poisonous world that they were trying so hard to get away from. He hoped they would meet up with the rest of the people who didn't make it, and somehow they would find a way to survive. But after what he'd seen at the hospital, he knew the idea was one made of delusion and waking dreams. The shrill, panicked tone was something that would haunt his darkest thoughts for the rest of his life. He put his arm around Blake and whispered, "Don't say a word."

"But they—"

"Think of Jackson. Do this for him. I'll teach you the rest."

With tears in her eyes, she nodded, and Drew pushed down the hate for himself that he felt, knowing that he had just made his best friend's daughter a murderer right alongside him.

CHAPTER SIX

POE (before)

Harper told Poe years later that she could almost feel the pale, freckle-faced little boy's cheek swell up before she hit him. The contact seemed to happen prematurely, like when someone lets a precious set of words slip out that they immediately regret. Poe knew it was impossible, but she couldn't help imagining the feeling of flesh parting from itself, stretching out into the air like a balloon being filled with water, sinking under the weight of it.

Their father had always told them to stick up for themselves, and they would deal with the consequences. He would say, "As long as you can sleep at night, you did the right thing." Harper had always slept more soundly than any of them, her fearlessness echoing in the thud of her fist and the snap of her voice.

Their mother rushed into the principal's office with a slick sheen of sweat on her forehead. Poe remembered how her face glistened, like only her cheeks had just been caught in a rainstorm, while the rest of her remained dry and pristine. "What happened?" her mother asked. She was used to Kate dispensing with pleasantries, but not that day. There was no time for "please" and "thank you" when your daughter's schooling is called into question. If Harper's education was put in jeopardy, her mother would certainly have something to say about it.

"I'm sorry to tell you this Mrs. Holloway, but Harper punched one of her classmates. His parents are very upset. They demanded to talk to you themselves, but I told them I would handle it." Like an F.B.I. interrogator, he tried to make it seem as though he was their friend, and not the person who was about to inflict punishment. Maybe that made him think his audience would dislike him less, when in actuality, it made them loathe him even more. To Poe, sugary words never made up for a cool, stiff heart, though it seemed to her in their time people liked to think so. She guessed she got that from her father. Sometimes she wished she could accept people as they were just a little bit more: just a sprinkle of it would go a long way to cure the darker stuff that pricked its way into her brain every now and again. But in that particular situation, she was glad that he had taught her to see through clouds of false friendship and fancy comments.

"What happened?" her mother asked again.

The principle seemed confused by the question. Perhaps most parents took their children's punishment as something that was not up for discussion: authority had spoken and it was their job to smile and nod. "As I said, Harper punched a boy on the playground. His eye swelled shut. It's all black and blue and looks just awful. Awful. We are going to have to suspend her." He glanced over at a picture of a woman and a young boy that was sitting in a black wooden frame on his shelf. She looked like the kind of woman who would marry a man before she figured out she had other options. She had a smile on her face, but it looked as if it was plastered there…the kind of smile you give when you are supposed to look happy but really there's a hollowness deep in your gut. The child had a completely different sort of grin. He had the kind that was blissfully unaware of the fights between his mother and father at night, the kind that, if a house didn't have thick, sound-deadening walls, would send a child to his fair share of therapists as he aged.

Poe would never forget the look on her mother's face, or what she said next. Her response made her love her even more than she already had. Even if there were a tornado coming toward them, Kate would stand tall in front and block its monstrous view. "Why?"

The principle crinkled his nose. "The why doesn't matter. There's never a justification to punch someone, especially at their age. As the adults, we need to instill in them early on that kind of behavior will not be tolerated, and violence is never a way to solve a problem." He leaned back slightly in his chair, as if he thought that would be the end of the conversation. He had obviously never met my mother, Poe thought.

Mom looked him right in the face. "The why always matters, Principle Finch. My daughter has never done anything violent in her life, not even while playing at home with her siblings. I am sure it says in her file that she's never even gotten a warning from any of her teachers. If she went so far as to punch a boy, there had to be a pretty substantial reason."

Finch paused, apparently weighing his next words, probably wondering what he could say that would get them out of his office as quickly as possible. "Apparently there was some sort of argument about your husband, your whole family in fact. The boy was just teasing her. Boys will be boys after all. Things were said and Harper reacted with her fist. You understand we can't have that here. Our students need to feel safe." Poe couldn't remember the last time she felt safe. To her, everyone in her school were just obstacles, dark, unpleasant little things that she would have to overcome until she could leave for whatever came next.

Kate's face hardened. "Boys will be boys? We're still hiding harassment behind that supposed excuse? I don't really think it's appropriate to allow children to insult each other either, wouldn't you agree?" Principle Fitch held up his index finger in protest, but her mother continued. "And I'd also assume that when you say the students need to feel safe, that includes my children as well? I'll assume you agree that there is a fine line between teasing and bullying, and making fun of someone's family certainly qualifies as the latter. I'm not sure how allowing that to occur under your watch helps you reach the goal of a safe environment." She looked at Harper. "I doubt my daughter felt very safe when that was happening to her." Finch looked as if he were inhaling to speak then closed his lips abruptly. Sometimes it's best to know when to talk, and also, when not to. From the words that Principle Finch used, Poe guessed silence usually served him better than sound.

Poe looked at Harper and reached for her hand. She squeezed it tight. "Harper was standing up for me. Joey called me a bi... the "b" word that we aren't supposed to say. He said our family was a bunch of psychos and when I said he was wrong he told me we probably worshipped the devil and killed hikers that passed by and that's why we lived in the woods all alone." She was always confused as to why, with so much sorrow in the world, someone would assume that there had to be a dark, deadly reason to withdraw from day to day existence. Judging from her experience, the world itself seemed to be a perfectly good reason all on its own.

Kate looked at Principle Finch with widened eyes. "And are you going to punish that kid for talking to my daughter like that?" She had been sitting in the chair at Finch's desk but at that, she stood up and started to pace back and forth with her hands on her hips. She was able to still keep calm, but her smooth veneer was cracking.

"Mrs. Holloway, sit down please." Kate hesitated, but obeyed, keeping her legs crossed and her arms folded. She looked like the poster of perfection: perfectly pressed skirt, and a blouse that looked like it belonged on an old Hollywood star. Poe always felt that she took her features from her father, where Harper took them from her mother. Though she'd never been jealous (she adored her father after all), she always knew that Harper would have an easier go at it—life in general that is. She often wondered if her mother had several suitors before her dad, then realized the answer was obvious. Her bright blue eyes and wavy blonde hair, with doll-like skin answered the question loud and clear. "Look, no offense, but the way your family lives, you can't expect people not to ask questions…to think certain things. If your family isn't willing to be a part of the community, people are going to talk." His tone dripped with condescension, seeping off his tongue like saliva from a dog in heat.

A laugh burst through her mother's lips. "Let me see if I understand you correctly. The community has decided that our family is, how did that kid put it, weird, because we aren't as involved as people think we should be…and people saying terrible things is supposed to make us feel more like part of the group? We're supposed to feel less like keeping to ourselves? Do you see the hypocrisy here?"

Harper and Poe looked at each other. She didn't think they realized at the time how critical the conversation that took place in that thick, yellow-armpit-stained man's tiny office would be in shaping the rest of their lives. Hypocrisy had a way of finding them, and ever since Poe had told people what they were at their birthday party, it's time-worn face seemed to appear wherever they went. And as her mother pointed out, there was nothing like hypocrisy to make you feel less and less like participating in the town's yearly ice cream social, barn dance, or whatever: insert trivial, small town event here.

Finch didn't say anything, just pursed his lips together as he folded his sweaty, pudgy hands on top of his desk which looked like it had been there since the two-hundred-year-old school opened. Poe imagined several men like him sitting there before him, all-too-willing to drop bombs on children and their futures.

Finally, after what seemed like a good few minutes, he spoke. "Three-day suspension. That's the policy." How completely unsurprising it was for him to hide behind "policy." Wars had been fought, unjust laws had been followed…innocent people ended up dead from all the way back to the Bible years all in the name of policy.

Her mother came over and grabbed Harper and Poe each by the hand, then said in the most graceful tone, "Sure. Suspend her for three days. Do what you have to do. But you know what we are going to do when we get home? We are going to have some ice cream. Whatever kind Harper wants. By our psycho selves. And we aren't going to kill any hikers on the way there either." She added a pleasant smile for good measure as they walked out of his office, with smiles on their faces and the pride in their hearts that her father had always told them should be there.

Harper and Poe unclasped their mother's hands and raced toward the car, and for a moment, the Earth was spinning on its proper axis once again. They buckled themselves in, and argued about which CD they should listen to on the way home: Seal for Poe, KidzBop for Harper. Their mother pretended to be cross with them and chose her own selection, but Poe guessed she just used it as a reason to listen to Celine Dion.

On the ride home, Poe had imagined Principle Finch still sitting at his desk, stung to the core from the verbal lashing that her mother gave him. She always admired that about her mother: that she could keep calm while still telling a person what's what, and making sure they knew just how wrong they were. Even when Poe was on the receiving end of such a tone, which she had been only a few times, she still appreciated the hardened certainty of her mother's voice. There was no guessing with her, no wondering if what you did had some gray area with which you hadn't behaved as badly as you may have thought. You knew you had broken a rule, and you were to be punished. And that day, Finch knew just how badly he had behaved, and like a scolded child, he sat in the corner as they marched out of his office, and they were as sure as ever that, despite what others thought, their family was wholly ordinary in the most extraordinary of ways.

When they came home, Poe had expected to run straight to the refrigerator to get some ice cream. She'd been fantasizing about the creamy freshness of mint chocolate chip for the entire drive. Instead, they arrived to see her father sitting on the porch steps with his face in his hands. "Where's Gabriel?" Her mother asked.

"Upstairs." Poe noticed a silent exchange between her mother and her father, the kind where parents communicate the need for privacy in a way they think only adults can understand. As Poe observed, Harper had walked right past them straight over to the fridge and started shuffling through their frozen goods.

"Girls, go upstairs to your rooms. We'll have ice cream

in a little while, okay? And Poe, shut the door on your way."

"But, Mom…" Harper protested from inside the house, having heard her mother through the open door.

"Harper…go."

Her sister sighed, but headed toward the stairs, with Poe following behind. Once she got to the base of the stairs where they were supposed to head to their rooms, Poe hesitated, Harper already four steps ahead of her. "You coming?"

"You go. I'll be up in a minute. I wanna see what they're talking about."

"It's probably something dumb. Come on." Poe stood fast. "Suit yourself." Harper continued upstairs, and Poe waited until she heard her mother sit down before heading back from the direction she came.

At that time, there was a screen door as well as the regular door. When Poe had shut it, she purposely only shut the screen door all the way, leaving the other door gently resting against it. It was just enough to allow her to listen to her parents continue talking. She had never done anything like that before, always one to obey the rules, but something in her father's face was different. So instead of doing as she was told, she crouched down so that the wall and the door would block her parents' view of her, and she listened. Something had darkened, and she couldn't bare another moment not knowing who was responsible.

"Those sonsofbitches. They showed up at the house."

"Who?"

"Child Protective Services. Somebody called and made a

complaint against us." He chuckled darkly. "Actually, according to the woman who showed up, it was more than one. Apparently a group of them banded together and made all their complaints at the same time in some messed up attempt to have more impact. It must have worked because I just had to endure that woman poking around in our home for three hours looking for evidence that we are abusing our children."

It was several moments before her mother spoke. "Did they find anything?"

"Of course not. Why would you even say that?"

"You know what I mean. Of course we don't hurt our kids but who knows what they could use to manufacture a problem that isn't there." For the first time in her life, Poe heard her mother cry. "I'm scared, Connor."

The sound of arms being wrapped around a terrified woman. "It'll be okay, Kate. You know I'd kill every last one of them before I let them take our children away from us." Even as a young child, Poe knew her father meant every word. Though she shook, and forced herself to hold back frightened tears that threatened to come, she knew that no matter what anyone said, the gigantic, spindly, horrifying thing she feared would never come to pass. Her father wouldn't let it.

She never told her brother and sister what she had overheard. When Harper asked, she had replied that she had been right after all. "Just something stupid. Exactly like you said." Though a few weeks later, her parents got a phone call saying that the case had been closed and no further action would be taken, for Poe, and for her parents, the damage was already done. They'd had the audacity to make a woman as kind and loving as her mother worry that she would experience the worst pain imaginable: having her children ripped away from her.

She knew her father well enough to know that there were certain unbendable truths in his world, rules that everyone needed to live by: you are supposed to respect those around you, you should never involve yourself in the lives of others unless invited, and you should never, under any circumstances, hurt the woman he loves. They had broken all three, and her father would never forget it.

And neither would she.

CHAPTER SEVEN

CONNOR

They ran inside like rats fleeing a burning building, only in reverse, as if instead, the outside world was on fire. All of the new people clustered together in the entryway, sticking to the familiarity of one another. Connor noticed that they subconsciously put the women and Jackson in the center of the circle, and was mildly insulted.

I could have killed any one of them a thousand times by now.

But no matter. They would learn what the rules were soon enough. And in a way, he hoped they'd have to learn the consequences of breaking them.

As the new recruits ran in, Kate pulled him aside, away from prying ears. "You weren't really going to send the child out there, right? Please tell me you weren't…"

He *had* thought about it, though he would never admit it to anyone, especially Kate. For Connor, Hammurabi's code of "an eye for an eye" was a principle that time should not have left behind eons ago. If it hadn't been, the people of present day might have been a little more kind to each other: people are more likely to behave well when they know they will receive the same treatment they inflict on someone else. Of course, it would have been terrible for the child: he had done nothing wrong. However, his banishment would resonate with those who witnessed it like nothing else could: show the care to the children of others as you would for your own, or find them lost to you. The ones he had picked had surely heard what Drew had done to him so many years ago, and the lesson would stay with them as they learned to adapt.

And maybe, just maybe, the child's mother would have hardened herself enough to keep her child alive. The necessity to hide him from death could have very well made Blake a little more like Connor, and in those times, there was no better gift that he could have given her. He admitted to himself what he couldn't admit to Kate: he wasn't sure if he had spared the child because he wanted to save him, or because he knew she would never forgive him if he didn't. He hoped, for his own soul, that it was the former. And not because he believed in God: he didn't, or at least he didn't think he did. He didn't want to think of himself that way for his own sake alone: so darkened by experience that the death of a child was something he could deal with if it lead to something else.

But, as he had many times before, he told Kate what she wanted to hear: "Of course not. I just wanted to make that sonofabitch sweat…just for a minute."

He saw Kate let out a sigh. With a small smile she said, "Well let's go inside and welcome them." He felt her hand on her shoulder, and knew that at least for the moment, her delusion of the kind of man he was remained intact.

He *would* welcome them, but perhaps not in the way she had envisioned. He had to establish authority early on, and he knew just how to do it. He had been silent for long enough, standing in the background, staying quiet while the town turned him into something monstrous. Now was his chance to speak, and he couldn't wait to see their frightened faces as they stood there quietly, listening to his voice ring out confidently and triumphantly.

Their supplies were strewn all over the main floor, suitcases having flown open in the chaos, bins with their lids half ajar showing off the canned goods inside. A couple of them had family photos inside, crunched by the rest of the contents, or folded into an almost unrecognizable mass of color. Between the antique furniture and plethora of vases and silver trinkets that Kate loved now lay the only possessions that the strangers had left from their previous lives.

Connor nodded at Poe, Harper, and Gabriel, and they knew instantly to gather the newcomers' supplies and disperse them to their appropriate storage areas. For the canned goods, they opened up a large metal supply cabinet, and arranged the cans in alphabetical order, so that they would know exactly how many of each item that they had in stock. The cabinet was seven feet tall, thick, heavy, and completely immovable. Once they were finished, they locked it tight. It was Connor's wish that even if somehow a group of invaders got into their home, that cabinet would remain impenetrable, and they would have a means to begin again.

Next, the three of them gathered as many guns as they could and headed upstairs, dividing them up amongst their parents' room and their own. He smiled to himself as Harper chose the guns that looked like they belonged in Al Capone's hands to stay with her. Those were always her favorite, and he remembered ordering one for her birthday a few years back. Evidently, her tastes hadn't changed.

Each room had a gun safe that could only be opened by the fingerprint of a family member. Connor would never have let any new people in without that precaution. The only person he knew well was Drew, and as their situation illustrated, knowing someone for years didn't imply they should be trusted.

Once Harper, Poe, and Gabriel returned, still carrying the weapons that wouldn't fit in any of the safes, he announced, "Everyone, I require your attention." His family seemed to know that they were exempt from his statement, and started going through the pockets of the clothing they found in the bins, making sure no one had smuggled in a weapon. After they finished, they did a pat-down search of all their new recruits, including the child. One never knows how far someone will go to take control in a situation where their own survival was at stake, even to the point where they may hide a weapon in the clothing of a four year old. Of course, if someone were to make an attempt on his life, they would be out-skilled and outgunned, but that didn't make a potential stab wound any less lethal. In their situation, an infection could be just as deadly as the pandemic sweeping across the country. Though he hated to admit it, Drew did have the potential to be a valuable asset to their group, perhaps more essential for the future of the compound than even Drew himself realized.

But he didn't need to know that.

"We have several sleeping bags set up in the far living room." He pointed to the room at the back of the kitchen, surrounded by windows with bars on the outside. "You will be situated in a room with a vantage point that covers a large area of the property, and I suggest you use it accordingly, sleeping in shifts. One person at this post needs to be awake at all times, especially now, when people are starting to realize just how, excuse my language, *fucked* they really are. Decide among yourselves how you will schedule your sleep, because if I find out no one is watching, I will decide for you, and you may not like it."

He glanced around the room, waiting for someone to protest. They had the sense not to. Even the doctor, whom he could tell fancied himself the leader of the new people, stood quietly and waited for him to continue his orientation. "The sun is about to go down, so we will assign you your duties tomorrow morning. Each of you will help with one aspect of keeping this place safe and secure, whether it be working on the food supply…" he looked at the doctor. "…or teaching us more advanced medicine." He wondered if the doctor would be clever enough to realize that if he taught one of his family members everything he could, he may wear out his value. He would have to be vigilant of that. Of course he couldn't teach anyone to do major surgery, but in the circumstances they found themselves in, anything too invasive was already out of the question.

"As you will learn, one of our cardinal rules is that no one leaves the house after dark except in very special circumstances, as decided by myself or, if I am occupied, the decision rests with my wife until I am available." Kate shyly raised her hand and gave a slight smile. Connor loved that about her: the lack of wanting to be the center of attention despite how much she deserved it. To him, she deserved to be gazed at, admired for the beauty that he knew she was even if she herself did not.

Again, no one argued, just stayed huddled together like the scared little children that they were. "As for some of the other house rules: all of you will perform the duties assigned to you, without question or protest. If you knew what you were doing, you wouldn't be here. Remember that. Second, no one goes in mine and Kate's room under any circumstances. Third…" he laughed, "and third is my favorite…if you are all thinking you might just come into our home, organize and kick us out of the place we worked so hard to build, I beg you to reconsider." He walked over to Cassius. "You are a police officer, correct?"

Cassius nodded. "Ten years next month."

"Ah," Connor laughed, causing an expression of barely-contained rage to spread across Cassius's face. "So, it would be safe to assume that you are the most skilled fighter of this new gaggle of recruits we have here, correct?"

"Absolutely."

Slowly, methodically, Connor removed the handgun that he had in his holster, watching as the rest of them stiffened in fear. "I want you to take this gun from me. Go on…if you can, the compound is yours. No protest, I promise." He grinned.

Cassius, overconfident little egomaniac that he was, hesitated at first, probably wondering what the catch was. Connor smiled, knowing full well that there didn't need to be a catch. "Come on now. Take it."

Connor breathed slowly and easily as Cassius, someone probably fifteen years his junior, lunged forward at him, hands reaching toward his weapon. Within seconds, Connor had knocked him toward the ground. "Again," he said.

Cassius got up, muscles tightening. Connor guessed that Cassius did not want to let the opportunity to get violent with him pass him by. Instead of lunging forward, this time, he wound up for a right hook. Connor had his gun back in his holster, and Cassius's arm bent backward against his chest before it was anywhere near Connor's face. "That's enough. Thank you for helping me demonstrate." He nodded to Darius who stepped forward and gently guided Cassius back toward the rest of the group. "As you can see, in preparation for the end of days, I have prepared my body as well as our home to stand up against adversaries. So have the rest of us." Poe and Harper grinned, both fixing their gaze on Cassius. "If I can beat your best, it would probably be in your best interest to behave yourselves."

He turned to his children and pointed to the extra weapons, which they had put back in the duffel bags. "Take these to where we keep the backup weaponry." They nodded, threw the bags over their shoulders and disappeared around the back of the stairs. Connor stood in the sightline of his new arrivals. "Maybe someday I will tell you where they are headed. But today is not that day." He watched them looking at each other. When Harper, Poe, and Gabriel returned, he said, "Family?" Kate and their children fell in line at Connor's side. He handed Gabriel two bags. "Gabriel, go down to the cars that our guests left behind. Poe can tell you where they are. Get there quickly before the ones who didn't make it in go back for their stuff. Make sure there's nothing there that they could use against us later." He watched as his son's face hardened. Before Gabriel could undermine him in front of the group, he took him and Poe outside, leaving Harper and Kate to guard the group. "What is it, Gabriel?"

His son glared at him. "You really don't want them to have any chance at all, do you? Now you want us to take their supplies? Why didn't you just shoot them here? It would have been better than letting them starve to death or suffer from whatever that thing is that's killing people out there."

"Gabriel..." Poe started.

Connor stepped closer to his son. "You just don't get it, do you? Those people know exactly where we are now. We don't need them coming back here." He inched closer still. "Is it that you want someone to hold a knife to your sister's throat? Is that it? These people owe us nothing. And now they have nothing to lose." Gabriel stood silently. Connor turned to Poe. "Show him how to get to the cars, then come back for dinner. I need you in here to help me keep an eye on them." She nodded and started back down the mountain, her brother following closely behind her.

After Gabriel and Poe were out of sight, Connor went back into the house. "I think our guests would love to make us dinner to show how grateful they are for our hospitality." He felt his wife's stare, the one that meant she did not approve. She tried to hide it, but they'd been married for far too long for her to be able to slip it by him. He ignored it, knowing that though she concerned herself far more about what others might think than he did, he relished in their obedience enough for the both of them.

"I'll help them, Connor. Why don't you go read one of your books? They don't know where anything is in the kitchen yet." He considered arguing with her, but relented. She was, after all, right, and he did want to have dinner sooner rather than later. He felt the other women staring at him, as if gauging his relationship with his wife by that one conversation. Let her have her fun, he thought. They may have thought they had an ally in Kate, but he knew she was forever devoted to him and him alone. She was merely being polite, a habit she couldn't seem to break no matter how much he told her there was no need for manners when you had the upper hand.

"Sounds lovely, Kate. You can help them familiarize themselves with the layout of the house and where the supplies are located." He walked over to the living room where all the sleeping bags were. The room had been completely cleared out of furniture, except for a large wooden trunk. He threw the lid open to reveal several books, and grabbed one of the ones off the top. He'd read it at least ten times, but the book itself wasn't the point.

He carried the book over to a chair that sat at a small desk in the kitchen. "Wouldn't you rather read upstairs? It will be very noisy while we cook." Kate said. A part of him suggested that she was trying to get rid of him, but he ignored it and shoved it away.

"I think I'll read right here. Thank you. Always better light down here." He smiled pleasantly as he sat down, pointing himself away from the kitchen area and resting his hands on the desk as he propped open the book. He didn't need to see their new arrivals; he just needed to hear them. He needed to be silent, because if he was, perhaps a part of them would forget he was there, and he would learn something about the new people under his roof, things that people reveal when they forget someone's watching.

The rustling of pots and pans being moved. "Vera, right? I'm Kate." *The slip of skin in a handshake.* "Yes, very nice to meet you." *The sound of pleasantries hidden by a nervous voice, the kind of voice that says 'in another life, we would have been in a parent-child playgroup together, or maybe a book club that used reading as an excuse to spend a summer afternoon drinking chardonnay in the sun. But this is not that life.'* "I'm happy to meet you too. We wondered if we would be the only survivors. I'm glad to know that there is life beyond our walls." *A laugh. Then awkward seriousness.* "Maybe not. Not anymore."

With Kate's assistance, the new group put together quite a feast: an hour after they started, they were all in various

109

places around the downstairs with a steaming hot bowl of venison stew, with a triangle of homemade bread wedged onto the edge of it. Gabriel returned just as dinner was served, and told him that the remainder of their supplies were locked safely in one of the many caches they had buried outside the property.

"Good thinking. We need more in those now that there's more people," Connor told him, more so that Kate would see him praising his son than for Gabriel himself. Connor remained in his chair, but he had set the book gently on the corner of the desk, and turned around to face his family and the strangers. He watched them all, paying attention to which people gravitated toward one another. Mostly, it was family with family, but a couple groups co-mingled. The youngest Melone brother sat close to Blake and her son, all three sitting cross-legged on the floor between the sleeping bags. Their interactions didn't seem to have a romantic element, so Connor could only assume he was being protective. Forever a cop, he thought. He watched as Blake's serious expression temporarily cracked, and both of them smiled at each other as they shoved the food provided by Connor and his family into their mouths. *So ungrateful...acting like they had the audacity to expect to be here*, he thought. He was the one who let them into his home when he didn't have to. They should be thanking him, but not one person had.

Not one.

He wondered why he would have expected anything different. They came from the same group of people that he had repeatedly asked for help (or even just the benefit of the doubt) ten years ago and who had all denied him. Instead, they turned little bits of words and phrases into something ugly, and made him out to be the devil. Perhaps it was *they* who were the devil. If letting a whole family be destroyed through pettiness and judgement wasn't classified as evil, he wasn't sure what would be. They had convicted him with hearsay and nonsense, assaulted his children with words and violence, and no one had stopped it.

And now several of them had already paid the price.

Connor had trouble keeping their names straight: Cassius and Darius. He thought it ridiculous to be so uncreative when naming one's children. Their names sounded like near copies of each other, so much so that they even rhymed, and he wondered if they equated their own identities similarly. His own children were born of the classics, with names that would make them stand out in amongst the rest of the world throughout time: Harper Lee, Gabriel Garcia Marques, and of course, the godfather of all things twisted, Edgar Allen Poe. Their names would help them stay strong when others were weak, and that would get them through whatever was coming next. He shouted to the brothers, and the crowd grew quiet. "Cassius, Darius, tell me, why did your parents name you such similar names? I can barely tell them apart. They are so alike that they seem to negate any importance that they would carry on their own."

Darius opened his mouth to answer, but Cassius cut him off. "Now, I have to tell you how wrong you are." A sly grin slid across Cassius' face. His brother looked at him, begging him with his eyes not to rock the boat that they barely just boarded. Connor wouldn't have been surprised if that particular expression hadn't crossed Darius' face hundreds of times before that night.

"Darius, his namesake comes from a Persian King." Slowly, Cassius rose to his feet and glided toward Connor. Connor mirrored him, leaving his book behind him on the desk as Cassius left his empty bowl sitting by Blake. As Cassius grew closer, his voice became quieter, though the room was small enough that everyone could still here. "Then there's mine: Cassius. I'm sure it carries meaning, of what I don't know, but it's stayed alive with the help of a very famous man, a man whose memory has stayed alive for thousands of years because of a single act. Of course you remember where that name comes from." The men stared at each other. "No?" He forced a fake-humored laugh. "Well, Cassius was one of the main conspirators that killed Julius Caesar. See, he knew that power can make a man turn into something evil… make him do things that most men wouldn't have the stomach for. So when the opportunity came…he snuffed him out."

Gabriel and Poe inched closer to Cassius, ready to restrain him if need be, but with a flick of his hand, Connor waved them off. He grinned, basking in the opportunity to expose the man who thought himself a lion as the lamb he actually was. "Oh don't mistake, Cassius, I am very familiar with my Roman history, as it sounds like you are. That must mean that you remember what happened to the conspirators that killed Caesar." He paused for a moment to look around at the faces staring at them, and saw that, as he wanted, he'd gained their full attention. All were frozen, and for a moment it seemed as though oxygen itself had fled their home, afraid of what the outcome of the conversation between the two men would be. "When the people found out what the conspirators had done, they were angry, and drove them from the city. Cassius and those who followed him died far away from the home that they loved in disgrace, away from the family and friends and the neighbors they thought they were protecting." His voice grew louder.

"You see, the people *wanted* Caesar to be in power. They wanted to be led by a man who was smarter than they were. They knew that Caesar was what they needed to prosper." He took another glance around the room. They were all still fixated on him, and he basked in it, turning his attention back to Cassius. "So the lesson we can learn here, is that history tells us, if someone is thinking of leading a revolt, then he must make sure the people he is liberating want to be freed…otherwise, he will just end up alone and dead, left to rot among the rest of nature's creatures that made very poor decisions."

Connor broke his stare with Cassius, leaving him standing in the middle of the living room alone. "Now, everyone pick a sleeping bag. We are going to have a lot of work to do in the morning." He ascended the stairs, and listened as his wife said goodnight to their guests. And that was exactly what they were: guests. He had to admit, he was impressed by Cassius' bravery. Yes, there was cockiness about him, but he saw a bit of himself in the man's certainty, his hardened stare. But there was only one thing to do with a guest who wears out his welcome. And if the time came, he was prepared to do just that.

***

5:30 a.m. came quickly. In a way, Connor was surprised how soundly he slept. But, he realized he shouldn't have been: seeing Karma fix what human nature had broken as he sat by and watched had given him the miraculous ability to sleep more soundly than he ever had.

He marched downstairs, followed by each member of his family in a single-file line: orderly, just how he liked it. "Up, up! Everyone up! It's time to get you acquainted with your new home!"

He heard moaning from the nest of sleeping bags in the living room. "We just got to sleep," one said. "Please let us be," said another.

"Well I guess your bodies will just have to adjust." Slowly, all of them began to rise, stretching and bending their way into alertness.

Once they were all up and dressed, Connor had them line up outside. He was slightly irritated that the men still stood ever so slightly in front of the women, as if they expected to be harmed, but as he remembered the faces of those he had sent away, he smirked to himself. He had all their well-beings held tightly in his grasp, and the power that they had taken from him, he now held with a steady, strong hand. "We are going to begin our tour in the barn. Follow me."

As they walked to the barn, Connor smiled to himself. How fitting, he thought. *All these people, people who thought we were crazy, are now following behind me; as they should. Ironically, coming here was probably the smartest thing they've ever done.* He smiled at Kate, who was walking next to him. "Wait until they see this," he whispered. "After this, they will understand the depths of their helplessness more than they ever have." He reached for her hand, but she stuck it in the pocket of her skirt. He blamed it on the cool morning air, and kept walking.

Poe and Harper slid open the doors of their barn, presenting their doomsday oasis to the rest of the group. Connor pointed to the left side: "Here, you will see we have pens of livestock: chickens, goats, and cows. There is a fenced field on the other side of this barn. There is a door where each type of animal can pass through to get to the field during the day, and they come back in here at night to sleep or to stay out of the sun. They provide us milk and eggs, and, in a pinch, protein." They stepped slowly through the barn, and Connor watched as they all studied the place that would give them the food they would normally find wrapped neatly in plastic at the super market. He wondered if anyone would have trouble eating an animal now that they had to look them in the face first. Most likely, they would avoid eating their livestock, but Connor knew from experience that some people had just as much trouble looking into the eyes of a deer or a rabbit as they pulled the trigger. Human guilt didn't discriminate between livestock and wildlife.

He pointed to the right side of the barn, where there were hundreds of plants and giant tubs of water with live fish swimming about. Some were rather large, while some were barely two inches long. "Here we have our aquaponics garden. The fish provide nutrients for the plants, and of course, give us protein and vital sustenance. If any of you paid attention to any of your fancy health magazines, you would know that your omega-3s are very important if you want to stay healthy. As none of you ever bothered to figure out, malnutrition can be just as deadly as any disease, and I need you all in peak physical condition. There will be no place for weakness here." Pointing to the plants, he said, "Lettuce, herbs…most plants that you can think of, and some that you've never heard of, are in this garden. They come from all over the world, and they all have a variety of nutritional benefits which we will need since going to the neighborhood drugstore is no longer an option." He laughed. "There are even some here that can kill you. If you're good, maybe I'll tell you which ones."

Every face in the group grew cold, and Connor smiled. He felt Kate glare at him, and turned to see her arms folded and a heavy stare aimed right through his eyes, but he pushed on. "Everything in here is put to use, including the waste. That contraption over there was made by my son Gabriel." He gave a proud nod to his son. "There, even the waste products are converted into compost or fertilizer for the outside garden. Nothing is wasted here."

He watched as they all took in their surroundings, when suddenly a buzzing sound interrupted their concentration.

"Perfect timing!" Connor said. He reached into his pocket and pulled out a handheld ham radio. "I want to introduce you to another member of our group: a very important one at that." He pushed a button. "Gordon? You there, buddy?" Gordon was the first person Connor ever felt comfortable enough to call buddy, and probably the last. That comfort probably came from the fact that they never had, and never would, meet face to face.

"Sure am! How's it going over there?" His voice crackled.

"Going well. Have some new people here now...just showing them around. You?"

"Good here too. Nobody new, but me and the Mrs. are doing well. Keep on keepin' on, that's what I say." Gordon's voice grew serious. "I don't think anybody new will be coming around here. Last I heard there isn't anybody new left." He sighed. "Looks like it's going to be just us."

Connor paused. "Hang in there, Gordon. I'll talk to you soon. Over and out."

"Over and out."

He addressed the rest of the group. "Gordon is from Maine, and keeps me informed on what's happening on the East Coast. I do the same for him. That way, even while we're here, we will know what's coming, and what we need to be aware of." He waved it in the air. "Extra safety precaution." Chuckling, he said, "Another precaution is that I am the only one who has this. So if you want to try to do anything stupid like tell people where we are because you find yourself with a case of the bleeding hearts, you're going to have to take it from me.

And you all saw how well the gun situation turned out."

No one seemed to protest.

***

As they left the barn, Connor wondered if any of them appreciated the magnitude of what they had built there, or if they were just happy they knew where their next meal was coming from. He whispered to Kate, "None of them have even paid us a compliment, or said thank you."

"Maybe if you hadn't scared them all half to death last night, they would." Kate had venom in her voice that Connor wasn't used to, and it stung him to the core. But it was gone as soon as it came, brushed back under her normal sweet and careful tone. "I'm sorry sweetheart. I'm sure they will thank you, it just might take some time."

He put his arm around her. If he didn't know better, he'd have thought her shoulders went rigid at his touch. "Thank you, honey. I'm sure you're right."

They headed back to the house, and Connor could almost breathe in the triumph he felt over his enemies, though they would serve whatever purpose he saw fit. Despite letting them inside his home, they would still only be just that, and one day, they would apologize for the pain they caused his family. Of that, he was sure.

CHAPTER EIGHT

POE

Poe awoke in the middle of the night with a throat as dry as burnt toast. She tried to swallow, but it didn't help much, the saliva in her mouth not quenching it as much as tickling it. The moon shone through her window, and the 3:00 a.m. hour seemed almost peaceful, until she rolled over and saw the gun cabinet next to her bed, hovering there as if keeping watch. When her father had first installed it in her room, she used to wake up in the middle of the night and, for a split second, see the black shadow standing there and think that someone had broken in to attack her, or worse. As she awoke, she would realize there was no danger, but not until after she had already broken out into a cold sweat. But as the years passed, she had grown used to it, and it lingered there like an old rocking chair. It reminded her not to let her guard down, that there was a group of strangers asleep downstairs that she had never met before today.

Except for one.

She wondered if the woman she now knew was called Blake recognized her. She hadn't thought so at first, but she realized that in the commotion which had spread like a fog over the afternoon, she couldn't be sure. Had Blake looked at her with knowing eyes? Did it even matter? She wasn't certain, but there was one thing she did know: she desperately needed a glass of water.

Instead of going to the bathroom right across the hall to get it, she opted to go downstairs to the kitchen. She could check in on the new people in the meantime: her father would be proud of her initiative. If they weren't sleeping in shifts like he had told them to, she would need to inform him in the morning. With her soft slippers covering her feet, she made her way into the hall and to the stairwell, careful to not step on the loud spots in the wood. Something as simple as a creak in the floorboards could give her away in an instant. Her father always taught her to know her surroundings, down to every grain in the floor. That would give her an advantage over any intruder: they would not hear her coming until her knife was at their throat and their blood was already spilt.

When she rounded the corner, she saw Darius Melone keeping watch as instructed. Something crept insider her like relief, but she wasn't sure why. She had no obligation to protect anyone but her family. Telling her father if they disobeyed should have been second nature, as natural as breathing. The people sleeping in front of her were only as valuable as their skills and their ability to adapt. If they lost one of those crucial ingredients, they would have to be dealt with, or everything that her family had worked for would be lost. There would have to be consequences, and if her father had his way, they would be swift.

There was no movement in the room, except for Blake, whose sleeping bag was right on the edge of the living room and the kitchen. She was tossing around inside it, flipping her gray, worn pillow from side to side, desperate to find a comfortable position. Her father hadn't bought them new pillows. Poe guessed that was probably part of their punishment.

It was a wonder how she didn't wake up everyone in the room, and after the day they had, it was a wonder anyone in the house slept at all. At first, Poe pretended not to notice, busying herself in the refrigerator even though the water pitcher was toward the front.

She told herself she didn't feel an ounce of pity for any of them. Her family had opened their doors, and would now give them the means to survive in a dying world. But Blake…Blake was different. Blake had saved her that day so many years ago, and her humanity should earn her more comfort than the rest. She had proven herself, and should be rewarded for being better. There had to still be some justice for good behavior in the world, otherwise, there didn't seem to be much point. "Can't sleep?" Poe whispered from behind the fridge.

As she closed the door, Blake answered. The jars and bottles jingled. "Trying to. Not having any luck." She glanced over at Jackson, who lay quiet and still, as if he was asleep in his own bed at what used to be their home. "If he could just bottle up a bit of that and give it to me that would be great." A sigh escaped her. "That kid could sleep through a train running through the house, I swear."

The words escaped Poe's mouth before her brain could catch them and tie them back up again. "Do you want to bring your sleeping bag up to my room? It's probably less noisy up there without so many people breathing hard and snoring. Plus this floor creaks a lot. It can sometimes lurch from a sneeze." Poe looked at Jackson. "He can come too." She heard her father's words in her head, telling her not to trust even the gentlest stranger. He would always remind her that rabbits are gentle too…until they bite. But she reasoned that she wasn't sending Blake away from the group on her own. Poe would be there, so even if she was wrong about her, she'd see it right away. Better to know right away rather than later.

"You sure? I'd really appreciate it."

Poe nodded. "Hand me your sleeping bags, and you can carry him."

As quietly as she could, Blake slid out of hers and carefully rolled it up so it could be carried easily. Darius gave them a quizzical glance then turned back to his post. "Thank you." It occurred to Poe that she liked Darius's quiet nature, and that he would most likely be the least trouble out of all the strangers they had let inside.

As they reached the base of the stairs, Poe warned, "Follow my footsteps exactly, or Dad will catch us."

"But—"

"Trust me, okay? Exactly."

Blake nodded and fell in behind her. Poe hoped Blake didn't notice that she held her breath as they passed by her parents' door.

Once their sleeping bags were laid out, Blake crawled in and stared up at the ceiling. Jackson curled himself up into a ball, and pulled the edge of the bag so far up that Poe could barely see the top of his eyelids. His lashes fluttered against the fabric. "He's adorable. How old?" Her father had asked during the introductions when they had first arrived, but Poe wasn't exactly adept at making casual conversation, and spit out the first question that popped into her head.

"Four. And thanks." There was a mother's smile in her voice.

For a moment, the girls just laid there, staring into the nothingness of the night. Just as Poe thought Blake had fallen asleep, she said, "Those kids who picked on you that day? A few years later they got thrown in juvie for stealing a car and wrecking it. They were drunk I guess. I think they moved away or something after that."

Poe smiled even though Blake couldn't see her. "You do remember." Despite the awful reason they had met, she felt warmth inside herself. It was a special thing to be remembered by someone who had crossed your path for mere minutes.

"Yep. They definitely got what was coming to them. Thought you'd want to know."

Poe leaned over the edge of her bed and looked at Blake. "Thanks. For back then."

"Absolutely. Too many people stand around and do nothing. I never want to be one of those people." She looked at her son. "And I never want him to be either."

The silence between them was now a comfortable one,

like that shared with a long lost friend, the kind that remembers you when you wore braids and drew pictures when you were supposed to be doing homework. And despite only passing through each other's lives for a few brief minutes, maybe that was exactly what they were.

But moments later, Poe's stomach turned. At first, she had wanted to keep the fact that she had known Blake from before a secret, but she then started to wonder if that was the right call. But it had been over twenty-four hours, and she was afraid the time window had passed where she could have told him without him being upset with her. She rolled back over to look at Blake. "Don't tell my dad, okay?"

"Why?"

"I don't know, I just…I think it will bother him. I can't explain it. We'll pretend we just met, okay?"

"Are you frightened of your father?"

Poe's jaw tightened. "No! Of course not. I just think he will wonder why I didn't say anything. Better at this point not to tell him at all."

"But why didn't you say anything to begin with then?"

Poe's voice grew higher. "I don't know. I just don't know, okay?"

Blake sat up and looked at Poe straight in the eyes, concern beaming from her face. "I'm sorry. I'll do whatever you want. It'll be our secret. If you decide he needs to know then you can tell him yourself. He won't hear it from me. I promise."

"Thank you."

Poe didn't mean to be short with her. She knew that

Blake didn't know any better. But that was part of their job as the leaders of this compound: to show them the rules so that they would all survive...even if she wasn't entirely sure what the rules were. Maybe her father would be fine with it. He probably would. Possibly. But for whatever reason, something deep inside told her to keep her friendship with Blake locked deep inside herself, like the gun cabinet next to her bed, only bringing it out when the time was right...if it ever was. Maybe a part of her wanted a secret to keep, or at least the trust that came with it; Blake giving her that responsibility, the weight of it, resonated with her in a way nothing else ever had.

Every moment of her life, she shared with her family: every meal, every quiet afternoon–every breath. She had a friend now, something that her father didn't know about. A feeling erupted in her heart that she didn't recognize: something like rebellion snuffing out a hint of shame.

And it felt wonderful.

Just as she was about to drift off Blake spoke again. "So, since I'm keeping a secret for you, maybe you can keep a secret for me?"

At this request, Poe felt compelled to not only roll over, but throw the blankets off of herself, get out of bed, and sit down beside Blake. She hoped she didn't seem too eager, but no one had ever told her a secret before. Her sister, yes, but family is different. Family has to trust each other, especially when living outside of society. But a friend telling her something no one else knew? That was a different experience altogether, something important that deserved her full attention. "Sure. What is it?"

Poe noticed Blake's eyes had become wet. "You can't tell anyone. Ever. Not your sister, not anyone. Okay?"

"Promise."

Blake took a deep breath. "I'm not an EMT. I cut hair. I'm of no use to anybody. Not here. Not now."

A lump formed in Poe's throat as panic enveloped her. She did not expect the secret to be something that could affect all of them, something that could, God forbid, mean life or death at some point. Keeping a friend's secret was one thing, endangering all their lives was quite another. "Why did you do it?" She asked, already knowing the answer.

"Drew was trying to keep me alive. And I didn't stop him. I watched that man and his wife get shuffled off into the woods to die and I didn't say a word." Tears drifted quietly down her cheeks, making wet pools on her pillow. "I don't know if I can live with that. Drew said to do it for Jackson. And I suppose I let it happen for him and Vera too. I didn't want them to get hurt for covering for me. But I don't know if I can live with it. How am I supposed to be a good example for him after allowing that to happen?" She got up out of her own sleeping bag and turned to face Poe. "I feel like someone has grabbed ahold of my chest and won't let go."

"He was right." The words came out, surprising Poe herself just as much as Blake.

"Are you sure?"

"Yes. You can learn everything you need to. And then it won't be a lie anymore. You just need a little time." As Poe said it, she knew she actually believed part of it in her heart.

She wasn't just trying to ease the mind of a new friend; despite the worry she felt, she truly believed that, as a mother first, Blake had made the right call. Maybe she had more survival instincts than anyone, especially her father, ever imagined.

"How am I supposed to get that? One of you is going to be watching us all the time I'm sure. I really doubt your dad is going to let us wander around unsupervised. They'll see right through me."

Poe let out a breath she didn't realize she was holding. She wasn't sure if she was trying to convince Blake or herself that they could undo what had started without anyone getting hurt. Blake *had* made the right call for herself and her son. But for the rest of the group? That answer would only come with time. As for herself, not telling her father the truth was simply a dressed-up lie, but she had never had a friend before, and she wasn't about to cut their friendship off at the knees before it even started. She hoped the situation could still be mended, and maybe they would be even better off for it; she just needed to figure out how. After a couple months, it would be nothing more than a blessing in disguise; *if* they were careful.

If ever there was a chance to pay Blake back for saving her all those years ago, this was it. "I'll help."

Blake smiled sadly. "Thank you, but how?"

Her reservations hadn't gone away, but an idea was forming in Poe's brain, a flicker of light in a room full of noise. There was a way to save her, but the deception would be deep. "I'll tell my dad tomorrow that I want to learn medicine. I'll explain that I can be the one who watches you and Drew while learning from you both at the same time." She smiled, for Blake as well as for herself. She hoped if she smiled long enough it would dull the pain inside her that came from what she knew she was doing to her father. "Drew can teach me, but he'll be teaching you too. My father will never know, and he'll never feel the need to check because I'll be with you both."

Poe jumped slightly as Blake threw her arms around her. "You'd do that? I don't know how to thank you. I…thank you."

Poe nodded then climbed her way back into bed. "It'll be all right. Get some sleep, okay? Everything will work out tomorrow. My father gets up at five though, so you have to be back downstairs before that." She leaned over and set her alarm clock. "I'll wake you up and get you both back down there before he knows you're gone."

Blake nodded and closed her eyes, and the night seemed a little less dark.

CHAPTER NINE

CONNOR (before)

"Emily," Kate said as Connor walked into the living room. She had the glow that people have when they are daydreaming. She was seated on their soft brown couch with a pale pink skirt on that gently draped over her legs and brushed against the top of her calves. The couch was the one she had insisted they buy at a garage sale on the way back from the grocery store one afternoon many years before. Connor had, of course, whined that they had no idea what had happened on it, or what people had sat on it before they came upon it, to which she replied, "Exactly. You just look at it and know it's got its own set of stories." Connor told her he preferred his stories to be in book form.

They bought the couch.

He sat down beside her and wrapped his arm tightly around her shoulders. She leaned into him, resting her head in the nape of his neck. "Good choice," He told her. "We don't have any poets in our brood yet."

She smiled. "Exactly what I was thinking. Emily Dickinson should feel honored; may she rest in peace."

"We're a pretty special lot." He could feel the pride she had in their other children beaming off of her. Gabriel had already demonstrated a sharp eye for mechanics. Harper's strength was her fearlessness, allowing her to still be a strong actress in their school play despite the constant name-calling from the other children, and even as a child, Poe was already demonstrating the ability to be the writer Kate had always dreamed of being. Connor couldn't tell if he was proud or disappointed that everything good and pure inside of them came from her. "Although you better stop coming up with anymore authors that you like. We're going to have to build a bigger house."

Connor laughed, and she lovingly stroked his cheek with the back of her fingers. "No promises." She released herself from his hold long enough to grab a baby accessories catalogue out of the basket of magazines they had next to the couch. After she grabbed it, she cradled herself right back to where she was—the spot where when they first started dating. They would comment how she always fit there perfectly, and through the years, it seemed to become truer with each passing day. "I know we won't need much new stuff, but it's always fun to look."

They took turns flipping the pages. He noticed that she stayed on a page with a lavender and lace crib for just a couple seconds longer than the others, and made a mental note to order it the second she wasn't looking. He would set it up when she was out, and he would watch her face light up at the surprise. "Our appointment is tomorrow at one o'clock right?" He asked.

Kate lightly slugged him in the leg. "Yes of course. How could you forget?"

He smiled. "I didn't. Just wanted to make sure we weren't late. I hate being late." He kissed her on the forehead and lightly placed his hand on her stomach. "I can't wait to hear it from the doctor's mouth. I mean I know those tests are pretty accurate, but it'll be real once he says it."

"Gosh I don't want to get my hopes up. I mean we had more "no" tests than "yes" tests."

He nodded. "I know, but I would imagine it's awful hard to get a yes if it isn't true. It wouldn't just appear out of nowhere."

Kate sighed. Maybe hearing Connor confirm what she hoped to be true made it all the more real for her, the same as hearing Dr. Matthews say it would have for him, in the way that a child is comforted when a parent tells them everything will be fine, even if they have no way of knowing if it's true.

**

"I'm so sorry guys, but the urine test came back negative." Dr. Matthews seemed genuinely disappointed for them.

Connor put his hands on Kate's shoulders and felt her lay a hand on top of his. "I don't understand, Doctor. How can we have a false positive? Doesn't it test a hormone or something?"

Dr. Matthews considered it for a moment. "Sometimes those little sticks can be very picky. I've seen many a person do it wrong, and I have to break the news to them too that their yes was just brought on by a user error."

Connor hated the way he said it, *user error*, as if a baby could be reduced to nothing more than a glorified computer glitch. Their baby wasn't a misread wire or bad code. She had a name. "Are you absolutely sure she's not pregnant?"

Kate chimed in. "Could we do a blood test?"

Dr. Matthews' expression hardened, like his smile was suddenly baked in the oven and turned into a stiff, crisp surface. Evidently, he was not a man who was used to being questioned. "I'm sure. The urine test was a negative." Suddenly he came back to himself, and his smile was soft and malleable once again. "Go home, get some rest, and try again. I'm sure it will happen for you soon. And above all, relax! It's amazing how many people get pregnant after they stop trying."

Someone knocked on the door of the exam room. "Who is it?" Dr. Matthews asked.

"It's Gina." Gina was Dr. Matthew's nurse. She had been in the position for several years, at least since Kate had started coming to the office for prenatal care when she was pregnant with Gabriel.

"Come in."

"I wanted you to come in and look…" Gina started to speak then noticed Connor and Kate as she glanced over. Her eyes grew wide then returned to normal. If Connor hadn't been paying attention, he may not have noticed. "Oh. Hello."

"Hello," Connor and Kate said. Kate added, "How are you?"

"Fine." Gina turned her attention back to Dr. Matthews. "I'll be in the other room when you're ready, Doctor." She left with a pleasant wave that seemed forced.

Connor wondered for a moment what he had done to make her mad, but then remembered: most of the town had now convinced themselves he was some sort of serial killer, cult leader, or at the very least, had something sinister to hide.

He didn't have to have done anything to her personally. His mere presence was enough to warrant suspicion.

Kate sat on the examination table for a moment then slowly rose to her feet. "Thank you for your time, Doctor." The disappointment on her delicate face spread quickly to the rest of her body: her shoulders slouched, and as they made their way to the car, her pace slowed. Even her curls seemed to grow limp in the hot sun. "I was so sure. I mean I just had this…feeling. I mean I *knew* I was pregnant."

Connor grabbed her hand and squeezed it, as he had done a thousand times before, but with even more meaning in that moment. "It's going to be okay, Kate. You'll get your Emily." He forced a chuckle. "Or maybe a Charles."

A hint of a smile appeared on her lips. "You know I hate Dickens."

Connor felt around in his pocket for his car keys. Finding just fabric and lint, he realized that he had left them on the counter when he had gotten his wallet out to pay for the appointment. "Just one second, I have to grab the keys. I left them inside."

He had made it to the entryway when he realized they

were talking about him. Impulsively, he ducked around the side wall that held the glass doors and listened. He could make out the words, but what really got him was the laughter. It was the only clinic in town, and he had to trust them with his own medical care and that of his family.

And they were all laughing at him. He peered out of his hiding spot for just a moment to confirm his worst fear: Dr. Matthews was there. He was standing within the group…and he was doing nothing. It was a good few minutes before he put a stop to the cackling, and to Connor, that was a few minutes too long.

He wished he hadn't allowed them to have that birthday party. Though eventually, someone would have decided on an answer to the riddle that was the Holloway family, the mysterious group who lived in isolation and only came down to drop their children off at school and to get supplies. But perhaps they could have lived in anonymity just a little bit longer, and the kids would have been older when they needed to start defending themselves. Connor had hoped the town would be perfect for them when they bought their land there: he could build a place to keep his family safe, yet it was in a feasible driving distance to town in case of emergencies. He had thought people would be too busy taking care of themselves to get in their business.

He thought wrong.

When they got into the car, he turned on Kate's favorite Celine Dion CD. She had told him once that Dion was the one that taught her how to love, and he told her that he owed Ms. Dion a huge debt of gratitude. "You brought it…thank you."

He took his eyes off the road to briefly glance at her. "Celine's good in that way. She can help you skip through a field of flowers or she can hold you while you cry. I figured either way, she'd be of some help." At that, Kate burst into tears. Without a word, Connor pulled over the car, and with a wooden fence and a field full of wheat swaying in the wind outside, he held her as she sobbed.

CHAPTER TEN

DREW

Drew's eyes seemed unwilling to close that night. Uneasiness crept over him, like a thousand needles pricking against his skin. He knew it was impossible for him to be the only watchperson on duty until morning, but even though Darius was in the position, he still felt a heightened state of alertness. Vera lay next to him, and it occurred to him how primal people's humanity becomes in an emergency situation: and what they were facing together was even more than that. For all they knew, it was the end of the country, perhaps every country for that matter. All sympathy for strangers flies away when the world is on fire, and the basic instinct to protect one's own takes over entirely. Darius would be concerned with Cassius alone, and vice versa. When something shifted forever, they would cling to each other as they clung to life. Drew's people were his responsibility, and he knew the idea that he should rely on anyone else to fulfill his duties as well as him would be a fatal mistake. A group can be cohesive during normal circumstances, but once disaster strikes, the truth reveals itself.

And the truth could involve everyone crawling on top of each other as the ship they called America sank into the ocean depths.

He looked over at Vera. She was still awake, lying there folded into a tight ball. Her jaw was clenched shut. "Are you cold?" he whispered.

"A little." For Vera to even admit that much meant that she was actually freezing. Her fingers were folded together toward her face, and in the moonlight, her normally almond-colored nails appeared to be the color of sand.

He reached out of his sleeping bag and pulled her close to him and wrapped his arms around her. "Makes you miss our soft wool blanket that we keep on the couch at home huh?"

She smiled. "That thing has been with us many a movie night. Remember our first Christmas together? We spent the entire night wrapped up in it and lying by the fireplace."

"Of course I remember." He kissed her forehead. Vera's face suddenly became sullen. "What is it?"

"It's just strange to think…that last movie we watched together could have been the last time we snuggle in front of a fireplace." She sighed. "How many other things did we do for the last time and not realize it? Was our last plate of fettuccini at Carmen's the *last* one?" She paused. "It sounds ridiculous to be concerned about, I feel ashamed that I thought of it actually, but I just joined that book club I told you about. Will I never again read a book that isn't found in this house? Maybe the first time I took a stroll on that trail by our house last week was also the last time: firsts and lasts all at once." As she spoke it struck him how quiet the world outside was. There was no chatter of wildlife, no hum of the city; just nothingness stretched out around them. He couldn't help but wonder if the disease had snuffed out every inch of earth except the part they rested on; the entire world now consisting of a small patch of land, an Eden covered with gardens and guns, shelter, and salvation.

But he couldn't let Vera know that.

He squeezed her tighter. "We will still experience life, just a little differently. We'll have new firsts, I promise. Our firsts might just be a little more unusual this time. First garden, first berry picking, first gun lesson…" He smiled and was grateful that she smiled back. No matter what happened to him during the day, even before their lives had changed forever, if he could put a smile on her face everything else seemed to fade into the background. That smile was enough to make him close his eyes.

The next time Drew awoke, it was to the sight of the back of Blake's head as she followed Poe up the stairs. He started to rise from his sleeping bag, but felt a gentle and firm hand hold him in place, steadying him as it always did. He turned to see Vera staring at him with a loving but authoritative expression on her face. "Let her go," she whispered.

"She shouldn't be anywhere alone with these monsters. You saw what they did to those people outside. They sent them away without a second thought."

"Blake's a smart girl. She'll be okay." Vera paused. "Besides, if Blake can make friends with one of them, all the better for us. God knows we could use an ally in this place. It's certainly worth a try."

Drew sighed and settled himself back into his sleeping bag. A feeling of acceptance swept over him, the kind that comes when you realize that the person you married is smarter than you are. The thought of letting Blake be alone with any of them made his head spin, but Poe especially. She seemed nearly as threatening as Connor: a protégé who seemed to have the same twinge of sadism that her father did. She knew what was going to happen when they reached the top of the hill that day, and she smiled as she led over half of them to almost certain death. If she had been a patient of Vera's, she would have been one of the ones that she couldn't quite shake even after the session was over.

But, as usual, Vera was right. If Poe seemed to gravitate toward Blake, for whatever reason, it could only work to their advantage. Maybe it would take some of the flame out of Poe's eyes that flashed every time she looked at the group. At the very least, maybe it would keep her and Jackson safe in a way that he couldn't. That realization made another thought sail through his mind: if Poe's friendship can protect them, maybe he should send Vera upstairs too.

He'd always been able to keep his family safe from harm. He'd never once needed someone else's assistance, and he had never thought that the first time he might require some help, salvation would come in the form of a sociopathic sixteen-year-old girl. He began to think of ways that Vera could win her trust too, in case she needed it someday.

A second voice startled him, deep and rasping. "Drew we

have to have a plan. These people are crazy. They don't care about us and they'll kill us without blinking an eye. The minute we walked in here we may have just traded one kind of death for another."

Cassius. His face took on a deep hollowness in the dark.

"Yes they might be thinking that about us, but that's more reason to avoid pissing them off!" a third voice hissed from a spot across the room. Darius turned from his post and looked at Drew. His eyes hardened as he looked for an ally. "What do you think?"

"You're both right." The brothers looked at each other, then at him. "But for now, they have the upper hand, so we have to play by their rules. We are at a complete disadvantage right now."

He heard rustling as Vera propped herself up in her sleeping bag. "The three of you have to remember something: we don't know a damn thing about surviving out here. I don't know rosemary from poison oak, and I'd probably shoot myself if I tried to kill a dear for food at this point. We have to keep in mind that we can learn everything we need to know from the people in this house. Let's take a second and be grateful that we're here in the first place. They could have sent us away with the rest of them."

"You're right. And that also means that we are valuable to them in some way. Let's make sure we remind them of that every chance we get." He gestured to the brothers. "Remind him about your assets... your strengths. Make them see that they made a good choice when they decided to keep you. For the time being, we need to all be polite and keep our heads down." Drew stared at Cassius. "*All* of us."

140

Cassius slammed his fist down on his pillow. "I'm telling you, they're crazy. They misplaced their humanity somewhere on this hill. Especially Connor. He's playing with us, taking pleasure out of this whole thing. It's sick."

Remembering Connor's face during his "selection" process, Drew couldn't help but nod in agreement. "You're right. It's the worst thing I have ever seen human beings do to each other." A cramp seemed to hit his stomach as the words came out, as if the lie had to crawl its way straight out of his bowels. He had seen something much worse. He had *done* something much worse. And that was before the world fell. "We just have to wait it out, gain their trust. He'll have his fun then we can all get back to the business of living our lives out here. They may even learn to trust us if we don't give them a reason not to." He directed himself toward Cassius again. "But we have to stick together and watch each other's backs."

"Agreed. And then when they least expect it…we take out the leader. It's the only way to keep us—"

"No!" Vera interrupted. "Don't you dare. If we do that, then we're no better than he is."

"I can deal with being just as bad as him if it means staying alive."

"Cassius, we can't do that. No matter how much we learn, he will always know more than us. Living off the grid has been his expertise for years. It's a lifestyle that's been engrained in all of them." Drew looked at his wife. "We just have to have a change in leadership. No one has to die."

Unexpectedly, while still gazing out the window from his post, Darius whispered, "Someone *always* has to die."

CHAPTER ELEVEN

CONNOR

When Connor wanted to, he could move like a ghost, weaving in and out of the background undetected, except for the little hairs on the back of someone's neck as they stood straight up. On the second full day with their guests, he decided to use this gift. That morning, he had grouped everyone up for lessons: Vera went downstairs with Kate and Harper to learn how to skin and prepare meat, Cassius and Darius followed Gabriel to the garage where he would teach them basic mechanical skills, and Blake and Drew went with Poe to practice medical training. He was originally going to assign Poe to teach Drew how to shoot (without live ammunition of course), but she had begged him to learn first aid. If it was important to her, he figured there would be plenty of time for shooting later, and left them to pull apart their stash of medical supplies. And, of course, he wasn't planning on giving any of them a gun any time soon.

His first stop was the top of the stairs that lead to the basement. He was careful to open the door and sit down after he could already hear the familiar ripping and tearing that came with shedding an animal of its skin. The deer they had shot was large and muscular, a perfect way to let Vera gain experience. They would be cutting, curing, and slicing for hours, giving him plenty of time to observe the other groups. Vera, with her calm eyes, and easy attitude, struck him as the kind of woman who could adapt well to any circumstance she found herself in: practical, and unyielding. How she had ended up with someone like Drew was a question he couldn't possibly answer. She did not seem like someone who was any cause for concern.

Some of the other guests were other matters entirely.

He propped his head against his hands and waited, listening. His breath came out steadily and silently, in and out without leaving a trace that would leave him detected. Though he preferred the quieter parts of caring for the compound, he was a hunter at heart, and could will his body to remain as still as his surroundings.

He heard the three women struggling against the beast before them, the first steps of preparing the carcass not going as smoothly as usual since a new person had joined them. "Ugh, do you ever get used to the smell?"

"I kind of like it." He heard the smile in Harper's voice.

"If you like that smell, we've been having you do this for far too long," Kate said with a laugh. "Better move you on to the garage with the boys. Maybe some chemicals would do you good."

"Naw, you know you'd rather have me down here with you than Poe. She'd probably name it before we cut it open."

"Not as easy to cut into Bambi as John Doe." Vera

chuckled. "I didn't even realize I made a pun just now."

Between more cutting and pulling sounds, Kate said, "Haha, very true. I like my food to remain anonymous." A pause. "You're doing very well, Vera, now that you're actually hanging on to everything."

"Yes, it definitely works better now that I'm touching it with more than one finger."

"You still got that sour look on your face though." He heard what sounded like Kate giving Harper's ribs a nudge with her elbow. "I mean you're doing great, Vera. Really great." Her voice dripped in sarcasm, but Kate let it go. As soon as he had enough noise to cover his movements again, he got up and shut the door to the basement behind him. There were other places that required his attention more urgently than where his wife and daughter were making small talk.

His next stop was the garage. There was a small, high window on the far side of it, which he could open slightly so he could hear, and where he could look through while standing on a ladder without anyone noticing if they passed by. As he gazed down into the garage, it struck him how much it resembled a medieval torture chamber: metal objects hanging from the ceiling, tool after dangerous tool lined up in alphabetical order on a peg board that stretched the length of the building, and of course, the truck that had been given its own suit of armor as a means of last-resort escape. The contraption seemed to have every scrap of material from every corner of the earth nail-gunned into it, but somehow, it looked professional. Gabriel always had a knack for building things, though Connor knew he didn't tell him that enough. The boy tended to get the idea that he knew best if he encountered too much praise, so Connor was careful to keep it to a minimum to avoid any conflict. He had to make sure that Gabriel understood who was in charge, and as he got older, that had become increasingly more difficult.

From his vantage point, he could see Cassius, Darius, and Gabriel hovering over a piece of metal and wood that sat on the workbench in the corner of the garage. Gabriel was furiously hammering away at it, forgetting to wear his protective goggles as usual. With one final swing, he picked up what he was working on and held it up over the workbench. "You see? You can make pretty much anything into a weapon?"

"What did this used to be?" Darius asked.

Gabriel's back was facing Connor, but he could hear the smirk in his voice. "Used to be an old mud flap and a chunk of fencing. A little more useful this way if you ask me."

"Looks great. What other stuff have you used?" Cassius surveyed the shop as he asked the question. Just curious? Connor doubted it. This was the kind of conversation he had been waiting for, the kind that would help him see who was just itching to take everything Connor had built and steal it for himself. He had guessed it would be Cassius, given the conversation they had already had the previous night, but now he would have an idea what was coming. *This* was why he paid attention. *This* was how he would keep his family alive.

Gabriel dug something out of a drawer and laid it in the palm of Cassius' hand. "Used to be part of a disposable camera. But if you rig it to a doorknob, an intruder's going to get quite a jolt. Won't kill anybody but might make them think about moving onto the next place. It gives them a little preview of what we've got going on here."

The three men had a chuckle, picturing an intruder getting an unexpected buzz as they attempted to enter the house. "That's a good one," Cassius said. "But what about something you can carry on you, like in your pocket, in case we're out on the property and see somebody?"

Connor hoped Gabriel would say he couldn't think of anything, or at the very least, tell him he'd build him something later and just conveniently never get around to it. But Gabriel did neither of those things. Instead, he opened the drawer again, and handed Cassius a piece of twisted metal that had a long flat section, with a piece that stuck vertically out of the middle, almost in the shape of a wine bottle opener. "I made this out of an old pair of glasses." He handed it over. "It fits perfect in a pocket and doesn't take on much shape there, not like some of the knives would. No one will even know you have it. But, if for some reason you were ever captured and got a pat down, you would get caught with it. I'm working on coming up with some other things, smaller stuff that might be missed if we were searched."

Connor watched as Cassius slid the device into his pocket. "Thanks man. I'm not exactly a skilled knife guy yet, and I don't think your dad's going to give me a gun. I just don't want to be defenseless. It doesn't really do much good for me to be here and help defend everyone if I have nothing to do but sit on my hands."

"No problem. The whole point is for us all to protect each other right? You can't do that very well without any weapons." Gabriel shrugged, completely ignoring the fact that he didn't know the man he had just given a stabbing implement to. He trusted the safety of his sisters and his mother to a man he'd barely met twenty-four hours before. How disappointingly unsurprising, Connor thought. "Just don't tell my dad okay? He'll freak out." Cassius nodded.

Connor knew that there was a very good chance that Cassius intended to stick that tool straight through his neck. He felt a twinge of pain tingle down his spine just thinking of it and the fact that his only son gave it to him made it hurt even more.

"I agree. Maybe you have something I could use too?" Darius asked.

Gabriel paused for a moment then started digging through the drawer once again. This time, he pulled out a small toothbrush that looked harmless enough, until one looked at the non-bristled end: it had been sharpened to a point. "Not as glamorous as the glasses, but put it in the right area of the human body and it'll definitely do the trick. This'll do until I make you something else." Connor had a difficult time not crying out in frustration, seeing that his son had just armed yet another person, and especially one related to the man he was certain wanted to kill him.

"Thank you, I appreciate it. As high up in the hills as we

are, people will be getting desperate I'm sure. You never know when somebody might come by."

"For sure."

Cassius turned away from the tools and gestured toward the truck. Connor noticed his strong arm muscles, and pictured him thrusting the weapon into his flesh. In his imagination, it plunged straight through to the other side, like it did when they hung animal carcasses up for curing. "So tell me about this. It looks like it's from a video game."

Connor watched as Gabriel's eyes lit up, eager to talk about his favorite contraption. "This is in case what will never happen happens. If for some reason we get overtaken and we have to leave, this will keep us alive, provided this thing isn't airborne."

"I'm sure it's not," Darius said.

"Why?"

"Because we would all be dead already." Connor had to agree. Though there was no proof, if they were wrong, he had to think they would know by then in one way or another. However, they also had no idea if the disease could mutate, in which case something that was not airborne today *could* be airborne tomorrow. Unfortunately, with a world on the brink of total annihilation, they would have to get used to knowing the answers they were so desperate for may never come.

Gabriel thought about it for a moment then continued. "It will carry all of us, cramped of course but it'll work. There's a secret supply storage in the floor of the truck, with water storage rigged in the cab." He patted the side of the truck with his hand. "It's my baby."

Cassius circled the truck, taking in every detail. Connor bit the side of his cheek to keep from yelling at Gabriel right then and there. He was supposed to be teaching their guests how to build fencing, vegetable cages....things that the family needed done but couldn't be used against them later. But instead, Gabriel was showing them ways to take over what they had built, and perhaps kill them all in the process. He thought of his wife and daughters, their faces under the knife of intruders; only the intruders had been invited in, welcomed with an open door and watchful eye.

"Well, we better go get to the not-so-fun stuff before we get caught in here." He handed Darius and Cassius each a tool belt. "We're going to go around the property and check everything: the fences, the garden, everything. If we see something that's loose, we tighten it. If we see something broken, we fix it. Pretty common sense stuff." He adjusted his own belt. "Oh, and I'm putting the finishing touches on another underground refrigerator that you can help me with."

"Underground?" Cassius asked.

"Yeah. The earth stays cool if you dig deep enough. You can make a storage area and cover it up with moss. It's a great way to have extra supplies and also keep them hidden. Pretty cool actually."

As they left the garage, Connor slowly climbed down the ladder. He would have to have a very urgent conversation with his son, but it would have to be at the right time. Common knowledge: never let the enemy see a chink in your armor. He would have to find a time where they could be alone, and he would put the fear back into his son that he had thought had been there all along. He was sure he had taught him right. Granted they didn't agree on every aspect of their lifestyle, but he thought when the situation was dire, Gabriel could be counted on to be smart.

Evidently, he was wrong.

As he headed toward the house, he didn't notice anyone behind him until he felt a tug on his leg. He turned around to see the top of Jackson's head at his waist. Jackson smiled as he looked up at him. "Hi, sir."

"Hello, young man. How are you today?"

"Very well. I just wanted to say thanks a lot for having us. It's really nice of you."

Connor felt an unfamiliar sensation. It had been so long since someone had been nice to him he had forgotten what it felt like. And to have it come from a child he thought of banishing for even the briefest of seconds made him wince. "You are very welcome, young man." He hesitated. "Did your mother tell you to say that? Does she even know you're talking to me?"

"Nope. And nope. But Mommy always says if somebody does something nice for you, you should say thank you. So thanks." And with that, he skipped away, bouncing a small red ball that he pulled out of his pocket. Connor watched as Blake came out from another corner of the compound. From that distance, it appeared that Jackson had run off and was getting a good scolding. As Blake shuffled him inside, she glanced up at Connor, giving him a slight nod.

Of all people, he thought. The two that he had thought

about sending away were the only two to show him any kind of courtesy. Jackson had impressed him that day too…very well-spoken for his age, possibly smarter than his own children were back then—and from what he'd just seen, *still* smarter than his own son. The girl must have done something right to have raised such a good boy. All those adults around and it took a child to do the right thing, the just thing. For the briefest of seconds, he felt a crack in his thinking, one that made him wonder what else he had gotten wrong.

He came back into the house briefly to get a cool glass of water. He seemed to get dehydrated more easily now, and he wasn't sure if it was the weather, the situation, or something worse. As he shut the door behind him, he noticed his wife shuffling through the fridge. As he stared at her, it still blew his mind that she chose him. She could have had anyone, but she chose him. He was unbelievably grateful for that, and vowed that even in spite of himself, he would never do anything to destroy it. "How's the meat coming?"

"Great. Vera has picked up on it pretty quickly, once she got past the smell."

"Is that right?" He laughed with her, not letting on that he already knew how the situation had gone. "It does take some getting used to. I can hardly blame her for that."

Kate wrapped her arms around him. "Definitely." She reached up and wiped her finger across his cheek. "You're dirty. What have you been up to?"

"Oh just tending to a few things outside." He gave her a warm smile. "I'm going to go past the gate and see if I find anything."

"Okay, be careful."

"Always." He kissed her on the forehead as he walked out the door. "Kate?"

"Yes?"

"I'm doing this for our family. You know that right?"

She looked at him, an expression of concern sweeping across her delicate features. "Of course, Connor. Of course."

He smiled as he shut the door, and a part of him realized that he wasn't just doing it for them anymore, but Jackson as well, the four-year-old boy with the heart of a man.

***

A few nights later, Connor decided it was time to act. Enough time had gone by that he was sure his son wouldn't catch on that he'd been spied on. Gabriel always came out to the garage after dinner, like clockwork. He'd work there until he went to bed. But this time, Connor would be waiting for him.

He heard his son come in and shut the door. He hesitated before he spoke, lingering in the dark like one of Gabriel's forgotten projects that had grown a fine layer of dust over the years. He let him set up his work bench and start hammering away before he spoke. "You're missing some things."

His son jumped back, in his startle letting the hammer land on the work bench with a loud clatter. "Dad, you scared me. How long have you been in here?"

Connor slowly emerged, his face lit by the weak lamp that rested in the corner of the garage. "I did an inventory of all your weapons, and there were some missing. What did you do with them?" He stared at his son, almost willing him to dare and utter a lie.

But he didn't. To Connor's surprise, the first thing out of his son's mouth was the truth. "I gave a couple to Cassius and Darius."

"Why would you do something stupid like that?" The clench in his teeth made each word hiss its way out of his mouth.

"Because they aren't any good to us if they can't defend themselves. There's no point. More people are probably on their way as we speak and they're sitting ducks right now. Just another couple bodies to shoot."

Connor felt as if he stepped outside of himself to watch as he pushed his only son against the wall. "They've barely been here for more than two days! How many times do I have to tell you…you can't trust anyone but your mother, me and your sisters. How many times?"

"YOU are the one who chose to let them in here! For what? To do our chores? Dad, what are any of these people supposed to do if someone finds us up here? God forbid they grab Harper or Poe. What are they supposed to do to help? Ask them nicely to go away?"

Connor slapped him across the face. "You will show me respect." As he looked at Gabriel, he thought for just a moment how easy it would be to let him win. It would serve him right if he gave up. Then when people turned on them Gabriel would only have himself to blame. But in the same instant, he knew he couldn't do that to Kate, Poe, and

Harper. He needed to protect them, not only from the new world, but from what he knew would follow.

As Gabriel rubbed his stung cheek, he said, "Maybe you should show me some too." Connor took a deep breath and let Gabriel go. He hadn't meant to strike him; Kate and he had never believed in that type of punishment. But a heavy feeling in his stomach told him that what he had built may already be coming apart, and his son could be the one doing the pulling. Of course Gabriel was right: eventually, the new arrivals would have to have weapons. But it would be on *Connor's* terms, at his own time. As he marched out of the garage, he heard Gabriel yell behind him, "I didn't even *want* to leave ten years ago; none of us did. That was all you!" He heard Gabriel spit on the ground. "You're going to have to give them a little trust eventually. Or this whole thing is going to go up in flames."

Connor was afraid the embers had already begun.

That night, after everyone had gone to sleep, or were at least in their beds, Connor crept down to the basement. He sat down at the table that they used for skinning and preparing their meats. The blood of a hundred kills had soaked through and dried, giving the table a permanent burnt red color, and a smell that Connor couldn't forget if he tried.

He couldn't go to bed, not yet…not before he talked to Gordon. Gordon was up at all hours too, and even if Connor caught him when he wasn't, he certainly didn't seem to mind talking. He suspected Gordon lived alone, even before the pandemic hit. Though Gordon had mentioned a wife, he never heard her voice in the background, or so much as a noise from the other side of the radio that would indicate that Gordon was anything but by himself. "Any news, Gordon? I'm sure the looting and rioting is getting pretty bad over there."

A long pause. "Nope. It's been so long since we've heard anything. I don't know if there isn't as much crime going on as we thought would happen or there's no one left to talk about it."

"Nothing from your family in Florida?"

"Nothing." For a long time, the two men sat with each other, somehow side by side yet thousands of miles away. "My niece has a birthday coming up soon. She'll be turning five. I can't believe how fast the time goes."

He thought he heard Gordon sniffle. "I'm sure you'll hear something by then."

Gordon forced a good-humored laugh. "I'm sure you're right. They have a radio too. No reason they wouldn't use it here pretty soon."

Connor didn't tell him the only reason he could think of that they hadn't used it, because the only thing he could come up with was that they were already dead. "Keep your head up, Gordon. Over and out."

"Over and out."

CHAPTER TWELVE

DREW (before)

The young boy wouldn't talk about what happened at first. He sat on Drew's exam table, averting his eyes and staring at a spot on the floor that had been there since a different patient had spilled grape juice years before. Since then, Drew hadn't allowed food or drinks in the exam room, no matter how much the parents begged him to. Grape juice, like blood, had a way of staying where you put it.

"Are you sure you don't want to tell me what happened?" The boy's parents were on their way, but they lived quite far out of town, and the beating was so bad that the school brought him to Drew to make sure he didn't have a concussion. The administration was afraid in the time it would take to get him to the big hospital a few towns over, he might pass out...or worse. So instead, a math teacher who had *not* been doing a stellar job supervising recess carried a boy named Gabriel Holloway into Dr. Drew Matthew's downtown office.

The boy remained silent. "Well, Mr. Samson already told me that you got into a fight at school, but I was hoping to hear it from you. I'd rather hear your side of the story than that of a guy who just happened to walk by."

At that, Gabriel looked up, his expression distraught. "A fight? Really? They came up from behind me. I was on the ground before I knew what was happening." He snickered darkly. "Not much of a fight. I'll probably get in trouble right along with them though." He sniffed and winced as he spoke, his nose swollen from the impact of the other children's fists.

"Were they in your grade?"

"I don't know. I don't think so." He paused and turned away. Drew guessed that he was trying to hide the tears that were forming in his eyes. "They looked much taller than me."

Drew sighed. "I'm sorry that happened to you."

Gabriel swallowed hard, and wiped the tears from his cheeks before he turned back, a little boy trying to be the man he wasn't expected to be, at least not by Drew. "It's all right. I figured it was coming."

Drew sat in his chair and wheeled himself over to the boy, trying to meet him as much at eye level as he could. "What do you mean you figured it was coming?"

Gabriel folded his arms across his chest. "People've been sayin' stuff for a while now. Stuff about my dad doing bad things and that's why we hide in the mountains." He coughed, and Drew could tell his chest ached too. "I always say, who's hiding?"

"Sometimes people just don't want to mind their own business."

Gabriel smiled slightly. "Well I sure wish they would. I mean we're just living. No big mystery. Just living. Why does there have to be something more than that?" He ran his fingers through his thick black hair and went back to staring at the floor.

"Good question. If you ever figure people out, will you let me know? I sure haven't been able to, and I've been on this planet a lot longer than you." Drew gave him a smile, and he was pleased that he got one in return.

Just then Gabriel's parents Connor and Kate burst into the room. Kate of course dove at Gabriel and threw her arms around him, squeezing his already-bruised ribs. "Mom, knock it off." His expression was one of a ten-year-old trying to assert his independence, but Drew knew it was pain masked in adolescent rebellion. He remembered being ten once, all sweat and dirt and nonsense.

She realized what she had done and released him. "Oh my gosh, honey, I'm so sorry. Are you okay?"

"Yeah, I'm fine." Gabriel shrugged his shoulders and attempted to sit up straight. Drew admired the boy for being so young but so aware that he didn't want to worry his mother any more than she already was. Boys seemed to always protect their mothers, no matter how young or old. It was a universal truth, the same as the world spun on its axis and children had an immense capacity for cruelty.

Connor addressed Drew. "What happened?"

"Apparently Gabriel was assaulted at school." From where they were standing, Connor and Kate couldn't see the grateful nod that Gabriel gave Drew when he called the incident by its true name. "They said it was a fight, but Gabriel said the other boys attacked him from behind. He suffered two bruised ribs, one black eye, and his right arm is sprained, but there doesn't appear to be a concussion."

"Can we take him home?" Kate asked. She ran her hand through Gabriel's hair, much the same way he had to himself earlier. Drew wondered if he had been mimicking his mother's gesture as a form of comfort accidentally or on purpose.

"Yes, but keep him awake for the next few hours, and monitor him throughout the night just in case. And of course, if anything changes, call me right away." He reached into his pocket and pulled out a business card, then flipped it over. "Here's my home phone number." Handing it to Connor, he said, "If anything changes; doesn't matter what time."

Connor nodded. "Thank you very much, Doctor."

Kate was already helping Gabriel off the table and out the door. She said thank you as an afterthought, but Drew understood. All she saw at that moment was her little boy, with the whites of his eyes red with blood.

After Gabriel and his parents left, Drew went out to the lobby to file some paperwork and saw that Mr. Samson was still sitting in the waiting room. "Jim?"

"Hi, Drew. Is Gabriel going to be all right? I tried to ask the parents but…"

Drew put a hand on Jim's shoulder. They had known each other since they were kids, though Drew didn't like him much. But the nervousness emanating off of him provoked some sympathy from Drew, and he gave in: only a little. "Yes, Jim." Drew started to walk away, but abruptly turned around: he couldn't help himself. "What the hell happened? What's going on at that school?"

Jim sunk further into his chair. "I don't know what happened. All of a sudden I just heard Rhonda Dailey's kid scream when she found him lying on the ground."

Drew sat down next to him. "I've heard the rumors going around town…about that kid's family."

"I know. Pretty sinister stuff. Patterson said he heard Connor's wanted in three or four states on the east coast. But nobody wants to call the cops on account of him being dangerous and all. What if the cops can't catch him? He could retaliate."

"Yeah that…or it could just be a family that likes to live out in the country, away from people." Drew suddenly felt the need to defend Connor, not for him, but for Gabriel. "Sometimes I think about getting away too. I don't think that makes me a criminal."

Jim scoffed. "Sure, Drew, sure. But I don't see you inviting those people over for dinner any more than I have."

Drew got up from his chair. He had conversed with Jim much longer than he was accustomed to, and much longer than he liked to. Sometimes, just a little kindness could make an outcast into a friend, or a monster into a mouse. There was a chance that was all Connor needed, just someone to reach out to him. "Maybe I just might."

But he never did.

CHAPTER THIRTEEN

POE

The first months after the new group arrived passed by with relatively little incident. Poe wondered if humans were so adaptable under normal circumstances, or did their adjustment come from the world's force of hand. Either way ended with the same result: a group of people from completely different worlds somehow blending together to help keep each other away from starvation and death.

As she thought about it, she twirled the ring that she wore on her thumb, spinning it around and around, liking the feeling of the metal against her skin. It was her grandfather's ring, one that she had stolen out of her grandmother's nightstand after his funeral. She never told anyone where she got it; evidently he hadn't worn it much. When her mom asked her once where it had come from, she said she'd found it on the ground at the park one afternoon. She'd kept it in her own jewelry box until her fingers were big enough to accommodate it, and ever since then, it remained on the thumb of her left hand. She'd never gotten to know him very well since he lived so far away from them. But for some reason, that day she'd been desperate to have something to remember him by. When she carefully took the ring out of the drawer, she noticed an inscription on the inside of it that read *Keep Your Friends Close, and Make Friends With Your Enemies*. She realized that inscription helped her know her grandfather more deeply than any story or visit ever had, and she promptly stuffed it into the pocket of her funeral dress.

Her mother and Vera behaved as if the fact they had never been friends previously was some universal, planetary oversight. They laughed like the world outside the compound was going on its merry way just as it had before, and that there was no reason it wouldn't continue on with the same delightful monotony that most people took for granted. As her mother helped Vera sew some new clothes for the women in the group while they sat in pink plastic chairs on the porch, she asked her about her life before, her love for Drew, and whether or not she believed rosemary to be better than thyme when they used it on chicken breasts. Watching them was like watching a magazine cover play out in front of her eyes, and Poe wondered if they truly believed everything would be okay or they were just very talented at pretending they did.

Her father hardly ever came to check on her, Blake, and Drew while they were supposedly teaching Poe basic medical first aid training. She didn't know whether to be happy about it or allow the guilt to swallow her whole. Knowing her father trusted her enough to make it easy to hide secrets from him left a gaping hole deep in the middle of her chest, and it sent a twinge of pain through her every time she saw him. Every hug, every smile cut her just a little bit deeper, and every once in a while she wondered if she would be able to keep her secret hidden forever like she planned. But every time she looked at Blake and Jackson playing happily, safe from the world that quietly shattered outside their borders, she knew she'd done the right thing.

Her brother had made the little boy some small wooden trucks from some old scrap he had lying around the garage, and the way they made Jackson smile told her that maybe the wounds were worth it. As most wounds were, because they signified a life lived. It occurred to Poe that she hadn't had any wounds to speak of since they had gone into isolation.

She thought about her past. Every child who had spit on her, every teacher who had looked the other way…they were all dead now. As she bit into a juicy slice of apple, she wondered where they were: did some get a funeral, with a crowd of crying faces staring at them in a big wooden box…were any of them even buried? Or were they forgotten like they had forgotten her? It seemed likely that for most, it was the latter. She expected to feel some comfort in that, and was surprised when she felt nothing at all.

Before Blake arrived, she couldn't remember the last time she felt anything.

Drew had taken her and Blake through every ointment, every suture, and every type of bandage that he could, and both of them were beginning to feel like they could make their way through the lie without detection. The feeling of a needle pushing through a piece of rubber that they used for practice skin felt familiar to them, and they both felt prepared for the sight of blood that they knew would inevitably come. But at first, the true test would come not in the form of blood, but the form of a scream.

They were practicing their stitching on an unlucky piece of cloth when the three of them heard Harper's voice from out the window: "Dad! Dad you have to come quick! You have to let him in!"

Drew, Poe, and Blake didn't say anything, just got up from the table and rushed outside. All their faces said the same thing: let *who* in? Who had found them so high in the hills? And if one person could get there, would more come?

They saw Connor running toward Harper, who was at the end of the drive, pounding on the main metal gate. Through the bars, they could see a young man who looked around their age, built like Cassius but with pale, Norwegian coloring, reaching his hands out toward her. One arm was bleeding.

"Harper, don't touch him! Stay back!" Connor shouted.

"It's Brian! You have to let him in Dad! He's hurt."

Poe looked at Blake, who replied "I'll get the first aid kit" without having to be asked. Poe breathed a sigh of relief for herself, though she knew that her new friend was about to have the first real trial of her medical training. She made her expression steely and unwavering. Their whole story rested on the injury before them. Every bandage or slight movement of Blake's own hand could expose them for the fraud that they were.

That is assuming Brian would get past the front gate.

Poe watched as Connor grabbed Harper and pulled her roughly away from the gate. "Who is this boy? How the hell does he know where we live?" His face became a bright shade of crimson, the shade of red he reserved for back talk and deep betrayals of trust.

Poe hoped she would never be the one to put that color in her father's cheeks.

By that time, Kate had heard the commotion and made her way up to them from the back corner of the property, between the barn and the blackberry vines. "Connor, calm down and let her talk."

Reluctantly, he released Harper. "Tell me what the hell is going on."

She cowered, shoulders slouching before him as if she expected to be struck. "I told him where we lived. Before the internet went out, before everything happened, he wanted to know about our family. So I told him. I told him everything." Connor stared at her with wide eyes. "I didn't even know he was coming. I thought I'd never see him again after everything stopped. I know I'm not supposed to tell anyone about us, Dad, but he's special. He wanted to know about me. We'd been talking for so long. I trust him! He thought I didn't because you wouldn't let me talk about anything! He knew *me*, but hardly knew me at all. I had to!" Her sobs came hard and fast, yet she still had the presence of mind to shrink away from their father.

Poe ran over and put a comforting arm around her sister, with Drew following behind. "Shh…it's okay."

"Connor, if you're going to let him in you need to do it

now. That cut looks deep and it needs to be stitched up badly." Drew's eyes hardened.

Harper ran back over to the gate and gripped the bars, as Brian went to place his hands on top of hers, but stopped as he thought the better of it. "Please, Mr. Holloway. My family's gone. I just want to be with Harper, that's all."

Connor went up to him and glared at him through the gate. "How do I know you're not infected?"

Drew looked at him. "Connor, from what we all heard on the news when this thing started, it only takes this thing a few hours. Even if he got infected in town, the journey on foot would have had him showing symptoms already."

"He needs to stay out there a couple more hours, just to be safe."

"Fine." Drew went up to Blake, who had returned with the first aid kit, and snatched it from her. "Then let me through so I can stitch him up. I'll sit with him until you tell us we can come back in." He placed a hand on Blake's shoulder. "Vera's sleeping. Don't tell her what I'm doing, she'll worry. Just tell her I'm out in the garden or something."

Blake shook her head. "I don't like this."

"I'll be fine, I promise." He turned from her. "Well, Connor?"

An odd expression spread across her dad's face. "Take Blake too. He's much younger than you Drew…looks tough too. I can't have him overpowering you. Blake can help you work on him and keep an eye on him at the same time. We need our doctor around."

Drew glared at Connor. "I'll be fine. She needs to stay

here. The less any of us are outside the compound, the better. Wouldn't you agree?"

Poe watched as the group looked at her father, waiting for an answer. She noticed the familiar stiffening in his cheeks, the tightening that happened when he really didn't want to answer a certain way but had been worn down by the teardrops in the eyes of his daughters, or the uncomfortable knowledge that someone was making a compelling argument. He took a deep breath, and one more look at Harper. "Okay fine, Drew. Just stay out there with him 'til dark. If he's fine, you can both come in."

Drew nodded and slipped out the gate. Kate and Connor sealed it behind him. Poe noticed that Blake was frozen still, apprehension seeping off of her like steam. "That was close," Poe said. "Are you okay?"

"What if he's wrong?" she whispered. "Drew's like a second dad to me…how am I supposed to tell Vera if he gets sick?"

Poe slipped an arm around her shoulder and smiled a sad smile when Blake gave her hand a squeeze. She hadn't even blinked when Connor had threatened to send her out too. Her only concern was for Drew. "You won't have to do that, I promise. Drew's right, Brian would have been sick by now." She gently guided Blake back toward the house. "Let's go get the vegetables picked; it'll help distract you."

Blake obeyed, but Poe didn't miss her glancing over her shoulder at Drew until the gate was long out of sight.

***

Between pulling the carrots from the earth and snapping off the broccoli florets, Blake stopped, orange flesh lying still in the hand. "Do you think he's right? It's not airborne?"

"I'm sure he is. You said yourself, Drew had gone to that hospital to see his friend and there were sick people everywhere. If it was in the air, he wouldn't be here right now."

"I know you're right. It's just scary. Really scary." A sound of a laugh that seemed to come from far away escaped from her and hovered in the air. "I mean every once in a while, up here, away from it, I forget what we left behind." She paused. "Then people with blood dripping down their arms show up and it's fresh all over again. I can't thank God enough that my son is here and safe."

Poe reached out, gently taking the carrot from her and stuck it in their basket of freshly-picked vegetables. "And he will continue to be. We're all going to be fine up here. This is what my dad designed this place for. He's known something like this was coming for years: maybe not in the form of a pandemic, but something. Put too many people on one planet long enough and it's only a matter of time before something snaps." She carefully pulled a tomato off its branch. "But for those of us who made preparations, the end is only the beginning. You'll see. Everything's going to be okay; different, at least for you, but okay."

Even as Poe said it, she wondered if deep down in the tiny midpoint of her heart there was a shred of doubt residing there, curled up and ready to crawl to the surface when just the right moment arose. But for Blake, she smiled.

A few moments later, Poe heard yelling from inside the house. The garden was a few hundred yards away, so she knew whatever was going on had to be heated beyond anything that had ever occurred in their house before. She was sure her sister was on the receiving end. Without a word, Poe looked over at Blake, and both girls ran up to the house, leaving their baskets of vegetables lying in the sun.

Poe threw the door open to see her father screaming at Harper. He had her pinned against the kitchen counter, one of his arms blocking either side of her. His face had reddened and Poe could see saliva spewing in little droplets out of his mouth. She watched as her father gripped the counter tightly, making the tiny veins in his hands protrude from his skin. "How could you have done this, Harper? How? You may have destroyed everything! And all over some boy! I didn't raise you to be so stupid!"

"He's not some boy! I love him and I'm going to marry him some day! You'll see I promise!" Tears streamed down her cheeks. "What was I supposed to do, just let him die? You can't do that to someone you love. It's not possible!"

Connor pounded his fist against the counter. "It's not our job to help everyone! We only need to protect our family and you completely threw that away!"

Harper stood silently, but a few moments later, her sorrow turned to rage. "He *is* my family too! He's all I have! You've kept us up here by ourselves for ten years! I don't have anything else. No friends, nothing! Did you really expect us to stay here forever?" Her face became a snarl. "Answer me! Did you really expect us to stay here forever?

Just to forget about the outside world and never want a life of our own? Just stay here with you forever? It's ridiculous! This whole thing is just you hiding and making us hide right beside you!"

Connor threw his hand back and slapped her across the face. Harper's hand immediately flew to her cheek. "You ungrateful little...you disgust me." In a low growl, he whispered, "Get out of my sight."

Poe had never imagined her father hitting any one of them, but she remembered once, after a particularly bad argument, Harper *had*. "I thought for sure he was going to hit me. I mean, I *knew* it was coming, except it didn't."

"He would never, I'm sure of it," she'd said.

Not looking Poe in the eyes, Harper had said, "It's just a matter of time. Is it really that hard for you to imagine? He keeps us up here, all alone. That's an abuse in itself. Do you really think it's that big of a stretch?"

In typical Harper fashion, in almost the same breath, she had moved on to another, less unpleasant topic, something so mundane that Poe couldn't remember what it was. What she did remember was Harper's voice fading into the background. Poe's own thoughts muffled the sound, covering it up with memories of stargazing with her father, the quiet of the night surrounding them like a warm blanket on a crisp evening. Those times with him made her think he was all the friend she'd ever need in the world, and that he was the only person who could ever truly understand who she was.

As Harper ran past Poe and Blake and up the stairs to her

room, Poe realized her father hadn't even noticed they were there. But instead of scolding them, he simply said, "Bring up the vegetables. Your mother needs them."

Poe hesitated, but her father's face was steadfast, and though she knew Harper needed her, she chose to listen to her father instead.

She always chose her father.

***

Dinner was over by the time her father let Brian and Drew back in. Vera threw her arms around him, by then realizing that he was not, in fact, picking vegetables. "I was sick. Just sick worrying about you." Her cheeks glowed pink, evidence of the crying that she had no intention of hiding from him.

"I'm all right. Don't worry." He looked at Brian. "We're both okay."

Brian held up his arm. "You're husband saved my life. I am...I'm grateful."

"It should heal nicely; pretty deep but we seemed to have gotten to it in time, and we cleaned it out really well, so it shouldn't get infected. You got lucky."

"Yeah." Brian smiled shyly. "That guy sure gave me a good souvenir though."

"What guy?" Vera asked.

"I headed this way after my family got sick. They're all gone now. On the way here some guy attacked me and took my supplies. I tried to fight him off but he gave me this." He pointed to his arm. "I guess I should just be glad I found you when I did."

Poe watched as her sister glided down the stairs, evidently finally hearing Brian's voice. Her mother was right behind her. She seemed to be hovering, perhaps worried that her father wasn't done screaming.

Harper threw her arms around Brian. "Oh thank God you're okay! I'm so happy you're here!" The couple kissed with the vigor that comes with distance and inexperience. Poe hoped her sister didn't see her wince at the sloppy, dramatic sight. When Harper finally broke free, she gave her father a hug. Her father stiffened. "Thank you, Daddy." Like so many other times that Harper didn't want to think of unpleasant things, she went on as though the fight that they had in the kitchen earlier that day never happened at all, but Poe could still feel a welt swollen upon her cheek. As evident from her mother's pursed lips and widened eyes, Poe could tell that she saw it too.

Connor just nodded.

She next turned to Drew. "Thank you for fixing him up. He'll be good as new right?"

"Absolutely."

Harper took Brian's hand and started to drag him around the house. "I want to give you the tour."

They didn't even make it to the corner of the kitchen when Connor stepped in front of them. "I don't think so. It's late and he's not going anywhere alone with you."

"Seriously, Dad? Really?" Harper desperately looked over at her mother, but Kate just shook her head. "Ugh…okay fine, tomorrow then. Here, I'll at least show you where you're going to sleep." She smiled. "I made your bed while you were still outside. It's just an old sleeping bag but it'll have to do."

Brian smiled. "Thanks, babe…Harper." Poe held in a giggle as she watched her father glare at him. She highly doubted that the pet names would ever come up again.

***

Over the next few weeks, Poe watched as Brian tried his best to become part of their routine. One particular morning, he started his day helping her mother make breakfast for everyone. Given how her father was when he first arrived, she was surprised he was even permitted to use the bread knife. After everyone had some oatmeal and toast made from the bread her mother had finished the day before, Brian followed Gabriel around as he checked the perimeter of their land. Poe went with them, still all-too-curious about the new member of their group who had traveled so far in order to be with her sister. She didn't say much, but she listened closely as her brother and Brian reinforced one of the guard towers as Cassius took his turn on watch. "If you're putting metal around the tree to make it slick, how does the person on guard get up?"

Gabriel smiled as a rope ladder flew out of the bottom of the guard tower, nearly knocking Brian in the face. "This. Anyone who is on watch carries a long pole with a hook attached to it that they use to pull the ladder down." He gripped the ladder and pulled himself up on a couple of rungs to demonstrate. "Easy. We can get up but no one else can. Both raccoon and human-proof."

"Awesome. I'm sure I won't be on watch for a while, but I'll know when the time comes." Brian rolled his eyes.

"Look, my dad's just trying to protect us. He doesn't know you. And quite frankly neither do I." Poe looked him up and down from his feet to his head. "We *all* need some time."

Gabriel put his arm around his sister. "Meet my sister, suspicious by nature, paranoid by nurture."

"Maybe, but I'll probably stay alive longer than your dumb ass."

"Aww, and she *sounds* like my dad too." They glared at each other for a moment, then broke into smiles. "Naw really dude, she's just trying to protect Harper. Lord knows Harper can't protect herself."

Brian's expression grew serious. "That's funny, Harper seems pretty capable to me. Intelligent too. She also tells me that she's the best shot in the family." He turned to Poe. "Maybe neither of you gives her enough credit."

Poe considered this for a moment. Though she was mildly insulted, the fact that Brian stood up for her sister, however wrong he was, definitely earned him a bit of respect.

At least for the time being.

***

A week later, it was Poe, Drew, and Kate's turn to go out hunting. Their meat supply wasn't nearly depleted, but Connor told them that they couldn't be sure if the deer would flee along with the rest of the human population. "It's only a matter of time before we're down to rabbits and squirrels. Hopefully they are dumb enough to stick around."

Poe didn't doubt that he was right; though hunting was the chore she dreaded most of all. "I don't like seeing their eyes when they die. That moment sticks with me for days afterward," she would tell her father.

"Every kill has a purpose, Poe. When you kill with no purpose, that's when you have something to feel guilty about."

"Right, but who decides what purpose is worth more than the purpose of another? I'm sure the deer have their own ideas about what their role in this world should be."

Her father didn't have an answer.

Brian decided to come along on the hunt, talking incessantly to Kate, asking everything he could think of about weaponry and finding game. When her father heard Brian was going to be out in the woods with his wife and daughter, he insisted he and Gabriel go with them, leaving Harper and her superior shooting skills to keep the group in line. Her father seemed exhausted from repairing one of the greenhouses, and Poe wished he would take a well-deserved rest instead. Her mother tried to convince him that they would be fine, but Connor would hear none of it. "I'm not leaving you two out there with the good doctor and the boyfriend that can't tell his ass from a hole in the ground." Poe was pretty sure Brian heard him, and she was also certain he didn't care.

Despite the hostile company, Brian smiled brightly when Kate handed him her bow and an arrow when they were several yards into the woods and away from the house. Each arrow was carefully handcrafted by one of the Holloways. Poe could always tell which ones she had made. She paid by far the most attention to detail as she carved, leaving intricate patterns on the stone.

Connor had always said they would eventually run out of bullets, and they would need to know how to hunt and defend themselves with weapons other than guns. Poe could use a bow and arrow, as well as a gun, but she preferred the knife that she always kept holstered at her waist. Her brother had made it for her and given it to her on her fourteenth birthday and it hadn't left her since, except when she went to sleep. And even then, it rested snugly under her pillow. "You're really going to let me try?" Brian asked.

"Of course. You're going to need to pull your weight around here just like the rest of us. Can't have you sunning yourself and sipping iced tea while the rest of us work can we?" She smiled and winked at him. He seemed grateful for the good-natured tease. Poe knew what it felt like to be the one on the outside, and though she still wasn't sure about Brian, she wouldn't wish that feeling on anyone.

Kate placed his hands in the proper places on the bow, and carefully slid the arrow between his fingers. "Now, see that tree over there? Try to hit it." Brian pulled back and let the arrow fly. It breezed right past, not even touching the bark. Drew gave him a pat on the back that seemed to tell him not to give up, while her father watched and snickered.

"Ugh, I'm no good at this."

Kate smiled. "It takes practice. Since we aren't seeing any signs of deer yet, let's keep working on it." She gave him another arrow, and lined him up again. This time, the arrow hit the side of the tree, only grazing it but it was enough to build Brian's confidence.

After about an hour, Brian was hitting the tree every time. Poe and Drew stood guard, ever careful of running into strangers who may want to turn into unexpected guests. Brian's arrival shook them up; not just her father, all of them. Afterward, every time they went in the woods,

Poe swore she sensed people moving through the trees, a shadow here, a whistle there. In between the chirps of the birds, she thought she heard voices, whispers of strangers that she did not care to know. In that way, Brian was a blessing: waking them up to the fact that no matter what, they couldn't afford to lull themselves into a false sense of security. The minute that happened is the minute they would lose everything.

Though sometimes, no amount of paying attention can prepare you for what comes next.

As they stood there in the middle of the quiet woods, Poe and Drew heard a loud crashing sound, like a bear smashing its way through the forest, and it was just enough for them to make another critical mistake. They would never find out what the noise was, but as they turned to investigate it, they lost their concentration and didn't hear the footsteps coming toward their group.

Connor had quick reflexes, but they weren't as sharp as they used to be. As the woman who they hadn't seen since the night they brought in their new arrivals ran toward him, he was unable to duck out of the way before he felt the sting of a knife blade through the skin on the side of his abdomen.

Gabriel leapt on the woman instinctively, using all his weight to subdue her. Poe recognized the woman as the wife of the salesman, both of whom her father had turned away. She realized in that moment that she hadn't even bothered to learn the woman's name before she had been kicked out. Despite her obvious anger at the woman for stabbing her father, she had to wonder what it said about herself that she showed more respect to the farm animals they slaughtered, giving them a name before they died, than she did another human being. A feeling that was something like shame flooded her, and she tried to shake off the nausea that came with it.

Possibly from the shock of being captured, the woman dropped the knife. "What the hell do you think you're doing, Anna? Huh?" Gabriel shook her as he spoke. Poe noticed that her brother *had* bothered to learn who she was, even knowing what her fate would potentially be. Evidently, there was more humanity left in her brother than in herself.

"It's his fault! My husband's dead and it's his fault. He lived a good life, never hurt anyone." She looked at Connor. "And you just sent him off to die…like he meant nothing," she sobbed under Gabriel's weight, and seemed to struggle for breath.

Poe was at her father's side, gently examining his wound. "He's okay. It's just a flesh wound. She barely made it through the skin." She helped her father sit on the ground, trying to give him a moment to recover from the shock. It surprised her to find him shaking, but only after the woman spoke.

"You could have killed him!" Gabriel continued to shake Anna, her head smacking hard against the ground as he did so. Just as Poe thought he was going to knock her unconscious, her mother pulled Gabriel up.

"Gabriel! No," Kate yelled. Anna took the opportunity to get up and run back into the woods from where she came.

"You let her get away!" Gabriel yelled at his mother. Poe had never seen him yell at her before and it made her stomach hurt.

Her mother put her hands on his shoulders. "I will not have you get blood on your hands. Not for this. There's going to be hard things that we will have to do now. We've already had to do things that no one your age should ever have to do." She glanced at Connor then turned her attention back toward Gabriel. "There may be a time where you have to take a life, but this is not that time. Even if all of them are still alive, now that we know it's a possibility, we will be ready."

Poe looked at her father. She expected him to be angry at Kate for letting his attacker go, but he wasn't even looking at her. He was staring straight at Gabriel. "Where'd she get the knife, Gabriel?" Her brother's face fell. The skin on his cheeks grew white. "She didn't have that knife when we saw her that night...she was wearing a dress. There were no bulges on her sides where a knife would be." Connor's voice grew low. "I'm only going to ask you one more time. Where did she get the knife?"

Gabriel avoided his gaze. "I'm so sorry, Dad."

"Say it."

He took a deep breath. "I never went back to the cars that night. I let them keep all their supplies." Suddenly, panic seemed to overtake him, and the voice that he could barely find moments earlier came out in a flood. "I thought they at least deserved a chance! I thought we would see them coming long before they could ever hurt us." He ran toward his father and knelt before him, like a subject to a king. "I'm so sorry. I never thought this would happen."

Poe found herself glaring at her brother. From her place at her father's side, she hissed, "*Exactly*."

Connor's silence hung in the air like the stench of death that no doubt permeated the town they had left behind. Poe just knelt there, frozen, unsure of what was about to happen next. Her brother and her father had never seen the world the same way, but this? Her father would see this as a complete disregard for everything he stood for. And that was something she wasn't sure either of them could recover from. It would certainly remain with her forever. She hoped that maybe, one day she could look at her brother and not have at least part of her see the gash in her father's side.

"Gabriel, take your father home. Blake can patch him up." Poe saw her pull Gabriel closer to her. "And talk to him on your way."

Connor shook his head and glared at Brian. "I'm not leaving you and Poe out here with *him*. Drew can fix my wound. I'm staying right here."

Her mother started to protest, when Drew jumped in. "Connor, Blake has more supplies back at the compound. Sure I can do a traveler's job, but you'd have less chance of infection getting worked on back there." Drew leaned over and spoke to him quietly, presumably so Brian couldn't hear. "Nothing will happen to your girls while I'm here. I promise."

Connor sat silently for a long time, staring into Drew's eyes. The exchange between the two men seemed deeper than the current circumstances. There seemed to be a wordless agreement between them, an interaction that Poe wasn't sure any of the rest of the group would understand—something that seemed bigger than a simple walk home.

Finally, her father spoke. "Keep them safe. Swear to me."

"I will."

Gabriel went over to his father and tried to help him get up, but Connor shook him off. As he headed back toward the house, Gabriel followed several feet behind, and Poe wondered if they'd ever walk side by side again.

When they were out of sight, her mother spoke again. "I know that was frightening everyone, but we still have a job to do. Everyone pick up their stuff and let's move on."

They went deeper into the woods, with no sign of a deer. Kate decided to have Brian use that time to practice some more. After about a half hour, Brian's arm began to cramp up, and they decided to move forward once again.

As they walked, Poe thought of her sister. She wondered if Harper would have leapt to Gabriel's defense, or flanked her father as she had done. After what her father had done to Harper when Brian first arrived, she guessed the former. If that had never happened, the answer may have been different. Harper had made an art form out of getting what she wanted, but it was always something trivial. When she had finally asked for something real, she had still gotten it, but it had come at a cost. It occurred to Poe that she may be the only one of her father's children that still had any desire to make him happy, and the pressure of that weighed on her like a thousand stars.

Just as they had gathered up all of the arrows, a deer poked its head out of a nearby cluster of trees. The group ducked down and slowly moved toward it, keeping their steps slow and deliberate. The deer seemed to sense them, and continued to move deeper and deeper into the woods, its dark coal eyes searching for them but unable to find where they were hiding. Though Poe was enjoying the smell of the forest after a fresh rain, she noticed that as they were stalking the deer, they were traveling much farther away from the compound than they normally did. "Shouldn't we turn back?" she asked her mother.

"Normally I would say yes, but we don't know how much longer we're going to be able to find game like this. We need to take advantage of this opportunity." Though something inside Poe told her to turn back, they pressed on.

Finally, the deer stopped long enough for them to get a clear shot. "Please, let me do it," Brian said as she started to raise her own weapon.

"Look, I know you're getting better, but…"

"Please. I…" Brian lowered his voice to a whisper. "I need this. I need to feel like I'm helping. I'm so tired of being useless. Please."

Against her better judgement, Poe relented, lowering her bow. "Just don't miss."

He didn't. The arrow plunged right into the deer's leg. Unfortunately, that did not render him immobile, and he bounded even deeper into the woods. "He's hurt! I can finish him off!" Brian took off after the wounded creature.

"Brian no! We don't know what's there. Slow down!" The rest of the group hurried after him, finding their cries ignored. Poe wasn't used to running through the woods, ignoring the loud crunch that her footsteps made which she would normally worry would scare away her prey. "Stop!"

The smell should have been enough. But Brian didn't stop until he was right on the edge of the embankment. The rest of the group gathered around him, wanting to know what finally made him stop his pursuit.

Poe didn't stop fast enough.

She was in the pit before she even knew her feet had left the ground. She saw Drew watch for a moment right before she turned her head and was met with the blue, contorted face of a corpse. The sight made the scream that she was feeling deep inside her catch in her throat, and she was unable to get out more than a rasp. She scrambled to get herself away from it, but as she did so, another shifted in the pile around her and landed on top of her, pinning her to the side of another. A dead hand rested against her thigh, as if inviting her to stay with him, to lie down among them because after the pandemic had chewed them up, that's where they would find themselves eventually, company among the dead and stories for the dying.

Poe knew she shouldn't, but she did it anyway. As she sat there, pinned down by a mountain of decaying flesh, she searched the faces for people that she recognized. Their town was small enough…she was certain that there would be someone in the pit that she knew, possibly several of them.

She was right.

She didn't recognize him at first, since she had only seen him once before: on the night that her father chose who would live and who would die. Lying on top of a pile adjacent to her, looking as though someone had dragged him to the edge and rolled him in, not having the strength to carry the full weight of him, was George, the man who her father had replaced with Blake.

Poe hoped it wasn't his wife who had to dump him there. Maybe the people her father had turned away had stuck together and some other person had saved her from having her last memory of her husband be the rubbery touch of his cold dead hands. His face was pointed toward the sky, and Poe thought to herself that while they weren't buried under the dirt, at night, they were buried under the stars, and maybe that counted for something too. If Tonya were there, she would have told her that, though Poe had a feeling Tonya wouldn't let her get that far. Poe couldn't say she would blame her. If someone had condemned someone she loved to death, no words would ever soothe the anger that would rest deep inside her heart. It would lay right beside the love for the person that she would have to spend the rest of her life missing with the fierce passion that came with a life cut short.

Her breath came in huge gulps, and she thought she was about to pass out when she saw Drew jump into the pit beside her, throwing the body off of her. "Are you all right?"

"My ankle…it really hurts." Drew seemed to ignore the blue and gray faces around them as he gently pressed the bone, watching as she winced. "The bodies…"

"Don't look at them, look at me." He made eye contact with her and held it, and despite who he was, she couldn't help but be grateful.

"It's not broken, but it's sprained." He yelled up to the horrified onlookers. She shifted her focus to Drew and her mother's screams seemed muffled. "Tie a rope to that tree and toss it to us." As he yelled the instructions, he glanced up and realized they were already wrapping the rope around the trunk. He turned back to Poe. "Now I'm going to squat down and I want you to wrap your legs around me the best you can, and hold on to my neck. I'm going to get you out of here."

Poe nodded. "Thank you…I mean really…" Drew waited for her as she tried to find the right words when she realized she had already retrieved them. "Thank you."

Securing his footing, he carefully pulled them up and out of the pit. A couple times, Poe watched as the crumbly dirt gave way and he had to find another step before he had planned on it, but after some meticulous climbing, they were back on solid ground.

She didn't tell anyone who she had seen.

Brian reached a hand out to Poe to help her off Drew's back, but she waved him away. Drew echoed her actions.

"Thank you very much for your help everyone. Now stay as far away from us as you can."

As the house grew closer, the first person Poe saw in the distance was her father. They had been gone far longer than they usually were when they went hunting, and the entire group was running toward them in a panic. Unfortunately, Poe thought, they had no idea how panicked they should really be.

"Stay away from me!" Poe shouted at her father, who was now at full speed. She struggled to stay propped up next to Drew while she simultaneously waved off the coming crowd. If she had caught the disease and he touched her before she could stop him, she would never forgive herself. "Stay away!" Her father only slowed his pace when he noticed that Brian and Kate were following Drew and Poe at a significant distance.

His already quite pale face grew white. "What happened?"

She looked at Drew. "He saved my life." She gingerly reached for his hand. "I fell in a pit…the place where they dumped…the people from town. He jumped in after me and saved me. He didn't even hesitate for a second."

Her father looked at Drew with an expression Poe had never seen before. "Is that true? You saved my daughter?"

"Her ankle was hurt. She couldn't get out. I couldn't just leave her in there."

Poe expected her father to say thank you, but he didn't. Instead, he got ready to do damage control, and to her surprise, glanced away like a wounded animal. She expected a bit more sentiment, but realized that her father was who he was, and not even a near-death experience would stop him from being himself. "You were both in the pit with the infected. You will have to stay out here for the night."

Drew glared at him. "Brian was only out here for a couple hours."

Connor glanced at her mother before continuing. "Yes, but he wasn't lying in a pile of the dead. I think the extra precaution would be wise. I'll call Gordon on the radio and see if he's heard of any other precautions for something like this." He stared at Poe. "You're going to be fine, sweetheart. I promise." She took his statement as the sentiment she'd been waiting for. Connor never promised things in the way most fathers did: the way where the child knows it's just a sweet yet futile attempt to make them feel better. Connor's way was different. When Connor said it, Poe knew he truly believed he could change the outcome of whatever situation. Like everything else he built through his own blood and time, he could mold it into whatever shape he wanted it to be. To her, he could move the stars if he wanted to badly enough. So when he told her she would be fine, she knew he would make that happen.

There was only a small voice whispering in the back of her head that said maybe her father didn't have as much control as she thought.

As everyone else went back to the house, as ordered by Connor, Vera lingered. Poe watched her try to come toward Drew, and saw him being ever-vigilant enough to not let her. "I don't care if I get sick. There's nothing here without you.

Please, let me come to you." The tears in her eyes were caught by her trembling lip as they slid off her face.

"I love you, Vera. You know I can't do that. I won't."

Vera stepped closer anyway.

"I will run down this mountain until morning, back toward those…people…if that's the only way I can keep you away from me. Please, go back inside." She still hesitated. "You know I'll do it."

With a heavy sigh, Vera seemed to know she was defeated, and ran back toward the house. They could hear her sobs for minutes after they lost sight of her.

***

That night, Poe and Drew built a campfire and stared up at the stars. After her experience, she couldn't help but think of George. "Feel anything?" Poe asked.

Drew shook his head. "No, you?"

"Nope. Nothing." A question lingered on Poe's lips. She considered it for a moment, then asked it. After all, she had no idea how much longer she would feel okay. Either never at all or in one minute, maybe ten, she could start to feel that something in her body was off: a tickle in the back of her throat, a dull ache at the base of her head, she had no idea. All she knew was something simple would tell her it was over . What would be the last thing she would tell her mother, or Harper? She considered deciding what it would be, but realized her last words would never be heard. Of course Drew would hear them, but they would never make it to the people they were intended for, because she would make sure they would never get close enough to say goodbye.

Rather than think of words that she hoped would never be spoken, she decided to ask her question. "If we make it, why do you think that is? I mean gosh, if anyone is going to get sick, it's going to be us." Drew looked at her. "Sorry…it's true though."

"I know."

Several minutes went by, and Poe thought she was never going to get an answer to her question. Drew just sat there, grabbing fallen leaves and ripping them into fine strips, one right after another. As he passed the time destroying foliage, she found herself getting lost looking at a shooting star.

Finally, Drew spoke. "If we don't get sick, there could be several reasons. If it passes through bodily fluid, we must not have any open cuts or sores." Poe did a quick scan of her own skin, and found nothing. Drew did the same and seemed satisfied that he was wound-free. "Or…there could be a genetic reason that some people get it and some don't."

"Like what?"

"I don't know, could be anything really." Drew got up and threw some more wood on the fire. "Could be something as complicated as a genetic abnormality that makes you and I immune, or it could be something as simple as us both having brown eyes. You just never know."

"Or maybe it's just dumb luck."

Drew laughed. "That could be true too. If so, I'll happily take it."

After about an hour of silence, they both curled up on the ground next to the fire and tried to go to sleep. But Poe had one more question for Drew, one that she knew he would probably not see coming. He may have not even known she knew what happened. Most difficult questions had a way of sneaking up on a person, like a shadow that falls over you like rain. "Was it your fault that the baby died?"

Drew had been stirring, but right then he lay perfectly still. Facing away from Poe, he whispered. "I don't know."

"Thank you."

At that, he turned to face her. "Not much of an answer. Why are you thanking me?"

"Because it was honest. You could have told me no. You had no reason to tell me the truth, especially now. I would have never known. But you said what you believe to be true. You aren't sure either. Thank you."

Drew seemed to consider his response then went with, "You're welcome."

Poe wondered if her question hovered in Drew's sleep, seeping into his dreams. In a way, part of her still hoped so, but most of her hoped he stopped wondering, and was sleeping with just a little bit of the peace she herself found so elusive. She looked up at the clear night sky, and as she picked out different constellations as she had only previously done with Connor, she began to wonder if the monster that he had created with his words was really just a man who made a terrible decision, one that cost her unborn sister or brother their life, but had cost *him* something too.

CHAPTER FOURTEEN

CONNOR (before)

Every now and again, Connor would be just going about his day, whether that meant tending the garden, or reading a book on the back porch, when he would hear Kate's scream from that day echoing in his head. It would ring out like a cry from an old forgotten battlefield, countless victims lying next to each other, their anguish being heard for miles yet heard by no one other than the dying. When the actual scream had taken place, he had thought for a moment that it was a bird caught in a trap somewhere on their land; until Poe came running out to the field where he was, her arms making fast, quick strokes at her sides. "Dad! It's Mom! Come quick! There's blood!"

Kate never slept in their bed again. That night, Connor dragged their first marital bed, the bed where they had conceived all their children, out to the burn pile. He threw it on top of all the branches and dead things that he had planned on getting rid of after the pile got bigger, but instead, the mattress completed it. As he heard the snap of the match as he struck it, he took one last glance at the giant wave of blood that had enveloped the middle of the mattress. It was still covered in their sheets, but there was no question that it was soaked through. He knew there would be no getting the stain out of the satin linens, though knowing Kate, she would have tried if he'd let her. So instead, he had left everything whole, and threw the flame down on top of it. As the red disappeared in a flood of orange, he had two thoughts running through his mind. One was that Kate had been right.

The other: the whole town could burn in hell.

He had heard the good doctor the day of their appointment a couple weeks earlier, joining in with his staff as they made fun of his family. "The hermits thought they were pregnant? Of course they did," that nurse had said. "Leave it to them to screw up a pee test," another had piped in. "They can build a bomb shelter, but they can't urinate on a stick properly!" one had laughed. "If you asked them how to kill somebody and use the body as fertilizer, I bet they'd know." He remembered the snicker on Dr. Matthew's face when he said, "Okay that's enough. Get back to work." That had been the extent of his scolding, and then he had gone on about his day. He didn't even blink when Connor had reappeared to get his keys. The others though—oh, how their faces changed when they saw him, their masks put back perfectly in place.

That night, Kate spent the evening lying in their new bed. The last thing he had wanted to do was go into town and pay anyone for anything, but he wanted to turn their room back to normal for her as soon as possible, and that meant not waiting for a mattress to be shipped. So begrudgingly, he went to the furniture store and bought the mattress, as well as new sheets. The look on the clerk's face said that he was considering telling Connor he couldn't shop there, but Connor's expression told him he'd be taking his own life in his hands if he tried. So instead, he and another member of the staff carried the mattress out to his truck, tied it in tightly, and quickly ushered Connor off into the darkness.

Connor spent most of the night sitting alone in the dark downstairs, thinking and wishing for things to rewind, to have turned out differently. When he finally pulled the sheets down to get into bed, he had thought Kate was asleep until he heard her soft voice: "Do you think…if we had been anybody else….would he have done the blood test? If we weren't who we are I mean? Would the baby still be here?"

"I…I don't know." The truth was, he *did* know. They had become victims of the mob mentality, the collective brain that had condemned them all. Somehow through the word of one little girl, he had become a killer in their eyes, or at the very least, someone who they thought of as less-than, someone who couldn't be trusted. The humiliation he suffered when he had been banned from the bookstore, the one sanctuary he'd had in that place, was nothing compared to what those imbeciles had done to his family. He and Kate had two children who were emotionally brutalized, one who had been beaten, and now another was dead. All because their neighbors harbored a fear of what they didn't understand. Connor knew that worlds had been built and destroyed by fear, and now his own world had crumbled alongside them.

They weren't the only ones to blame, however. He should have insisted on the blood test, he knew that in his heart. *He* had failed Kate, right along with Dr. Matthews, right along with the town. But if the opportunity ever presented itself, he would not fail her again. He made a promise to himself and to her that once the time was right, they would all pay for the child that no longer was.

CHAPTER FIFTEEN

CONNOR

It was a strange and cruel thing to have the person Connor hated most in the world be the same person to save him from the precipice, to see the same person who destroyed his world make it whole again.

Connor would not have believed that Drew saved Poe's life if he hadn't heard it from her mouth. Anyone else could have told him, even Kate, and he would have called them a liar. He would have assumed Kate was trying to make peace, putting the cohesiveness of the group ahead of the truth, prettying up a helpful hand into a heroic act. Anyone else in the group would have clearly had other motives. Cassius would have been trying to undermine Connor's authority, and Darius, he would have just been doing his brother's bidding. Harper or Gabriel would have just been exaggerating to prove they were right all along, using it as an opportunity to prove that they were grown up and had ideas of their own. But Poe...when she spoke of matters she knew to be so close to his heart, he listened.

He couldn't imagine it, watching her die; and he would

have watched. The only thing more unbearable to him than her dying would be for her to do it alone. Before the internet had gone out, he had seen the pictures: faces devoid of humanity, flesh sinking into bone, all races becoming one pale, dead, tone: becoming the color of the dolls in Harper's room, harboring the same empty eyes. Poe was supposed to be exempt from that; he had built the compound to guard against such a tragedy. And one simple slip on loose dirt had almost destroyed it all.

When Poe and Drew returned from their quarantine and entered the compound once more, Connor promptly made his way to the opposite end of their property. As much as he wanted to see his daughter, after coming so close to losing her, he knew an important conversation with Drew was coming, and he simply wasn't ready for it. He and Kate had planted a circle of Japanese maples and stuck a bench that Gabriel had made out of a fallen log in the middle of it. Whoever sat on the bench could not be seen from the house, and that's exactly how Connor wanted it. He could look up at the crisp crimson leaves and lose himself, if only for a few moments before some responsibility called him away, and he was once again the organizer of the chaos.

He had wondered shortly after Drew first arrived if he would be the one: much to his dismay. It had never crossed his mind, until he saw Drew lie in order to save Blake's life. Connor hadn't even made up his mind if he was going to give Drew a spot in the compound at all, and if he had decided to, the purpose would have strictly been for his medical knowledge, and for the opportunity to make him pay for killing their child with his criminal negligence. But Connor had seen time and time again that the only thing certain in life was uncertainty, and Drew had certainly surprised him.

Drew had condemned another man to death in order to save one of his own, a man that he had probably known all his life. He looked into his reddened face, and listened to the screams of his wife, a woman who probably had never done anything to him at all, and said the words that were necessary to seal both their fates. That was the kind of purposeful cruelty that Connor would need, the kind that no one in his own family possessed.

Though that had caught his eye, there was more than one criterion that he was looking for. And Drew had just checked off the most important one. It was evident that Drew was willing to do whatever he had to save someone he considered family, but would he do the same for *Connor's* family?

It now appeared that the answer was yes.

Connor leaned forward, resting his forearms on his legs. The day before, Drew had crawled into a pit of the dead in order to pull his daughter out of it. Last they heard, the government still had no idea how the disease was spreading. With communication down to those who had ham radios and so many people with medical knowledge dead or dying, exposing oneself to the disease in any way was to dangle one's own life off the edge of a cliff.

Drew jumped into that hole to save Poe, not having any idea if he would make it home to see his wife that night. For all he knew, he could have gotten sick right then, and he wouldn't have even been able to tell her goodbye. He would have had to leave his final words with Kate, and he would have been lost to the earth.

Poe would have been gone too, his daughter becoming one of the many victims of the indiscriminant disease that didn't care how much he loved her. It didn't care that her favorite meal was spaghetti, that she nursed a baby bird back to health when she was five, or that Gemini was her favorite constellation. It didn't care that her sister would be a hollow mass without her, wandering aimlessly without her compass to tell her which way made sense, so that she would know to do the opposite. A person needs a direction, even if it's wrong.

Her mother would have never recovered. Losing one child was impossible: losing another would have made her implode on herself, and he knew he'd never reach her after that. He would have spent the rest of his days watching Kate, afraid that if he turned away for a precious second she would use it to take her own life. He wouldn't be able to leave her alone in the kitchen, worried that the minute his back was turned she would take a steak knife through an artery, or if he left her to take a bath she would sink down into the water, purposely inhaling it deep into her lungs.

Drew prevented all of it. The man who had stolen one child from him had saved another. What did that mean for Connor? Was he now required to forgive? Not necessarily... but as with everything else, he had to make sure his family's safety was at the core of every decision he ever made.

Especially the next one.

After dinner, Connor guided Drew away from the rest of the group. He found himself having to corner him, since Drew had been spending every minute since he had returned from quarantine talking with the rest of the group. Understandable, he supposed. He'd imagine that, at least for most people, excluding himself, when someone thinks they may die, they want to be around other people, partially from joy, and partially for distraction from what may have been. "Will you come walk with me? Alone?" He sensed Drew's hesitation. "It won't take long."

"I've been away from Vera for quite a while..."

"Please..."

Drew looked over at Vera. Though she looked anxious, perhaps Drew's curiosity got the better of him. "Okay."

Connor often took a walk around the property after dinner, though almost never with anyone else. It was normally time he used to think, letting the sounds of nature soothe the anxiety that always lingered in his heart. He wondered what Kate thought as he and Drew walked out the door. Surely there would be some questions for him when he returned, but for now, he still took pleasure in the fact that Drew didn't have the slightest clue what was about to happen. Of course in a way, neither did he. "You know, I built most of this place myself, out of things that no longer had a purpose. The house? Old shipping containers and wood. They all had some sort of perceived defect, so I got them cheap. They're all still perfectly good though. The barbed wire on the top of the fence? Stole that from the abandoned prison a couple towns over."

Drew nodded cautiously. "What about those poisonous herbs? The ones you grow with the other normal plants?" His face appeared cautious as if even as he said the words he wasn't sure he wanted to. The sun was turning the sky blood red, echoing the sentiment that maybe, just maybe, he didn't really want to know.

Connor smiled proudly. "Now that, that's the real kicker." He lowered his voice to a whisper, though there wasn't anyone around to hear them. "Anybody will sell you anything for the right price. You'd like to think they wouldn't, but trust me...even the most angelic person can be bought off with enough cash." Connor tried to read Drew's face, but Drew somehow managed to keep a vacant expression.

Impressive, he thought.

They reached the edge of the property and took refuge in the circle of Japanese Maples where Connor had spent that morning thinking about the next step. "Sit," he said. He tried to keep his tone polite, but he couldn't help his words coming out as a command. Nevertheless, Drew obeyed, sitting down on the one part of the bench that creaked under any form of weight. Connor noticed him look around self-consciously at the sound.

For a few moments, the two men sat silently. Drew's whole body had tightened as rigid as tree bark, but Connor remained loose.

Or at least he thought he had.

"Connor, what's this about? You look as nervous as I feel. Why did you bring me out here?"

Connor massaged the palm of one hand with the other,

looking at the lines in the hopes that maybe they would tell him what to say next. No matter how little you valued the person you were talking to, it was always hard to say something you weren't prepared to acknowledge yourself. And from the looks of his situation, he valued Drew quite a bit more than he thought.

"I'm dying."

Silence.

"I found out right before the pandemic hit that I have a bad heart." He laughed. "Imagine being so prepared…every detail planned down to the wire, only to be hit with that. That's the one thing I couldn't figure out. Sure, I hoarded as much medicine as I could, but there was only so much I could get my hands on. No time. Unless we find out different, most everyone's dead, and I really doubt there will be many people taking the time to make pharmaceuticals."

"Why are you telling me this?"

Connor locked eyes with Drew. "I knew Blake was useless from the beginning." He paused. "Actually she'd proven to be quite the fast learner, but I knew when you arrived that the only skills she could offer the group was helping to keep us all groomed."

Connor watched as the other man grew pale. "Don't worry, it impressed me. Made me think you weren't such a worthless person after all."

"If you knew, why'd you let her come?"

"It wasn't about her. It was about you. You saved her. You killed a man and his wife to save her. I need someone like that here, someone with the instincts of a survivor. Especially now." He looked up to see the sun was completely hidden by the mountains, and the bright red was replaced by a dark blue. "I had to be sure though. Had to be sure that you would do that for the other people here, for not just your people…*my* people. And you proved that." He paused. "How did you do that exactly? Jump into a pit of dead people for someone in the grand scheme of things you barely know?"

Drew hesitated. "I don't know really. Instinct I guess… and I tried not to look at them."

"How could you possibly not look at them?"

"Because I knew if I looked at them I couldn't un-look at them."

Connor pondered his answer for a moment. "That actually makes sense."

After what seemed like several minutes of silence, Drew pivoted to face him. "What exactly are you asking me to do?"

Connor suddenly felt sick. He didn't want to have to depend on this man to keep his children and his wife safe. That was supposed to be his job. He'd built his whole life around that task, and he felt it slipping away. His stomach twisted, and before he realized it, vomit fell across the tops of his shoes, and he felt unsteady. His mouth became dry and he ached for just a precious sip of water. Drew grabbed him by the arm. "Are you all right?"

He wiped his hand across his brow. "I need you to be in charge here. After me. Keep them all alive."

Drew released him. "Gosh…don't you think someone else may be more suited? What about Kate? Darius? Or maybe Cassius?"

Connor grabbed Drew by the shoulders and shook him. "It has to be you. It has to."

"But why?"

"Because you're the only one who can. Cassius just wants to be in charge for the sake of it. Darius wouldn't want it, and Gabriel…Gabriel's not ready and he may never be. The girls are too young. Kate…Kate's the most kind, forgiving person that ever walked this earth." His sudden display of emotion made him feel vulnerable, and his head began to hurt. "Somewhere inside, you know as well as I do that kindness will be what ultimately gets them killed, without me to tell her no." He paused. "And besides, you owe me." He felt Drew attempt to lean back away from him. Desperation charged through his blood and he felt hot. "Please!"

"Okay. I'll do it. Of course I'll do it."

Connor sighed in relief. "Thank you."

A long silence hung in the air between the two men. All they could hear was the mosquitos buzzing in their ears and the frogs croaking at the nearby stream.

Drew was the first to speak. "You need more medicine. We need you around as long as we can have you."

Connor sneered. "Why, Drew, I didn't know you cared."

"You know more about this place than anyone. And besides…" He trailed off.

"What?"

"Your children. They deserve as much time with their father as they can get."

Connor was surprised that he agreed with anything that Drew said, despite what he had just asked of him. Turning off years of bitterness with one conversation was impossible, though if he was going to get Drew ready, he would have to do it anyway. "What did you have in mind?"

"Well first, where do you keep the keys to that heap of metal you call a truck?"

***

The two men waited until everyone else went to bed. Connor kissed Kate on both the lips and the forehead the same as he had every night since their wedding. He didn't know what ritual Drew and Vera had, but he was sure that they had participated in one of their own as he met him at the door to the kitchen. He saw Drew take one quick look over his shoulder as they stepped out into the night.

The warm, wet air hit both of them like a Colorado autumn, suffocating them for just a moment before they steadied themselves. He took a moment to realize that they would never make it to Colorado, family vacations being one of the things lost forever to the disease. Or at least that's what Connor told himself. A small part of him acknowledged he'd had no intention of ever taking Kate there to begin with, no matter how much she wanted to. So selfish, he knew, but the desire to stay away from throngs of loud, sweat-ridden tourists had overridden his desire to please his wife. He hoped there wasn't a slew of other dreams of hers that he'd forgotten in order to feed into his own desires.

"I'm putting her through too much," Drew said.

"Then why are you doing this?"

Drew smiled a regretful smile. "Like you said, I owe you one."

Connor slid into the driver's seat and turned the key. "Let's get on with it then."

He watched Drew watch him as he drove the car toward the opposite direction of where they had come from that first day. "Where are we going?

"You'll see."

They drove around toward the back of the property. Just as Drew thought they were about to drive right through part of the wall surrounding the compound, a section of it slowly started to open. Connor reached over, opened the glove box in front of Drew's seat, and pointed to a small red sensor that was hidden in the back of it, barely noticeable. "There's a sensor on the wall that reads it."

"God, I couldn't even tell that section opened."

"That's the point. It blends in seamlessly. That way, there's always an exit strategy."

"Why are you telling me this now?"

"You know why."

The gravel road threw them about the cab with the sudden sharpness of a firework, and shot pains through their bodies like being punched by an angry child. The truck was built to act functionally, not for pleasant Sunday drives. Connor reiterated that if you have to get out of somewhere quickly, there was no time for creature comforts. Drew complained that surely, there was enough room for at least an old towel to sit on.

They rounded the bend and the town greeted them with an image different than they could have ever imagined. Only a few months had passed, yet the town looked as if the earth had been scorched years before, leaving abandoned buildings with doors that had long since been left open swaying gently. The night was rather still, so Connor had an uneasy feeling as he wondered where the doors had found the breeze with which to move. Drew rolled down the window just enough so that they could listen for anything that would give them an idea that they were not alone.

No sound drifted in.

As they drove to the clinic, they looked at all the homes, and Connor could almost picture how they were supposed to look: in his mind's eye, the porch rocking chairs still had people in them, knitting or sipping lemonade. Old women were gossiping and men clinked their blonde ales together, probably while discussing their high school glory days where they were more than a father or a friend, or at least they thought they were. The hot dog stand on the corner still had forty-year-old-with-a-grilled-cheese-gut Freddie Johnson waving his tongs at them as they drove by, a big smile on his face, his red and white striped apron stained with golden mustard. The park was still sprinkled with loud children, where it was impossible to distinguish if any of them were laughing or screaming.

They parked the truck in the back of the clinic, careful to lock it and keep the keys with them. "There's no one here," Drew said.

"Don't get sloppy. That's when you make a mistake. You can't make mistakes when you are…" he swallowed and looked at the ground, then regained his composure. He wasn't ready to say the three words that had flowed through his head like acid: *when I'm gone.* "Let's go."

Connor had expected to break a window, but Drew pulled out a set of keys from his pocket and held them up for him to see. "I didn't imagine that I would ever *not* need to come back here. Even as we were driving away it didn't seem real." He separated a little silver one with a red rubber marker encircling the top and plunged it into the lock. Connor had expected him to fumble around like an idiot, making too much noise, but Drew's certainty reassured him. If only a little.

As Drew moved to thrust open the door, Connor caught his hand. "Be careful. We go in quietly, no matter how it looks."

Connor expected some protest, but received none. He noticed that he suddenly felt a need to take time to instruct Drew on the more detailed aspects of survival, the tiny shreds of material that he hadn't taken the time to teach the other people in the group. Drew would need detail as much as large scale knowledge in order to take his place. Connor hoped that he would absorb all new information quickly, and he had noticed the further they got away from the normalcy of the pre-apocalyptic world, the louder the ticking clock in his head had become. It pounded in his ears during conversations with his wife, as he tended the garden, even in the quiet of the forest as he hunted for their next meal. What was once a soft tapping now rang out like a pounding drum.

The sickly feeling returned again. Connor wasn't ready, though he knew he had to be. Nothing can prepare a person to instruct someone how to carry on after they're gone. It's an odd paradox of hoping they don't fill your role as well as you do, yet also hoping that they do. More than most, Connor had to force his way past the first feeling and into the second. "Did you bring a weapon?" he asked just before they entered the building. Drew would always need to remember a weapon from now on. He wondered what the doctor would pick: a gun, knife…he struck him as more of a large object kind of man, something that could knock someone down but that would allow him to not get blood on his hands. Drew would have to learn to accept the burden that came with deliberately taking life, a very different circumstance than if someone happens to die on an operating table, and be able to thrust himself back into the world a moment after. He could not afford weeks of wallowing, no one could—not anymore.

"You don't let us have any. Remember?"

Connor let the realization sink in for a moment then retreated back to the truck. Carefully and as quietly as he could, he opened the trunk with his own key and pulled out a four-inch thick piece of wood that had several nails sticking out of the end of it and handed it to Drew. He would start him off slow, but not too slow. "Aim for the vitals."

"What if they mean no harm?"

"They always mean harm, whether they know it or not."

Drew opened his mouth, perhaps to argue, but closed it again and followed him back to the door, where Connor pulled out a switchblade knife from his back pocket. "Come on."

Carefully, Connor searched the building with Drew

following closely behind him. He hoped Drew was paying attention, watching the way he moved, with soft, cautious steps, and looking around…always looking.

The office looked very different at night than during normal working hours, the blackness seeming to fit the sinister thing that happened to Connor's family there. What was once a peaceful, beige-and-flower-covered family practice looked more like a deserted mental hospital in the darkness, the roses on the wallpaper looking like a dead bouquet left on a gravestone.

Connor preferred it that way.

Despite finding no one, he continued speaking in a whisper. "Where do you keep the samples?"

"In the back." Drew took him to the back room behind the front office and unlocked it with another key, this time, one with a blue rubber label encircling the round part of it. The lock on the door was a substantial one, large and gold. The door itself was thick and metal. He noticed that there seemed to be some dents in it, as though people had tried to break into the room before they had arrived and had no luck.

"Why such a high-security door?" Connor asked.

Drew struggled for a moment as the door stuck, damaged from defending its contents against the intruders. "Before this, I came from a practice that was situated in a bad neighborhood. We always had people trying to break in to steal medication. I told myself the minute I had my own practice, the first thing I would do would be to buy a medicine cabinet that would protect our stuff." Drew went inside with Connor close behind him.

Thank goodness for petty criminals, Connor thought.

The room had no windows, and was lined on both sides with metal shelves. Connor picked up a bottle at the beginning and realized it was not alphabetized like he had hoped. "How the hell do you keep these straight?"

Drew moved toward the middle of the room and picked up a bottle. "By ailment." He held up a bottle. "See? Heart. H. Middle."

Connor snatched the bottle. "This isn't what I take. Did you just take me here to pick out something to kill me quicker or what?"

"Don't be stupid." That was the first time the good doctor broke his calm veneer. Connor liked it. "Grab that plastic bag over there and just dump them all in. See if your medicine is in here, but if not, just take it all and you can keep the ones you don't recognize as a last resort."

Connor started sweeping everything in the "heart" section into the plastic bag. As he was doing that, he saw Drew leave the room and come back with a large, black leather bag. Throwing it open, with one swift motion he pushed everything on the first shelf into the bag. "What are you doing?"

"We might need these too at some point."

Connor smiled. "What if other people come by and need them?"

"I guess they will have to look somewhere else."

"Good answer." Drew was adapting already.

After he filled up the first bag, Drew grabbed two more bags that he found around the office: one briefcase, and one backpack that he said his assistant's son had left there the day they first heard about the plague. By the time they were done, the shelves were empty. Drew loaded them into the car. When he came back, he found Connor sitting on the floor just outside the medicine room, his back against the wall. Not saying a word, Drew slid down beside him. They just existed next to each other for several minutes, letting themselves become part of the atmosphere: not disturbing it, just being in it like the air around them. Finally, Drew broke the quiet in two. "You know, you can live a long time with a heart problem."

"Maybe. In normal circumstances."

"Connor, you've made existing in this world possible. You decided that your family would live. And they did. Now decide that you will too."

"They aren't ready."

"You aren't giving them nearly enough credit."

Connor stared off into the darkness. "What would you do? Would you tell them?" He didn't expect to ask the question, and the words stayed in the air as if they had appeared on their own. More, he didn't expect to care what Drew's answer would be.

"You mean you haven't yet?"

"No. I think it would be too much for them."

"I'd tell them."

Connor sneered. "In that case, I'll keep it to myself."

They continued to sit in the dark for several minutes. When they would normally be assaulted with the sounds of nighttime: honking cars, the soft whir of a gas pedal, they were met with nothingness. "You know, I never actually said I was sorry."

"No, you didn't."

"I'm sorry, Connor. You were right. It *was* my fault. I'm truly sorry about the baby…*your* baby."

Connor stood up a little straighter, and noticed a peculiar feeling sweep over him, something like relief, both from the crushing weight of hating someone and from the absence of needing acknowledgement of his suffering. He remembered something a teacher had told him once: do not say *it's okay* after someone apologizes, because *it's not okay, is it?* So he opted for a different response. "Thank you." He paused. "And thank you for saving my daughter. I—I don't know what I would have…" Connor caught himself. That was not the time for an emotional break. His family need him to be strong now more than ever. "Thank you."

Drew nodded, and as he sat in the building that had changed his life forever, amongst the folding chairs, nameless drugs, and children's candy, Connor wondered if he felt a little lighter too.

CHAPTER SIXTEEN

POE

Drew and Connor didn't think anyone saw them leave the compound, but they were wrong. After narrowly escaping death (though in their situation they could never be sure for how long), Poe was unable to sleep more than a few hours, and lingered at her blue velvet window seat long after night had fallen. Blake caught her staring out the window. "Were those headlights I saw?"

"Yes. I think it was my dad and Drew." Poe tried to ignore the sinking feeling in her stomach. Her dad never liked anyone to leave the compound, except to hunt, and he wasn't hunting at night. If they left in that big of a hurry, there had to be something wrong. And for him to be leaving with Drew? Whatever it was had to have shaken him to the core, and the idea of her father being thrown off balance sent her teetering too.

Blake rubbed the sleep from her eyes. "Any idea what they were doing? Where would he be taking Drew? I'm sure he still hates him even though he saved you. That much animosity doesn't just go away."

"I don't know." Poe moved away from the window and sat back down on her bed. She peered over the edge and for a moment watched Jackson as he slept. "I couldn't sleep…even before the apocalypse. I guess you were right…he could sleep through a train driving through this room." She kept her voice normal, but her insides were still shaken.

"I hardly sleep anymore. It's true what they say…that when you're a parent, you never sleep again. Even when you get past the SIDs danger zone, there's still plenty of other things to worry about."

"Like what?"

Blake smiled. "Oh, just pick one. It's amazing the stuff you can come up with as a mother." She grabbed a toy off the floor, and put it back on a small section of shelf that Poe had cleared off for Jackson.

"Could his father sleep?" As soon as Poe said it, she wished she could take it back. "I'm sorry. It's none of my business."

"It's okay."

A question swirled around in Poe's mind, and she wondered if it was an appropriate one. After some thought, she decided she had already broached the subject, and she might as well continue. "It's just…you never talk about him. Where is he?"

"In St. John's Cemetery."

Poe leaned back, the weight of that answer knocking her off balance as much as her father's mysterious errand had, if not more. "Oh my gosh I'm so sorry. I had no idea."

"Poe, it's okay, really. Not many people do." She got up

and took a seat next to Poe and slid her feet under the top blanket. "His name was Julian." A smile spread across her face. "He was going to be the best father. He was amazing. We were going to get married after he finished his second year as a cop. I had picked out the place and everything." Poe smiled as Blake spoke, despite knowing that the story ended with a fatherless child and a wife-to-be who was married to the pain of her loss instead of the man she loved. "It was going to be in this little garden… you know the one by the community center that the kids put together? I think it was there when you guys were still around."

"I do remember. We went there on a field trip once."

"He volunteered there as part of an outreach program at the precinct. He helped every one of those kids plant a flower or a vegetable in that garden. He had such a good memory that he could have told you who planted what. His mind…if he hadn't been a cop he would have been a fantastic lawyer."

"What happened to him?"

Blake still smiled, but she wrung the sheets of Poe's bed with her hands. "So stupid. Just a routine traffic stop. Some guy had a tail light out…and also an arrest warrant for armed robbery. When Julian was on his way back to the guy's window after running his license through the system he opened fire." She paused. "They left him there. On the side of the road."

"I'm so sorry, Blake. It's so unfair." They sat silently for a moment, Poe holding Blake's hand and Blake letting her. Poe hadn't held someone's hand before, at least not someone who wasn't related to her. She liked the warmth, and the closeness that it seemed to symbolize. "Do you ever… nevermind…"

"No, what?"

"I can't imagine having to raise a child without his father. I think it could be the worst thing in the world. Do you ever wish you'd just never met?" She hoped Blake wouldn't take her hand away.

Blake nodded. "Not a day goes by where something doesn't happen that I wish I could tell him about. The time Jackson learned to throw a ball, his first word…all of it." Her chin trembled a bit. "There were so many nights where I would put a smile on my face for Jackson, and just ache for the minute he went to bed so that I could curl up on the couch and cry. When someone you love dies, every inch of your body physically hurts: your lungs, your muscles, every bit, inside and out. I ached every morning when I got out of bed and every night when I crawled back in, if I ever did. Sometimes I didn't sleep at all. But there *is* something worse."

"What?"

"To not have experienced that love at all. Even if it was only for a moment in the grand scheme of things. It's a moment that will sustain me for the rest of my life." Blake tucked a curl behind her ear. "He was just the best person and he still is."

Poe looked at her, still unsure. If the situation were reversed, Poe knew she would have crumbled long ago. Blake was somehow still standing, and it made Poe feel a weakness inside herself that she never knew was there and didn't like one bit. She wondered if it had always been there, the story just bringing it to the surface, or if somehow the story itself placed it there. "You don't think it would be better? You don't think it would hurt less?"

"Of course it would hurt less. But then there would be nothingness in its place." Her voice started to quiver. "He was my person. And he gave me that precious little boy. I see Julian looking back at me every time I look at him. And not just his face, but his laugh, the way he loves hockey and hates vegetables. Little bits of Julian pop up right in front of me every single day."

Poe gave her a hug. "Thank you for telling me."

"Thank you for making me want to." She sighed. "I haven't talked about him in a long time. Seems wrong not to…I never want to stop talking about him, even if it hurts. It hurts *not* to." Blake got up and crawled back into her sleeping bag.

Something stirred inside Poe that night. Like the weakness she had already felt, she could never be sure whether it had always been buried or if it had just been born after hearing Blake's struggle. All she was certain of was that she wanted to experience love, the kind that Blake was talking about: the all-consuming, makes life worth living kind of love that buries itself in your soul and never lets go.

And she knew she would never be able to do it if she stayed at the compound.

She was about to talk to Blake about it if she was awake, and purposely wake her up if she wasn't. But a loud sound from outside let her know that it would have to wait, and the multiple sets of headlights slowing to a stop in the driveway let her know that things were about to change forever.

CHAPTER SEVENTEEN

DREW

The day Drew found out about Kate Holloway's miscarriage, he was sitting on the back porch of his office, drinking a cup of herbal tea and eating the tuna sandwich that Vera had packed for him that morning. He inhaled the tea's rich aroma of ginger and honey and held it in for a moment, letting it out slowly as he took a sip. There were little blue birds on the tea bag tag and he wondered why they had switched brands. A moment later, his nurse opened the sliding glass door, and the look on her face told him that whatever message she was about to give him couldn't wait. He'd only seen that look on a handful of occasions, and each time had left a tear in his soul that would never heal. The thought of having to live with another made him weary. "Connor and Kate Holloway are here. They are sitting in the waiting room and won't leave until they speak with you. I could call the police if you want." She hesitated, and Drew waited for the other part of the news. "The wife looks a little pale." A tingling feeling swept over Drew's body, and somehow he knew that whatever happened during the conversation he was about to have would stick with him for the rest of his life.

He put his lunch down on the stoop, not bothering to hide his sandwich from the birds who had been eying it the entire time he had been sitting there. As he rounded the corner and walked into the waiting room, his hands started to shake, though he wasn't sure why. He knew in a few short moments, he would find out. "Mr. and Mrs. Holloway, what can I do for you?"

Connor's face was rigid. "I just wanted you to have the opportunity to face the woman whose child you murdered."

Drew felt the eyes of the other people in the waiting room fall upon him, and for a moment, he froze. He wondered if they would wait for his answer to convict him, or if they had already decided he had committed the crime he was being accused of. Either way, after hearing such a thing, a part of them would always wonder. He knew he would have if he were in their position. "What on earth are you talking about? I didn't kill anyone."

"Oh, you don't remember?" Connor's laugh sounded like that which rang through the halls of mental asylums: unbalanced and desperate. "Of course, why would you? We're the crazy people who hide up on the mountain right? Can't even pee on a stick correctly…" He gestured toward Kate. "Tell this woman why you didn't give her a blood test to see if she was pregnant. Tell her that it's your fault that she lost her baby." He paused and gestured to his audience. "I looked it up. There's a chemical in a pregnant woman's body that is there very early in pregnancy, but if it's really early, it might not show up on a urine test every time." Facing Drew again, he said, "Why did I have to look that up, Doctor? All I did was type that into the internet, something that you should have already known. Did you know? Or did you just assume since you're the doctor and all, you would know the answer?" He paused again, and Drew felt as if he were on trial in a court of law. Maybe he was, and the prosecutor was closing in. "Or…did you think we were crazy, so instead of relying on medical science, you relied on your own opinion?"

Drew looked at Kate, and immediately recognized the pain that he'd only seen once during his years as a doctor. The first time, he was working as a resident, and it wasn't his fault. This time was different, the burden falling solely on his shoulders and he felt himself break apart like the ground after an earthquake. As much as he wanted to defend himself, he knew he had to focus on Kate. He didn't do right by her once; he would now. "Oh my God. Kate, I'm so sorry for your loss." Even though it wasn't professional, he reached for her hand. She pulled it away. "Please, let me take you inside so we can make sure everything's okay with you."

Connor stepped between them. "Everything is most certainly not okay. And she's not going anywhere with you."

Kate looked at her husband. "Connor, I need to get looked at. Just to be safe."

Drew watched as Connor squeezed her hands between his own. "We'll take you somewhere else." He glared at Drew. "We'll have you see someone we can trust."

"Connor I want this to be over. I just want to get seen

and then go back to the house and never talk to any of these people again." He hesitated, but as Drew motioned for her to follow him, he stood fast and didn't stop her.

As he started to close the exam room, he heard Connor shouting at the other people in the waiting room. "What are you all staring at? Each one of you helped make this happen. All of you! You're all poison. You spent your time spreading vile rumors to each other and your misguided opinion of us cost a child its life!"

Drew motioned for Kate to sit down and he went back out to the waiting room. "Connor, please come in." He tried to keep his voice low and steady. As he spoke, an image flashed in his mind. When he was ten, he and his father drove over a bridge on their way home from a neighboring city and saw a man standing on the edge of it, clearly thinking about jumping. Drew's father didn't know it, but as he tried to talk the man down, Drew had rolled down the window to listen.

This was how Drew spoke to Connor.

"Kate needs you. Just come with me." His voice grew louder than he had planned. "Come with me."

"What's the matter? No one here can handle hearing the truth? Typical. Or is it that you just don't want anyone to hear what you did to our family? Is that it?

"You're a joke, Matthews, a joke. All these people, they may not believe me now, hell, maybe they do and don't care. But you're all going to pay for what you've done to that woman in there. You're all children, and you're going to find out one day just how fragile you are!"

Drew had enough. He couldn't have a person who was

clearly not in his right mind standing in the middle of his office threatening the rest of his patients and staff. One of the other patients was a rather muscular man who Drew had known since he was young. He glanced over at him, and both men seemed to understand each other. As Drew moved toward Connor, so did he, and together, they managed to grab one arm each and push him out the door, locking it behind him. He spoke to Connor through the glass. "I will send Kate out when we are done. You're going to have to wait out here." He turned away, and tried not to listen to the pounding fists that echoed behind him.

He considered calling the police, but didn't. Maybe it was because he didn't want to incite Connor's rage even more than it already was. It was a small town, and Connor could find out where Drew and Vera lived very easily. He probably already knew. Or perhaps it was because somewhere deep inside him, he knew Connor was right.

When he arrived back in his exam room, Kate was sitting in a white paper gown with her hands folded in her lap. Her wedding ring sparkled in the fluorescent light. "Was that Connor?"

"Yes."

Drew assumed Kate would apologize for her husband's behavior. She didn't. Instead, as she stared off into some unknown space only she seemed able to see, she said, "We were going to name her Emily. After Emily Dickinson, the poet." As he listened to her heartbeat with his stethoscope, she added. "It's a nice name, don't you think?"

He willed his voice not to shake. "It's beautiful."

***

Vera asked him why he was so quiet when he got home that night. She wrapped her arms around his neck, and what would normally make him feel better felt in that moment like she was stealing his air. He gently pushed her arms off and got up from his chair. "I don't really want to talk about it if that's all right." She seemed perplexed, and he couldn't blame her. They talked about everything, from the mundane trivialities of their daily routines, to whether their belief in God waxed and waned with the passage of time and circumstance. So to be told he didn't want to talk about it would certainly make Vera very concerned. But despite his desire not to upset her, his mouth remained closed, and he journeyed upstairs. "I'm going to take a shower."

"Okay, sweetie. I'll be up soon," she said.

Vera had always seen the best in him. They'd fallen in love in college: a doctor of the mind attracting the attention of a doctor of the body. He would make up friends with mental problems in order to have reasons to talk to her, and she would let him. Years later she told him she always knew. He asked her how. "No one can have *that* many mentally ill friends."

How was he supposed to tell her what had happened, he thought; especially as hard as they had tried. Vera had wanted children more than life, more than oxygen itself. So how was he to tell her that his careless mistake had cost a child its life? How would he tell her that the mother had been certain she was pregnant, only to have him tell her she was wrong? Mother's instincts are one of the most certain, proven forces in the world. How dare he assume he knew better? What harm would it have done to just humor her and give her the blood test she had asked for? He tried to think back to that day. Was he slammed with paperwork? Were his appointments getting backed up? Had he, as Connor claimed, let the town's prejudice against his patient make him think it was acceptable to rush her out the door? The more he tried to remember, the more he realized that it didn't matter what had distracted him. He clenched his fist and pounded it on the grainy white tile in the shower, then cursed himself, worried that Vera would have heard it and come in the check on him. He couldn't face her, not right then. He needed to be alone, partially to save himself, partially for his own retribution. He deserved to be punished, but he wanted to be alone as he did it.

Tears stung his eyes as he squeezed them shut, trying to keep them in, afraid that if he started letting them go he would never stop. He slid down the wall of the shower and folded his knees up to his chest. As it became obvious that the crying was coming whether he asked it to or not, he folded his arms across his legs and buried his face down upon them as tightly as he could. Perhaps between the rushing water and his arms muffling the sound, Vera would stay unaware of the terrible mistake he made for just a little while longer. Then again, he knew he should have just told her right away: no amount of holding it in would hide the pain in his eyes. Even if he stuffed it down, Vera had a way of seeing it bubble over, out of the depths of his very soul. So with heavy limbs and a heavier heart, he reached up and turned off the water, dried himself off, slipped on a t-shirt and jeans then asked Vera to join him on the window seat in their bedroom.

Even though he was sure she knew that night would be different than any other, she appeared with a glass of white wine for each of them, just as she always did, perfectly chilled with condensation running gently down the glass. "What's on your mind?"

Of course, she would get directly to the point. Drew took a long sip of wine, a stall tactic to prolong his journey into the inevitable. "I made a mistake; I made a mistake and because of it, someone died."

Vera gently put a hand on his knee. "I'm so sorry honey. Truly."

He took a deep breath and exhaled slowly. "A baby."

Her face started to change. "It's horrible of course. But please understand that in your profession, you're not going to get it right every single time. It's tragic, but it was going to happen at some point." Her mouth said the correct words, but as he said the word "baby," he noticed a slight coolness in her eyes. No matter how many niceties she came up with, no matter how much she comforted him so perfectly, he was different to her now: that baby was gone, snuffed out before it even had a chance to decide if it would be a saint or a sinner. As she reached over and squeezed his hand, giving him the most loving smile, he was certain he felt her press against his fingers just a little too hard, and he saw just the slightest strain in her cheeks. "Please, Drew; you need to get some sleep. A good night's sleep and I'm sure you'll see clearly in the morning."

He wondered if he'd ever see clearly again, or even if he'd ever seen clearly at all.

CHAPTER EIGHTEEN

POE

"Get up right now!" Poe yelled at Blake and Jackson. They hesitated, and were perhaps going to ask for an explanation, until Poe whipped the rifle out of her gun safe and chambered a round. After that, no story was needed.

Blake grabbed Jackson and knelt down in front of him. "Now I need you to hide in Poe's closet like we talked about, okay? And don't come out for anyone that you don't know."

Jackson clutched the stuffed bear he was holding. "Mommy, I don't want to. I'm scared."

"I know, sweetie, but remember what I've always told you? I'm not going to let anything bad happen to you, not ever. Right?"

Jackson nodded, but threw his arms around his mother. "I love you, Mommy. Please be okay. Don't leave like Daddy okay?"

Blake's eyes watered. "I'll never leave you, you know why? Because Daddy's watching over us and he's always going to protect us. He'd never let anything happen to me." She kissed him on the forehead then gently pushed him toward the closet. "I love you, baby. Now go."

Jackson knelt down behind Poe's clothes and quietly opened a compartment that was hidden in the back. As he slid in, he waved and wiped a tear from his eye. As Blake closed the door behind him and shut the closet, Poe knew she had to shove away her own fears, and get ready for the war they always knew would come.

Poe stared at her. "You have to keep it together, you hear me?" She handed her the knife that she had grabbed from under her pillow. "Keep it out in front of you, just like we practiced, okay?" Blake positioned it as she was told. "Good. Now let's go."

As they ran through the hallway, she banged on Gabriel's door with all her strength. "There's people outside! Grab your gun and get in position!" When Gabriel opened the door, he already had his rifle in hand. "Get Harper and tell her to get in position by the front door. If they get in, she'll be waiting for them." Gabriel nodded and turned in the opposite direction.

Once Poe had Gabriel going she turned back to Blake. "Get everyone up. Tell them to grab anything they can find that would work as a weapon."

"But the gun cabinet's locked!"

"I know." Poe swallowed hard. "I have to get to the roof. We'll get through this, I promise. Go!"

"Please be careful!" Blake said as she ran down the stairs. "I will."

As Poe took her position on the roof, she thought about how thoroughly she didn't believe they were going to get out of their situation alive. She'd always believed in her father, but looking out at the unfamiliar vehicles as they parked in front of their house, any trace of doubt that had been hiding out inside her mind came to the surface in a flood. Her father's lack of trust had rendered every ounce of preparation that they had useless. She watched as more and more people with guns, six men and two women, got out of the three trucks that were parked outside their home.

Dad, where are you?

She, her mother, Harper, and Gabriel were the only ones with weapons. Clearly, they were outnumbered, and all they could hope for would be to out think them before they were all dead. Just as she hoped the new people wouldn't be able to get through the reinforced metal gate, she saw a figure coming from their house start walking across the driveway.

Who is that?

In the dark, it took her a moment to recognize him. The scar on his arm was barely visible in the moonlight, and it seemed to wink at her as he unlocked the gate.

Brian was letting them in.

She could see from her vantage point that he was speaking with them. He threw his arms up in the air, and she heard whoever he was talking to yell back. She pointed her scope at Brian's head, putting the little read dot in the very center of his head. *He would pay for this*, she thought, until she saw her mother leave the house and go toward them, with Vera and Blake close behind, all making the long walk toward the group of vehicles and people that Brian had now given free access to their house.

She'd hoped Gabriel had time to rig his shocking device to the doorknob of the front door. If that didn't work, Harper would be waiting for them on the other side. If they came through the back, Gabriel would be there, though he wasn't nearly as good a shot as Harper. Poe had to hope that with mere feet between him and his target, Gabriel would come through.

Her mother stood in front of Brian, looking directly up at Poe. "Everyone, stand down. I want to hear what these people have to say, and you should too."

A woman who Poe guessed was the leader of the group came forward and stood directly across from Kate and Brian. She looked muscular, someone who could give even Cassius a fair fight. She had a handgun in a holster at her waist, but, to Poe's surprise, she left it there. Her hand wasn't even hovering over it. "My name is Shannon."

Kate addressed Brian instead. "Who is this woman, and the rest of them. How do you know them?"

Brian glanced back up at the house. Poe wondered if he could see Harper from where he was, and what new lie he was about to spin. "Everything I told you before was true. My family did get sick, and then I headed here." He looked at Shannon. "But I got to a point where I was running out of food. I thought I was going to die for sure. I met up with them and they took me in." They squeezed each other's hands. "When they found me I was malnourished, my clothes were in rags…I was a real mess. They saved my life."

"And you didn't bother to mention any of this before?" Kate asked.

"I'm sorry." He continued. "They offered to let me stay with them, but I said I had to get to Harper. I told them about this place, and I thought maybe we could all stay here together." He gestured toward the new group. "These people, they're police officers, firefighters, and their families. They'd all be really good additions to the group. They could help defend this place."

Kate sighed. "You should have told us."

"I was going to. But Shannon just told me they are in a bad state. Their food is extremely low and they don't have many bullets left. I was going to wait until Connor trusted me more and then present the idea to him. But they're at a place now where they either have to be let in or find some other source of help fast. It was just taking too long."

Shannon finally spoke. "We don't mean any trouble, ma'am. We can pull our own weight. We just can't be on the road anymore. When everything first happened, a couple of us at the precinct decided we would stick together. We were ready before anybody else even imagined the disease would get this far. At first we just took shelter at the station. But when we ran out of supplies, we started traveling, sticking to the small towns and as far away from other people as we could. We scavenged and managed to make our way."

Poe looked at each member of the new group and noticed that she was the only person with her gun drawn.

After hearing Shannon speak, her mother smiled. "Call me Kate." Poe winced, shocked at how quickly and easily her mother accepted Shannon's story, and Brian's explanation for why he had just left them vulnerable to attack, one which, thanks to her father, they were not prepared to fight. She had noticed her mother drifting from her father for some time, not directly, but in the little things: the way they didn't hold hands anymore, the way she contradicted him, even in the way her eyes never stayed connected to his for very long. They were changing, and her mother had picked the worst time to completely leave his side.

Just as the rest of the group got out of their vehicles, she saw another set of headlights coming up the driveway.

Her father was back.

He and Drew jumped out of their truck, barely pulling it to a stop.

Their guns were aimed right at Shannon.

She imagined she could hear her father's footsteps on the earth, pounding like that of a god coming down to bestow his wrath upon those below him. She wondered if Shannon and Brian would share that burden alone, or if some would be aimed at her mother. A part of her hoped for the latter. "What the hell is going on?" He kept his gun pointed at Shannon. As he did so, the rest of the new group drew their weapons with the quickness of trained professionals. Apparently *that* part of Brian's story was true. "I don't know who you are but get off my property, or I'll shoot you, I promise you that." Poe was surprised he hadn't done so already, but then realized that even her father knew they were outgunned.

Brian stepped between them. "Connor, no! I know them. They're friends. Please—"

Her father moved his gun and pushed it against Brian's

forehead. "You lead them here…I should kill you where you stand."

Poe looked around at the faces of each group. The new people had their guns aimed at her father, Drew, Vera, Blake, and even her mother. When she heard the commotion, Harper emerged from the house and put Shannon in her site line. Gabriel came up from the back of the house and did his best to cover the rest of the group, aiming at clusters of people rather than individuals. Blake, Vera, and now Cassius and Darius stood behind him. Poe noticed that now since no family members were watching, Cassius and Darius had each grabbed large kitchen knives, and had them pointed outward and at the ready. Yes, they were no match for the guns that were pointed at them, but they were better than nothing at all. And maybe, just maybe, if they played the situation right, they could get close enough to use them. She whispered a *'thank you'* to them that she knew they'd never hear. "Connor, right?" Shannon said in a smooth, even tone. "I couldn't wait to meet you."

"I don't care what you want, lady. As you can see, we are all trained to deal with people trying to take what we have." He gestured to the rest of the group, and aimed his gun back at Shannon. "You are in way over your head here."

Poe looked around at each face through her viewfinder. No one blinked. Beads of sweat dripped down the cheeks of every individual. She had a terrible feeling creep over her that her night was going to end very badly.

She was right.

They would only find out later that the sound they had

thought was gunfire was actually an explosion from something Gabriel was working on in his shop. They would figure it out after they found the remnants all over one of the back shelves, red grime solidified on the walls, putting the pieces together much later, too late to save her.

They all heard what Connor assumed was the crack of a gun going off. It didn't matter that it actually ended up being something else. In his head, in that moment, it was a gun. So when he fired a shot clean through Shannon's head, the war had started before her body hit the ground.

Poe aimed her rifle at the man closest to the front of the invading group and fired: direct hit. As he was down on the ground, she started aiming at the other people as they got closer. Each shot was precise, right in the chest, but for some reason, the people kept coming, only being deterred temporarily by her bullets. As Poe saw the first person on the ground start to get up again, obviously in pain but very functional, Poe realized her mistake. She squinted enough to see a slight bulginess in each of the invader's clothing, as if there was another layer behind their shirts: when they left the police station, they had taken some very important supplies with them.

All of them were wearing ballistic vests.

As they neared the house, Poe saw four more people getting out of the trucks; they must have been sitting in the back, because she hadn't even seen them until they emerged. She started aiming for the head, but it was a much smaller target and she only managed to hit a shoulder of one of them. As they made their way closer to the rest of their team,

Poe nearly dropped her rifle. The last four people were wearing riot gear.

There was no way to stop these people. They were going to get inside the house.

They had to evacuate the compound, and they had to do it now.

She was just about to throw open the door on the roof when she heard two women screaming. The first sounded like Vera. The second was her mother. For a moment, it struck her as odd that she didn't hear Blake among them. As she went back and peered over the side of the roof, she figured out why.

Blake was clutching her chest, and slowly sinking toward the ground.

Suddenly, the firefight stopped, and the quiet that filled the air was suffocating. She ran down the stairs and out the door, joining Vera and her mother as they surrounded her friend. Drew was working on her furiously, using a jacket to put pressure on the wound. Poe listened as he took quick shallow breaths. "You're going to be okay. You're going to be okay, you hear me?"

Poe had always been very aware of death. Even as a child, she understood it. Most of the time, when people grew old, something broken inside them would be more than they could handle and they would slip away. That was how it was supposed to work.

Time was so fickle though. Anyone could be driving home one night and be hit by another car, and they would be gone forever, or someone who ran marathons and ate nothing but vegetables could be snuffed out by a brain aneurism. She could lose anyone she loved at any moment.

But it wasn't supposed to be Blake; not her, not yet.

She grabbed Blake's hand and squeezed it. She wanted to tell Blake everything was going to be fine, to have it within her to make it pretty, like Drew. But Poe saw the waves of blood pouring out of her, and saw the chill that had flooded her cheeks. Let Drew tell her falsities, she thought. *I will comfort her with the truth, the best gift that I can give her now.* "I will take care of Jackson. We all will." She brought Blake's pale hand up to her lips and kissed it gently. "We're going to tell him how beautiful his mother was…how strong…and how we can see her every time he smiles, and how she's with his father now. And I'm going to tell him how brave you were, and how he should want to be just like you when he grows up. Like I do."

Blake's voice gave out in a whisper, and she let the words *thank you* slip into the atmosphere, along with her soul and everything in between.

Poe's heart shattered like a vase thrown on the ground when she realized someone would have to tell Jackson that his mother wasn't coming back. He was just a baby, and he was now going to grow up an orphan. Yes, there were people that loved him, but Blake…she was his mother, and a light all her own that made everyone around her feel special. At least she had done that for Poe, and she knew her son must have felt it too. How was anyone going to measure up to her? No one ever would. He would have to grow old wondering what might have been if that night never existed, and the thought made Poe's knees start to shake.

Drew and Vera had to be carried inside. Cassius and Darius pulled Drew away, while her mother held tightly to Vera. What they were doing could not be called crying; they were letting out screams that seemed to come from all life, as if nature itself understood the loss they had suffered, and it had manifested into the sound that Poe knew could have been heard for miles, if there was anyone left alive to hear it.

The people with guns ushering them inside seemed invisible. As they passed through the front door, Poe looked back to see a man cradling Shannon, with several other people holding each other as their tears fell.

***

The man who Poe shot first whose miraculous recovery clued her into the Kevlar vests was the first to speak. "You, sit down over there next to the others." He used his gun as an extra finger, waving it in the direction where he wanted Poe to park herself. For the moment, she listened, taking a seat next to Vera. On the other side, Vera had her arm around Jackson, who had heard all the commotion and come downstairs despite his mother's orders, and as soon as Poe sat down, Vera wrapped her other arm around her. Poe lost herself in the gesture for a second, feeling like part of a group that had nothing to do with her own family. Vera's grip was tight, and Poe was sure she wished it was Blake she was clutching instead. Gabriel was on her other side, while Cassius, Darius, Drew, and her mother were seated on the floor.

Her father was nowhere to be seen, and the realization made her grow cold.

She looked over at Jackson. No one had told him what happened to his mother, but the tears were streaming down his face nonetheless. He may not have been told in words, but when his mother was nowhere to be found and Drew and Vera were sobbing uncontrollably; he figured it out on his own, and buried his face against Vera's side.

As much as everything inside her hurt in a way that made her imagine a ball of yarn, long, spindly things twisting and turning in on themselves, Poe pushed it away. She knew that if she let the insanity that death brought take hold of her, she would be of no use to the rest of her family and they might as well lie down and accept their fate. So instead, she paid attention. She would keep her word to Blake, and she would make sure they would make it through what lay ahead, and the people who had taken her from them would soon be crumbling at their feet.

Poe noticed that they hadn't restrained them in any way. Apparently they figured there was no need since she and her family were on the receiving end of their weapons. She took careful inventory of each group member: one man had his gun in a holster that was too big for it. It was an easy guess that he was not one of the police officers that Shannon had mentioned. He had to be a spouse or a family member, which meant he would be an easier target than some of the others. Another man was wearing dress shoes, which meant wherever he was he had left in a hurry. The group immediately started taking off their gear and tossing it in a pile in the corner of the living room.

Poe wondered if they would notice if one of the vests went missing.

She studied the faces of her fellow prisoners. She hated to use that word in their own home, but that was exactly what they were. Darius and Cassius seemed to be watching them as carefully as she was. If she could only get one or both of them alone, perhaps they could formulate a plan. Her mother was only paying attention to her own children, alternating between watching Harper, Gabriel, and herself. She seemed to be inching closer to Harper, and it wouldn't be long before one of their captors noticed and pushed her back to square one.

Darius spoke first, much to Poe's approval. If it had been Cassius, they may have all found themselves thrown into a second round of the war that just ensued. "I'm so sorry about your friend, but we have to work something out. There's so much all of you don't know. We didn't know how hard this would be either. You need us, and I think you know that…or you would have killed us all already. Please, just let us bury Blake and we can figure this out right after."

The man who Poe guessed was second in command after Shannon snarled at him as he marched toward them. "You tried to kill us. We were just talking and he just shot her. Like she didn't matter at all!" His voice was loud but shaken. "Bury her? After what you did to Shannon? We're going to dump that girl in the woods and leave her for the predators to finish off." Vera screamed at the thought of it but Poe pulled her close, afraid that she would antagonize them further and find their rage turned towards her.

The man watched as two others dragged her father inside and threw him down on the floor with everyone else. The man threw himself on top of her father and shook him furiously. "She was my *wife*! We just wanted some help, that's all! What the hell is wrong with you?" Poe tried to get up and pull him off of her father, but one of the women from the other group stood in front of her and shoved her back in her seat.

Harper glared at him. "What do you mean? You are the ones who fired first. And now Blake's gone because of you!"

He stopped beating her father and slapped Harper so hard she fell down. "Shannon gave the orders you idiot. If she didn't say fire, then we didn't fire. None of us." He turned back to her father. "Nobody in our group shot at anyone until you slaughtered my wife like an animal." He spit toward her father's face, and it landed right on his forehead. He tried to get up, but the two men who had dragged him in pushed him back down. Shannon's husband looked around. "You didn't even bat an eye when that girl bled out." Wiping the sweat from his brow, he asked, "Which one is your wife? Which of them?" He stepped around and looked at Poe and her siblings individually, then at Vera and her mother, studying their faces and waiting for one of them to give themselves away. Poe clenched her jaw, determined not to make any sudden move that may reveal herself. In her mind, she willed her siblings and her mother to do the same. If he couldn't figure it out, then she hoped he would stop before anyone else was hurt, though she knew deep down that the pain for the evening wasn't over. He stopped in front of Kate and stared at her. "It's you, isn't it? You—"

"It's me. I'm his wife. Me." Bile rose from the middle of Poe's stomach as Vera shoved Jackson into her arms.

"No! It's me! She's lying I swear!" Kate cried…screamed with all the strength she had, but his attention was on Vera.

"Well, one of you is lying." He looked between Drew and Vera. "You two were the inconsolable ones when you saw that poor girl die, not him." He moved toward Kate, but as he turned, Vera spat at him.

"It's me you stupid sonofabitch. Me." She glared at him.

Wiping the spit from his shirt, he threw her on the ground. With Drew being held back and screaming in the background, the man beat Vera so hard that Poe thought she may have been dead. He slammed his fists down on her once-strong body, and by the time he was done, her face had swelled into an almost unrecognizable form. When no one was looking, Gabriel pulled her mother up to him and held her close to his chest as she cried.

There were a couple precious seconds that the group neglected to pay any more attention to Vera, leaving her in a heap on the floor of the room. Poe used those seconds to hunch down and whisper in her ear. "Why did you save my mother?"

With her eyes closed and a weak smile on her face, Vera said, "Because my daughter's gone. I'm dead already."

When Shannon's husband, who Poe figured out was named Justin was finished with Vera, he approached her father again, this time hovering over him and grinning. "Take him to the barn and lock him in with the livestock." He stared at Connor. "I'm going to kill him. But he's not going to know when it's coming. I want him to feel it…all of it." Her mother was inconsolable, lying against Gabriel like a frail child hiding from life itself. Poe had never seen her mother so weak…and it scared her deep down in her gut.

She tried to read the expression on her father's face, but the blood made it impossible. She thought about crying out: her heart told her to scream and cry and tell them to leave her father alone. But she listened to her head instead: begging was not going to work. Only careful planning was going to save them now. The time for negotiations had passed in a hail of gunfire and survival was the only thing that they could afford to concern themselves with now.

Justin gestured to a woman and a man to his left. "Lindsey, Tim, take that girl and drop her somewhere in the forest. I don't want her attracting any vermin."

Drew fought against the two men who were still restraining him, trying with all his strength to get to his injured wife. Crying for Blake had made his eyes swollen, small slits of the deep brown peeking out from the lids. "I'll kill you! I'll kill you for this! She didn't do anything to you! Neither of them did! I'll kill you for this."

Justin pulled Drew toward himself. Their faces were inches from each other. "Take him to the barn too."

Suddenly, Gabriel ran at Justin too, winding his fist back as he went. Though he aimed at his face, a shove from one of the invaders threw him off and he knocked into Justin's shoulder. "Gosh, you all are just itching to get tied up…take this sonofabitch too." One of the invaders grabbed him by the neck and shoved him toward her father and Drew. "And make sure you search all three of them." They patted all three of them down right then, and found the knives that both Gabriel and her father kept around their waists, tossing them toward Justin. As punishment, Justin punched both of them hard in the gut as his men lead them out the door.

As four of the invaders took Drew and her father out to the barn, the rest of them started to make themselves comfortable, with no visible acknowledgement that they were in a house that didn't belong to them. Some started going through the bags they brought in, while others were responsible for keeping Poe and the others subdued.

Poe liked the way Justin moved. In fact, she liked the way they all moved. They were too aggressive…nothing about them was methodical, which to her, meant they were a sloppy group that happened to have had one good idea. They hadn't thought past getting the gear from the police station and had let their grief talk them into invading the compound. After that…they would have nothing. Sure they had survived for quite a while, and maybe they would have been a formidable opponent for a different group, but there was some flaw in how they operated that allowed them to run out of supplies in the first place. They didn't pace themselves or think through their actions. They were not going to be a match for her and her family. Sooner or later, they would make a mistake. And that mistake was going to cost them their lives.

***

Poe stayed awake all night. She watched as those who watched her changed the guard, noticing every twitch in their faces, and every nervous finger-tapping. She studied them, timing how long it took between shifts. She noticed that one of them, a man with a mole on his left cheek, always stopped at the kitchen sink for a glass of water right before he was done with his shift. Perhaps she could exploit that. She also noticed a woman who the others called Regina tended to nod off a couple times during her turn to watch them. If she could just get to her gun…

Darius stayed awake too. When their captors' backs were turned, he and Poe would communicate silently, pointing to certain people and elements in the room and nodding at each other, willing one another to look at things by moving their eyes a certain direction. They studied the room together, looking for items that could be used as weapons if they could just get the chance. Poe wondered if his years as a pilot were what gave him such a calm air about him, or if it had more to do with growing up as Cassius' brother. She decided both factors played a part, making him into a cool, calculating asset to any escape plan they came up with. She decided she would mention his behavior to her father the first chance she had, and hoped that he would start to see Darius as an asset on a personal level rather than just another body he could use to defend their home.

That morning, she heard screaming from outside. "Where the hell are they? What the hell did you do?"

Another voice. "I tied all of them up, I swear!"

The first voice, which to her sounded like Justin's. "He's a survival expert, dipshit. Of course he knows how to get out of a knot! Why didn't you use the handcuffs like I told you to?"

The sound of flesh hitting flesh.

"I'm sorry, all right?"

Poe smiled to herself. Her father was going to fix everything; he always did.

Three nights went by, and she hadn't heard or seen anything that would give her a hint as to where her father, Drew, and Gabriel were hiding. But she didn't need it. She knew they were working on something to get their home back, and she was certain they would put that plan into action soon. But in the meantime, she and Darius could be working from the inside out, as her father and Drew worked from the outside in.

On day five, she got her chance. During day four, she heard a couple of their captors talking about two missing group members, two that went on a supply run and had never came back to the compound. They ended up sending one of their men out to look for them.

He didn't return either.

That afternoon, an invader with pock marks on his skin and dark eyes grabbed Poe by the hair on the back of her head and ushered her downstairs. Her skin started to tingle when she saw that Justin was waiting for her. "I know they're watching us. All of them. That's why you're coming with me." He pulled her from the other man's grasp and pushed her outside. Once they got to the center of the drive, he shoved her to her knees, and she could feel the sting of the sharp rocks against her flesh. The world fell silent and all she could hear was the snap of his finger taking the safety off his gun. She felt the end of it against the back of her head.

So this is how I go– kneeling on the earth under an open blue sky.

"I know you're out there," he yelled. "One of you at least will see this. Tell the rest." As she heard the gun fire, she imagined her life slipping away, watching herself drift away from the earth to join Blake, wherever she may be.

Then she opened her eyes.

Dust swirled around her from where the bullet had hit the ground next to where she was kneeling. "If you don't stop killing my people, the next one's going in her temple." With those parting words, he lifted her up and shoved her back toward the house.

Her mother was there, waiting with outstretched arms. "Oh thank God," she said as she threw her arms around Poe. "Are you all right?"

"Yes, I'm okay."

"If I'd lost you…" She felt her mother cling to her harder.

Harper ran inside next, an invader close on her heals, with Brian even further behind. "I heard the shot! What happened?"

"I'm fine," Poe said. "He was just trying to scare Dad."

The invader that was chasing Harper finally caught up. "If he's smart, it worked." He reached over and grabbed Harper by the arm. "You're coming with me. You're not done getting the meat out of that refrigerator. Move!"

Brian glared at him. "Don't talk to her like that."

"Don't you dare act like you care about me. This whole thing is your fault." Harper attempted to rid herself of the invader's grasp. "You're so tough, why don't you just shoot us? You're going to kill us eventually anyway…just do it already and save the theatrics."

"Harper, stop it."

She ignored Brian's pleas and continued to taunt her assailant. The man snarled and shoved her to the ground. "Go ahead! Do it."

"Don't test me, bitch."

Just as he drew his gun and aimed it at Harper, her mother released Poe and dove in front of her, putting herself in the path of the weapon. "Please. She's just upset. My husband's the one who you're really mad at. Please, just leave her out of it." Poe watched as her mother stared into the eyes of Harper's attacker. They seemed to be in a battle of wills, and when Poe saw the shine in her mother's eyes, she knew who would win. After what seemed like several moments, but was probably only a flicker of time, the man put his gun back in his holster and walked away, slamming the door behind him. Brian followed him, scolding him all the while. Poe heard a few key phrases about how they needed to be treated better and that he better be kinder to Harper especially or he would be sorry.

Too little, too late Brian.

Though Poe was happy her sister wasn't hurt, something dark lingered in her head. Perhaps it was just a natural fight or flight response…survival instinct on behalf of her offspring. Or maybe it was something more. She had already abandoned her father morally when it appeared she was going to let Shannon and her group stay with them, but to risk his life? Her mother had pointed the man's anger at Harper in a different direction: at her father. Of course, Poe wanted her sister safe, but she couldn't help but feel a hint of rage toward her mother. Her father already had enough wrath aimed his direction—he didn't need any more. Kate had always protected him, with every ounce of strength she possessed, but not that day. She'd stood by him through a whole town turning against them, violence against their children, even the loss of a child. They'd been together since they were Poe's age, holding hands in the sunshine, writing each other letters of love. But *that* day, something had changed, heavy and daunting, and Poe wasn't sure if the thing that had shifted would ever go back.

The next day, since they were down three people, they were not able to watch the entire perimeter of the compound, or guard each of their prisoners every moment. So when they allowed Poe to go outside and gather more food for them from the garden, she heard a whistle coming from the back woods. Careful to not be seen, she waited for the gap in shift changes and raced toward the sound.

Drew was waiting for her.

"Drew! Are you all right? Where is my father? Where's Gabriel? Are they okay?"

He hugged Poe tightly. Poe was slightly surprised, but

even more so when she felt herself hugging him back. "They're fine. We heard a gunshot. Is everyone okay? How is Vera?"

Poe gave him a reassuring nod. "Everyone's okay. I thought Justin was going to kill me, but he was just trying to scare you guys. Vera's staying strong. Worried about you of course but staying strong." She paused. "I've never seen someone hold themselves together as well as her, especially after…everything." It seemed too soon to say Blake's name out loud, yet also not soon enough.

Drew sighed. "Thank God."

"Why isn't my father here? Or my brother?"

"I thought it best if I come, and Gabriel agreed. We didn't know if, God forbid, someone had been killed, but we had to figure that if Justin had killed someone, it would be one of your family members." His tone grew uncomfortable. "I thought…I thought your father may do something crazy, something that would possibly get more people hurt if he came to talk to you and got bad news. Gabriel agreed, so I came in his place, and Gabriel stayed to make sure your father didn't leave the second we did."

She nodded. "That makes sense. I miss him, but that makes sense."

He stared at Poe for a moment, and she could tell that what he was about to say, he didn't entirely want to. "Poe, your father wants you to do something. He wants you to…help him draw them out."

Poe wasn't sure where his request was going. "By doing what?"

"He wants you to set the place on fire."

Drew may as well have pushed her toward the ground. "What? You aren't serious. You can't be." Frantically, she tried to think of an alternative. "What about the arsenic in the kitchen? We could poison them instead…"

"We thought of that—it won't work because they will get suspicious when none of our group is eating at a particular meal. It could result in them forcing one of us to eat the tainted food. We can't risk it."

She thought she heard some people at a different part of the compound yelling, but she couldn't be sure. They were right. If they poisoned the food, one of their own may die in the process.

Drew continued. "He says if you start it in Gabriel's bedroom, it will be fine. Since each room is made from a shipping container, everything should take quite a while to burn. After we get them out, there shouldn't be very much that we will need to rebuild."

"But he's never burned any part of it before. How does he know?"

"If you start it in the back, it will create enough of a diversion that you will have time to isolate some of them and overpower the rest long enough to get to the weapons. There will be time to take them all out and put the fire out before the rest of the house is engulfed." Poe didn't miss the fact that he avoided answering her question. She was always confident in her father, but that time, a part of her wondered if desperation had clouded his judgement. His mistake with the weapons had already got them invaded—now he wanted to start a fire? What he had asserted as truth was nothing more than a somewhat educated guess and she hoped the rest of them wouldn't have to pay the price. It was bad enough that the place she had called home for so long was going to be partially destroyed; she couldn't imagine if something went wrong and it took a family member along with it.

She took a breath and tried to absorb what she was being asked to do. She tried to shake off the uncertainty, but questions kept whipping through her head like machine gun fire. What if something went wrong? What if the fire moved too quickly and their whole home was burned to the ground? Suddenly, she heard footsteps running toward her. She turned around, and Darius was standing in front of her. "Poe, they are looking for you. You need to come back now."

As unsure as she was, she decided to do as her father asked. Despite the major error that put them in the position they were in, he had cared for them their whole lives. He had kept them alive that long and he deserved a chance to fix it. She pushed any doubt deep down inside herself, though she could still hear an echo of it in the back of her mind. "Tomorrow, at noon. That's when everyone comes inside and we all eat lunch. They watch us. Everyone will be in one place."

Drew nodded. "We will be there." He reached in his pocket and handed her a small, silver key. "Hang back. Some will leave, some will go fight the fire, and some will stay guarding you. When they are all distracted, some of you take down the ones who don't go try and fight the fire. We will be on the other side waiting for the ones who run outside. Arm everyone. Only come out after you do in case we get overpowered." He put his hand on her shoulder. "Be careful."

Darius grabbed her hand. "We have to go. Now."

Poe nodded at Drew as Darius dragged her away.

***

As they ran back to the house, Darius asked her what Drew was doing. "Something's happening, isn't it?"

"Yes. At noon tomorrow, be downstairs. Tell Cassius when you can. You won't see me until you smell the smoke."

"Smoke? Oh God, Poe, what are we doing?"

Before she could explain, one of their captors marched toward them with her gun drawn. She recognized her as one of the ones who had taken Blake's body away. "Where the hell have you been? And where are the vegetables?"

Poe felt butterflies form in her stomach. In her excitement about seeing Drew, she had left the vegetable basket down at the edge of the garden.

Darius interjected. "There was a fox down there. We chased it up a tree. Before we could go back for the peppers we heard you all calling for us." The woman stared at them for a moment then seemed to accept their explanation.

"Well now that we know where you were, go back and get them." Poe started to turn around. "Not you, him."

Darius jogged back toward the garden, and Poe thought she felt him periodically look back at her.

"I want to talk to you," the woman said.

"Okay."

"Come with me."

Poe didn't want to. Her insides were screaming that she didn't want to be alone with any of these people, especially one of the ones who disposed of her friend's body so disrespectfully. But she followed the woman to a couple chairs they had on the back porch. She sat down and folded her hands in her lap, squeezing them together to keep them from shaking, all the while thinking *if you only knew what you had coming.*

The woman slouched as she sat, and Poe noticed her black hair hung in pieces over her shoulders. It wasn't a hot day, so she thought maybe the sweat could be blamed on walking the perimeter of the compound: another reason this new group was not suited to go up against them. "I need your help."

"Why would I help you? Any of you?" Poe surprised herself with her own bluntness.

The woman sighed. "Look, if you just give me some information, I'll try what I can to make this whole thing easier, okay?" Poe looked at her without responding. "Everything just got way out of control. As much as I loved Shannon, I do believe your father genuinely thought one of us had started shooting at you. If all hell hadn't broken loose, maybe we could have all worked something out." She looked down at the porch under her feet. "We just got desperate. Haven't you ever been desperate?"

Poe folded her arms across her chest. Thanks to her father, she had never found herself in that position.

Until now.

"What do you want?"

"I wanted to know how much you think your people can produce, of all the meat and produce and stuff. I was thinking I'd present it to Justin that we start trading with some of the surrounding groups of people. If you did that, I could make the case for your group to be treated better, maybe even get some of your freedom back."

Poe searched for her next breath. "What do you mean? Other people?"

The woman looked at her quizzically. "You didn't think you were the only survivors did you?"

Poe considered the idea for a moment. "Yes...I guess I did." She felt as if her mind had become three sizes too big. The new information came with more questions than answers. She supposed it had been silly of her to assume that they were the only people left, but her life of isolation hadn't lead her to think any differently. Her world consisted of only her family, and that was before the disease had hit. "You mean to tell me there are other people out there? Communities that are functional like ours?"

"Wow...you really didn't know." She caught a slight smile on the woman's face before it disappeared. "Yes. They are pretty far from here. Yours seems to be the only one in this town, but a couple hours in any direction and yes there are other people."

Poe's heart hurt. "I thought....I thought everyone was dead. I can't believe it." She hadn't realized she had been aching for people she had never met. She wondered if that had been brewing before the disease hit too.

Now the woman smiled and let her see it. "Believe it. I'm going to be straight with you, not very many people made it. But some did. And those people need meat and produce too."

Poe smiled. "I think we can handle that." She made the agreement, knowing that very soon, they would never have to fulfill it.

"I'll tell Justin."

As the woman got up, Poe asked, "What's your name?"

"Lindsey. My name is Lindsey." She paused. "You're Poe, right?"

"Yeah."

"You look an awful lot like my daughter." Lindsey stared off the deck and down into the field below.

"Where is she?"

"In the bottom of a pit somewhere." She had her hands folded in her lap much like what Poe was doing. Poe thought maybe she was trying to hide that she was trembling too.

"I'm so sorry."

"She was my baby. It happened during the first part of the outbreak. They didn't know what to do with all of the bodies so they just dug a big hole and dumped them all in. Like garbage. A landfill for all the loved, broken, and lost." She sniffed. "She was the sweetest girl. Always made friends at school with the kids that had none. She deserved better."

Poe remembered her terrible moments in the pit. She remembered the dead hand on her leg, and the vacant, foggy mist in all the eyes that were looking at her, but not at the same time. Something rose up inside her, and in spite of herself, she ignored the gun between them and threw her arms around Lindsey. "It happened here too. They all deserved better."

Lindsey sniffed again. "Thank you." Both women looked at each other for a brief second, realizing that maybe they understood each other a little more than they thought. "You better get back to work before the rest of them catch you."

"Okay. Thank you."

Lindsey nodded and started to walk away, but turned around a second later. After looking around, evidently to make sure she wasn't heard by the rest of the group, she said softly, "We didn't dump your friend. When Justin wasn't looking, we found some shovels in that shed. We gave her a proper burial. Tim even made a cross for her so maybe, when everything calms down, you can find her again."

Poe's throat hurt. The relief swelled up inside her like a storm and threatened to slip out, but she held it in, afraid she would attract unwanted attention and get Lindsey in trouble after she was so kind. "Thank you. Thank you so much."

Lindsey nodded, going back the way she came, and Poe found herself alone on the porch.

Poe sat there for a moment, ignoring the fact that she would probably be on their radar even more than she already was if she didn't get back to work. Let them watch me, she thought. Because Lindsey had just changed everything.

There were other people still alive, and nearby. A part of her knew it was a possibility (she wasn't stupid), but she'd never fathomed that it could be a reality. Thinking that way would have been too painful if it had turned out she was wrong. With other people came other realizations: all things were now possible. Life was possible. Maybe, just maybe, she could someday have a love like Blake's. Maybe she could be a mother. She hadn't even realized she was interested in being a mother until that moment. And right then, she knew she would do anything and everything to make sure that would happen, even if that meant starting a fire in her own home.

Lindsey seemed to be a good person. She risked her own safety to do right by Blake, a person she'd never met. She was caught in a situation she couldn't get out of just as much as the rest of them. Poe vowed that if she could, she would find a way to make sure her father spared Lindsey's life. But if she couldn't, after noon tomorrow, she would do whatever needed to be done to stay alive and live long enough to leave the compound and find the life that she hadn't known she wanted, and now that she did, it fell upon her like an embrace that warmed her deep down to her bones.

CHAPTER NINETEEN
CONNOR

Connor watched as Drew stared out into the middle of the barn. There seemed to be a mist of hay particles floating in the air and he could feel them as he inhaled. He listened to the sounds of the animals mix with the gentle splash of the water as the fish swam and thought about how he never expected to end up there, trapped in his own compound next to a man he thought he despised.

Their captors had tossed them into the pigpen: some sort of figurative point about their lack of moral character. They were both half sunk into the ground, a combination of mud and shit and leftover food that Connor and his family had prepared from their own scraps. He felt it seep under his fingernails, and he knew that when they got out of there, the smell would remain on them for days. They had tossed Gabriel in the corner of the stall, and he watched out of the corner of his eye as he tried to wriggle free.

Connor had never killed anyone before. He'd never had a need to. He always knew he could, and he would, when the time came, but thinking about it wasn't the same as actually doing it. Pulling the trigger and ending Shannon's life almost seemed like two different things, though he knew they weren't. It would take a while for his subconscious to link the two: the slight, insignificant clenching of a muscle and the blood that came with it. He couldn't have prepared for the moment after, the moment when he knew that he had snuffed out a life and it would never light up again.

Blake's death wasn't supposed to happen…a perfect example of why he was supposed to always be in control. He was the only one who they could depend on to make the most sound, rational decision, the one that was best for his family. If he had been there from the beginning, the people who were now occupying their home would have never made it past the front gate, and he would have subdued Brian before he had even made it past the steps by the door. And when he had found out what Brian had done, he would have sent him back from the direction where he came. He would have told Harper that Brian would be okay, knowing full-well he wouldn't, and he would have felt almost at peace with that fact given the troubling emotional attachment she had to the boy. He was just that, a boy, completely generic and completely replaceable, though he knew Harper didn't know that. Not yet. How could she? He had been the only one she'd ever gotten to know and Connor knew that was his own doing. Perhaps he had created the monster that left the door open for the bigger, meaner one. But no matter. He would fix it. He always did.

Drew looked as if his brain had left his body entirely, and all that was tied up alongside Connor was his outer shell. He imagined if he had seen someone else's child grow up, he would feel the same love, and the same biting loss that Drew was feeling now that Blake was gone. But Drew would need to recover, and quickly. That would be something he would need to learn if Connor was going to count on him to be in charge. He couldn't let the grief swallow him. There would be time to mourn Blake, but today, they needed to save their families, and today, that meant getting themselves free, and making it to the weapons cache that Connor had hidden just outside the property. "Drew, we need to get out of here. They could come back any minute and then we're done. We need to get out and we need to do it now."

No answer.

"Drew, please." He hesitated. He was never good with words: Poe and Kate always knew the proper thing to say. When most people spoke of unpleasant things, he would stay silent, hoping he could communicate the right things with a look or a glance.

It nearly never worked.

This time, he would have to try harder, he thought. "Drew, I know this is awful." He took a deep breath. He wasn't accustomed to saying something positive about anyone but his family. He couldn't remember the last time he praised someone who was not related to him,...then he realized he probably never had. "Blake was a strong, lovely girl. It seemed like she really cared for Poe, and that's something she's never had outside our family before. It's safe to call them friends. Poe never had that, even before we stayed here. I'm truly sorry that she is gone." His stomach churned a bit, but he felt like those were the right words, at least the closest he could get. He was shocked to realize he may have really meant some of them too.

Drew finally looked at him. "I feel…so much hate inside of me. I feel like I may explode. I've never felt anything like this. The ugliness."

"Then use it. Use it to help me get us out of here."

"What are we going to do? There's too many of them."

"We know what we're doing, they don't. They don't know this place like we do. They only made it this far by luck alone. They aren't thinkers."

"How do you know?"

Connor smiled. "Because they needed us."

Drew's face changed. "How do you deal with it?"

"What?"

"The rage. The all-consuming anger. I don't feel like there's room for anything else."

Connor paused for a moment. "I don't know what you mean."

Drew stared. "The whole town turned against you. The things I heard…it had to just make you so angry."

"That's why we left."

"Sure you left, but the feeling is still there. It's obvious. The way you acted when we first got here…after today, I can't blame you for it. How do you walk around with that feeling every day? Doesn't it eat you alive? I already feel like something's taking little bites out of my soul, and it's been what, an hour? What am I going to be like a year from now? Two? The grief, of course it will never stop. But the rage…the magnitude is so huge I don't know how to carry it."

Connor considered arguing with him, but couldn't come up with anything to negate what Drew had said. He couldn't deny it. The evidence was in every wrinkle on his face, every step that he took, the way he carried himself. It had become a part of him, a memory and a presence as much as his wife or his children, a companion that was his and his alone. The feeling was there as they made dinner at night, there when he kissed Kate on the forehead, even there when he smiled listening to Harper and Poe laugh as children. It was there. Always there.

"You just do. It sits there, and you move about your day, and it just curls up inside you and stays there. It's a part of you just the same as the oxygen in your lungs or the blood pumping through your veins."

Drew didn't respond.

"What?"

"I don't want to live like that."

"Sometimes something happens and it's so bad that there's no other way to live. It's either carry it with you or die to escape it. And no one wants to die."

Suddenly, Gabriel's voice echoed out from the corner of the stall. "Maybe we should try and get out of here and chat later."

Connor's focus shifted to his son. "What do you think I'm doing? And what the hell were you doing putting yourself at risk like that. They could have killed you. I'm going to beat your ass when we get out of here." Connor snapped, slowly trying to loosen the rope on his hands. His skin was becoming raw with the effort, and he worried that it would be difficult for him to hold a weapon with such frayed flesh and aching wrists. Even a small knife would become heavy in weakened hands.

Gabriel grinned. "Do you think this might help?" After he spoke, he scooted around so that his father could see the razor blade he was holding between his fingers.

"Did you come up with that yourself?" Connor stared at him.

"Yeah. It dawned on me that if we ever got caught, we might want something that would probably be missed in a pat-down. I've been keeping it in the small pocket in my jeans." He paused. "I came up with it trying to think like you."

For the first time since his knife attack, Connor smiled at him. "Well done, son. Well done." And for the first time in even longer, he meant it.

After scooting over to his father, he began to run the blade down the rope that tied his father's hands. When he was free, he took the blade from Gabriel and repeated the process. When they were both free, they went over to Drew. As Gabriel worked the blade over the rope that bound his feet, Connor pulled the knot free from the rope that tied his hands. Without a word exchanged between them, Connor held out his hand. After only a moment's hesitation, Gabriel took it and smiled.

As Drew kicked his feet free from the rope that now only sat loosely around his feet, he said, "Promise me that they will pay for what they've done. Promise me that."

Looking at him and seeing something of himself in the other man's eyes, Connor said, "They will."

***

The morning that they would attempt to take their home back, Connor, Gabriel, and Drew woke up as the sun started to rise. It peeked over the mountains and slowly illuminated the world before them, one that would start off with a dead peace, and later, turn in to the site of a war that neither of them were sure they were prepared to fight. He had lined up six guns from the weapons cache, two for each of them, with appropriate holsters. They had been sleeping in one of the guard stations where Poe would sit with her shotgun, like three children hiding from their parents in a neighbor's treehouse so they could pretend to slay dragons and conquer countries just a little bit longer.

Connor stepped outside of himself for a moment and realized the irony that despite everything he built for his family, he never built his children something as innocent and simple as a treehouse. He'd rarely done anything in his life where the only purpose was to bring happiness to another person. There was always an agenda, always a reason behind every lesson: he taught his children to shoot guns to protect themselves, not to spend time with them. He taught Gabriel to fish not to bond as father and son, but to make sure he would be able to feed himself when society fell. "You're lucky, you know," Drew said.

Connor hadn't realized Drew was even awake. "How do you mean?"

"You are a stubborn, difficult, brute of a man. You have every single person in your life stuck firmly under your thumb." He looked at Gabriel, who was still asleep. "But your children love you. That kid could have got shot last night, but he risked it to save you."

"I know that they love me."

"Do you?"

Connor didn't answer. Love wasn't something he was comfortable talking about, especially not with Drew. Knowing that Drew had never gotten to be a father made an odd feeling sweep over him, guilt mixed with shame mixed with longing. He wondered if he had gotten the father part of his life right, but not so much the "dad." He looked around, and noticed there was nothing there but himself, Gabriel, and Drew: no books, no music, nothing. His children had done as instructed. They'd eliminated distractions, and had been prepared for any incoming threat. But in doing so, did they run out of time to experience Vonnegut, or hear *Les Misérables*? Where was the small box of special toys that every child had, the one they thought their parents didn't know about? It was certainly not up in that guard tower, and Connor began to wonder if one existed for any of them. He watched as Gabriel rubbed the sleep from his eyes, realizing that his son had become a man much earlier than he should have, and that Connor only had himself to blame.

Connor felt a pang in his heart as he thought of his daughters as well, especially Poe. Given his medical situation, he wasn't sure if it was physical or mental. Maybe both. It was all up to her now. No sixteen-year-old girl should ever have so much resting on her shoulders. In a brief flash, he thought about the life he took her from, the life he saved her from: mundane high school nonsense, first dates, pointless graduation rituals. For a second, he wondered if he had made a mistake, but the thought was gone almost as quickly as it came.

In other circumstances, he would have never asked her to be involved in something so life-threatening: it would never have crossed his mind. He preferred to take on the most important responsibilities that came with caring for his family on his own, but he knew he was not in a position to save them by himself. As much as it pained him, he knew they would have to risk their lives to save themselves, or they would be ruled by the outsiders and their leader forever.

The grief that Justin was feeling had sent him on a rampage, and there was no telling who would be on the receiving end of his anger next. He had already threatened Poe. They had to act before more of their people died. "I know she can handle this...I just don't want her to have to." He didn't share everything that he was thinking: how he felt that the very fact that they were even considering the plan in front of them was his fault and his alone; that if something happened to her, he would never forgive himself, and it would not be hard for him to walk into the pond by their house, lie face down, and never come up for air again.

"She's a tough one, Connor. She'll come through." Connor knew he was right; his brain knew anyway. His heart was another matter.

Poe was the strongest of all his children by far. Somehow she had been born built for the hard stuff; the times that made most children shrivel up into a heaping mass of emotion. He remembered once when he explained to her that her grandfather had died, and she would never see him again. They hadn't been particularly close with Kate's father, but enough that he would sometimes dress up as Santa for Christmas, coming to their door with a twinkle in his eye, and send them cards every year on their birthdays. He wasn't someone they saw every day, but he was involved enough to give them a collection of happy memories.

For his other children, he prettied it up, telling them about the castle in the sky where he would get to reunite with his own grandparents, and the love of his life that he knew long before their grandmother...but not for Poe. For her, she took comfort in facts, figures. So instead of telling her about how he was at peace and was not suffering anymore, he told her that Grandpa had gone into cardiac arrest the night before, and though his body was alive, his brain was dead. "Is he going to donate his organs?" she asked. Connor replied that he would. "Good."

They waited at the edge of the woods toward the front of the house. Since they knew the group would be gathered in the kitchen, when they smelled the smoke, they would leave through the closest door: the front. Nothing else would make sense. Even people as ill-equipped as they were would know that much: when there's a fire, use the closest exit, not the one on another floor. As the smoke came billowing out of Gabriel's open window, Connor's skin started to tingle.

He looked at his son's face, where he expected to see tears of mourning as he watched the place he spent his childhood fade into smoke. Instead, he saw the stone expression of a man who knew what had to be done, and that he was the one who had to do it. He put a hand on his shoulder. "It's time."

They hadn't counted on one of the intruders coming up from behind them. Whether he was going for a morning walk, or looking for them so he could be a hero and recapture their fugitives, they would never know. All Connor knew was when he looked around and saw a man coming up the driveway he had to be kept quiet. As Connor met the eyes of the man coming toward them, the stranger promptly started shouting and running toward the house. Connor and Drew started chasing him while Gabriel kept watch in case there were more on their way, and Connor could tell that between him and Drew only one of them was sure what he was going to do when he got there.

Connor got to him first. "Stop! Connor, no," Drew begged. Connor wondered what it would take for Drew to lose his sympathy for those who hadn't earned it. If seeing his wife almost beaten to death didn't do it, and watching the girl he considered his daughter get gunned down didn't, he wasn't sure anything ever would. A part of him admired that, but another part knew if he didn't break him of that, it may get them killed.

"We don't have a choice, Drew. It's him or us."

"Maybe there's another way."

Connor looked at him. "Vera's in there. You saw what

they already did to her. We are way past trying to negotiate. Do you really want to take a chance on them hurting her again? We've already lost one…" Drew hesitated, and Connor tested him. "Tell me not to do it one more time and I won't."

Connor watched as Drew opened his mouth to speak. He waited for a moment, but Drew remained quiet. As Connor felt the bones crack in the other man's neck, he tried to ignore the panic in his eyes as he realized his last seconds on earth had come to pass.

They managed to make it back to their hiding spot, dragging the body behind them, just in time. They had caught the man far enough away from the house that the others had not heard his calls for help. Guilt crept up on Connor as he rolled the body into the bushes, quickly covering him with any twigs and branches that he could find. He looked Gabriel in the eyes. The calm expression he had before had been replaced with wide, scared eyes. But there was no trace of the contempt that Connor had expected. He just nodded at his father, and Connor saw that his son finally understood: though he would do anything, commit any sin to protect his family, that didn't mean he was safe from the scars they left behind.

As Connor was about to walk away, he did something completely unexpected, even to himself. Before they put their plan into action, he uncovered the man's face for a brief second, and gently pushed his lids shut with the tips of his fingers, noticing that his eyes were brown like his own, and like Poe's. He wasn't sure if it was more a gesture for the stranger or for himself, but he hoped that once his eyes were closed, the picture of his last seconds of life would leave Connor's mind forever.

As they quickly made their way up to the house, he realized it hadn't worked. But when he looked up and saw Gabriel watching, his son said two words that would stay with Connor for the rest of his days.

"It's okay."

The fire started to empty the house of its occupants. Two men came out first and then two more. They stood near the house and looked around, perhaps thinking they must have missed something, while Connor and Drew waited for more to walk into their firing line. They couldn't risk shooting until everyone was out, because the gunshots would warn those who remained inside about what was waiting for them on the other side of the door, and they may take the time to arm themselves, taking the house back before they ever lost it.

Then nothing.

Drew looked at Connor. "Where's the rest of them? There's supposed to be more." Both men stared at the front door, almost willing more people to come out and face what was coming to them. But none emerged.

Connor's attempt to answer was interrupted by the sound of gunfire as he saw Cassius storm out of the front door with one of his military-grade guns. The last time Connor saw it, he was locking it in the weapons cabinet, so he knew at least that part of the plan was happening as they had imagined it. Cassius had shot one before two more rushed him, attempting to grab his gun. As Connor and Drew ran out of the woods and toward the fray, they saw him knock one down with the barrel of his AK-47. The last remaining man had somehow managed to wrap his arms around Cassius' neck when Connor put a bullet in the man's head.

Justin was the last to fall.

Connor stared down at him, the man who had tried to take everything from him. He'd expected to want more, some chance to yell at him, to punish him for what he'd done. But as he looked at the vacant eyes staring up at him, he realized that he was minutes away from getting his family back, and this time, that was enough.

Between them, they were able to kill all the people who had left the house. He looked toward the upstairs windows and noticed that the fire had seemed to move past Gabriel's room. The blood in his veins felt hot as he realized what that meant: they had taken too long. "Where's the rest of them? Where's Poe?"

As he asked the question, Harper threw open the door. "They went to try and put the fire out before we could get to them! They made Poe go too! She's still in there!"

Connor ran full speed inside the house, with Drew and Gabriel close behind. When he entered, the smoke hit his lungs like the fire it came from, burning as he inhaled it. As he glanced around, he saw two women trying to wrestle a gun away from Kate, who was cowering on the ground, and he heard it fire in an aimless direction. They didn't see him come up behind them. He pulled both of them away from her easily and pushed them toward the ground, shooting them both as they lay beneath him. As he pulled Kate up, he said, "Run. I'll find Poe. Get Harper and Gabriel out of here."

"No way," he heard Gabriel from behind him. "Mom, get the rest of them out of here. Dad and I will both go get Poe."

Kate reluctantly agreed when she noticed Harper lying on the ground, clutching her arm. "Mom…they got me."

There was blood.

Connor looked at Drew, and he seemed to understand what he was being asked to do. Drew lifted Harper up, Kate hovering close beside them. Vera picked up Jackson and clutched him tightly as they opened the door, letting the sunlight help illuminate the smoke-filled room.

Quickly, Connor counted the members of the invading group who had been subdued lying around them: two were dead, but one more, Brian, was very much alive. As far as Connor was concerned, Brian was one of *them*. He lay there with his hand on his head, and a large knot forming on his left temple. That meant two were still missing. He knew immediately where to find them.

Poe.

The smoke wrapped around them as they ran up the stairs toward Gabriel's room. It grew thicker the closer they got, and Connor started to have a hard time seeing Gabriel even though he was right beside him. He squinted downward and noticed the two missing people, both looking either unconscious or dead, each with fire extinguishers in their hands. If he hadn't nearly tripped over her, he may have missed Poe entirely. He looked down to see the person who understood him most in the world lying nearly lifelessly on the ground below him, curled in a ball like before she was born. "Gabriel! She's here!"

Both men pulled her up, one on each side. As they headed back down the hallway, they barely heard a muffled voice from behind them. "Help…"

Poe stirred. "It's Lindsey. Please. She tried to help me. Don't leave her behind."

Connor looked at Gabriel. "I can take her by myself, Dad."

Connor hesitated, but there was a certainty in his son's eyes that made him trust him in a way he hadn't experienced before. It was clarity of purpose, something that had eluded him since Connor could remember. But after what Gabriel had done for him in the barn, and earlier when he had comforted him so perfectly, he realized something: perhaps that clarity had always been there, he just hadn't bothered to notice.

"I'll take care of her."

Carefully, Connor transferred all of Poe's weight to Gabriel, who picked her up and started carrying her down the hall in his strong arms, stronger than Connor's had ever been even in his youth. He shuddered, seeing one child with her head slumped over, being carried in the arms of another, both of whom he had been unable to protect no matter how hard he had tried. Connor picked up Lindsey and caught up to them, hoping she was still alive and he would be able to accomplish the one thing his daughter had ever asked of him.

As they left the smoky house and were greeted by the rest of their family, they tried not to notice the bodies lying around them. Connor saw that Brian had somehow made it out of the house, and he was hovering around Harper. He went over to her to make sure she was all right. One of the outsiders had cut her in the struggle, but despite what to Connor looked like a gaping wound, Drew said that she would be fine.

While he was beside her, he managed to ignore Brian entirely. As much as he wanted to put a bullet in that kid's brain so he would never bother them again, he knew there were more pressing matters. He thought to himself that there would be plenty of time for that later, now that they had successfully taken back their home.. Fire would always trump revenge, and now that their place was their own again, he had to make sure there was something left.

Connor looked back toward the house. He thought he could handle it, seeing it burn, if it meant his family was safe, even if the worst happened and the entire thing was reduced to ash. But while he watched everything he'd ever built, everything that was as much a part of him as anything or anyone else disappear behind a cloud of smoke, he realized he couldn't. The compound was his life's work, and if what he had dedicated every waking minute of his days on earth to became nothing, what did that make him? Would he, his memory, disappear right along with it? "I'm not losing this," he whispered.

In the chaos and the blood, no one noticed as he went back into the house, hidden by the thick blackness of the billowing smoke and his own will.

He picked up a fire extinguisher that was in the shed along the way. In the back of his mind, he realized that so much time had gone by during the struggle that the fire had become too dangerous to fight, which was why Poe and Lindsey had ended up unconscious. It was a miracle that he and Gabriel had gotten them out at all, and while they were outside regrouping, the fire had gotten a chance to grow. But he ignored that thought as stubbornness outweighed common sense and headed back up the stairs.

By the time he got there, the whole back part of the house was covered in flames. He managed to put out some of it. But as he turned around to look back at where he came from, trying to make sure he had a path out, part of the floor gave way and his leg fell through, pinning him in the hall.

There was nothing, Connor was sure, that made a person feel quite as small as being trapped, watching their own house dissolve in a blanket of fire around him. Connor watched the flames twirl like little orange tornadoes: up the wall and onto the ceiling, and he thought about how everything he had worked for his entire life had all been taken from him: and by his own hand.

Yes, Poe had set the fire, but it was his plan that she had put into action. Perhaps he had acted too rashly. Perhaps he had let his emotions quicken his pace, and if he had slowed down, he could have thought of a better plan. Desperation had made him dangerous, and he would never get the chance to say he was sorry. He had let control slip from his fingers and now he would pay the price, and give up the few precious weeks, months or years that he had left. As he slipped into unconsciousness, he saw the outline of a man hovering over him, and hands closing in.

"Wake up! We have to go!" It was the voice of the last person he expected to see. Brian was pulling him out of the floorboards and onto solid ground.

As he stood on his own two feet, he asked. "Why did you save me?"

"You're a stupid, ignorant asshole, but, God knows why, Harper loves you…and you're welcome."

He looked in his eyes, and through the thick smoke, uttered the words he never thought he would say to the second man who had almost destroyed his life. "Thank you."

Brian helped him make it to the top of the stairs, letting Connor lean against him. When they got there, Connor pushed himself up, wanting to walk unaided. Connor started down the top step, but turned back to look at him. Both men stood there for one precious moment, staring at each other with something bordering on respect.

Connor will never know why Brian hesitated to follow him. But because he did, Brian paused long enough to look up and see that a beam was about to crash down upon him. He had but a second of life left, and he used it to say four words. "Take care of Harper."

Then he was gone, slipping into the wood crevice that

had formed below him, swallowed up by the house and the earth and the flames.

When Connor stumbled out, Kate was there to greet him with a huge smile and a tearful embrace. "Thank God!" He wrapped his arms around her and let her sob into his chest, and he fought the urge to cry too. He had gotten everything so wrong.

If a man dies saving another man's life, the living man carries the weight of that responsibility. But if that man is terminally ill? That loss weighs heavier still. Brian had his whole life ahead of him, a life that he had planned to spend taking care of Connor's daughter. Given his own circumstances, Brian dying and Connor living didn't make sense. In a logical universe, Brian would have lived, and Connor would have been the one lost to the fire. But that wasn't what happened, and if it wasn't, what did that say about the world that he was going to leave his children in? Someone he had just figured out was a good man had lost his life saving his, and what he had tried to save was about to burn up anyway. But as the house came crashing down in front of them, he realized that losing it didn't matter. He hadn't lost control because he never had it to begin with. It was just an illusion, something that could be snatched away in an instant with something as simple as a single match.

That evening, the group piled into the small bunker that Connor had built just in case something ever happened to their home. It was similar to their house: a shipping container that he had rigged to give them oxygen and had buried below the ground. He'd never thought they'd need to use it, but he was certainly glad he had taken the precaution now that the place he loved had been reduced to ash-covered rubble. He sat in one of the white plastic chairs that he had placed there and looked around: cans, water jugs, blankets…it would be enough to last them a couple months. With as many people as they had, they would need to get more supplies, but it would be a good start as they began to rebuild.

That evening, he had gone outside to call Gordon on the radio to give them an update on their situation. When he came back inside, a heavy knot formed in his stomach. Gordon had given him something to tell his family a long time ago, back before they were invaded in fact, but that was not the time. The news he had heard would have to stay with him and him alone. There were other matters to attend to, ones that couldn't wait a moment longer.

After they had all eaten a meager dinner of canned soup, Connor steadied himself for a conversation with Harper that he knew he was unprepared for. She was lying down on top of a blanket, curled in a ball and staring at the side of the bunker. He grabbed a chair and scooted it next to her and as he sat down, he gently rested his hand on her shoulder. "I'm sorry about Brian."

She shook his hand away, as if his touch burned. "No you're not. You hated him from the start."

"You're right. I did." He took a deep breath. "But after what he did today, I can see I was wrong."

She rolled over and looked him straight in the eyes. "He's dead now. It's a little late for platitudes."

Her devious eyes, the ones she had used to manipulate him from the moment she was born, were now swollen with tears and rage. "Absolutely." He hesitated. "But you know what? I know now that what you felt for him was real. You deserved the chance to feel that way, and I'm sorry that I tried to take that away from you."

She looked at him silently for several moments. Finally, she said, "You really do mean that, don't you?"

He took comfort in her tone: more of a declaration than a question. And when she gave him a slight, approving nod, he knew he had gotten through to the fearless child who may never know the absence of fear again.

He wasn't sure if the tears he allowed to come were for the man he had misjudged, or for the daughter who would never be the same. If he had to guess, he would say what finally broke him down was a bit of both. Brian had died rescuing a man whose own life was slipping away, and the look on his daughter's face said that he had taken a piece of her with him. For that, he deserved to be remembered with positivity, and maybe for the optimism that had led him to open their doors to strangers. So, for just a brief bit of time, he could allow himself to openly grieve alongside her for the man who had tried, in his own way, to save them all.

The next morning, Lindsey took them into the forest. Connor hesitated, but when the rest of the group followed, so did he. He had saved her life, and after Brian, he had to think that someone who he'd saved wouldn't turn against him, at least not immediately. He certainly wouldn't have.

She took them to a small clearing, a place that seemed

man-made but wasn't, perfectly sheltered by massive trees that had been there for hundreds of years. At the base of one of them was a small cross made of two sticks tied together. "I wanted you all to have a chance to say goodbye," Lindsey said.

Relief filled Connor's heart when he realized what he was looking at. Blake's body hadn't been left unburied. She was right there, resting in peace, undisturbed in the woods that had protected them for so long. Drew deserved that much.

So did Poe.

Vera spoke first. "Baby girl, you're with your daddy now. And Julian too. May you find comfort in the arms of God and those you love the most. We will miss you forever and love you always."

Drew was next to say goodbye. "I taught you how to ride a bike, now Julian can teach you how to fly." He kissed two of his finger tips and placed them on the end of the cross. "I love you forever." He seemed composed, putting his arm around Vera, and mouthed a *thank-you* to Lindsey. Connor suspected it was only his love for Vera that kept him standing, and if he didn't have her to be tough for he would have lied down right beside Blake, letting the rain gently mist down upon them both.

Poe knelt in front of the cross, not caring about getting her jeans dirty. "Thank you. You know what for." Connor wondered what she meant by that, but even without saying, he understood it was none of his business. A part of him felt left out. He and Poe shared everything. But maybe there were things about her that he wasn't meant to know, or never could. And maybe that was okay, because as she got up, she stood tall and strong. He hoped he had contributed to that strength, but was suspicious that she had possessed it from the moment she was born, and he had just been lucky enough to call her his.

Finally, Jackson came up, and Connor felt himself break apart watching the young boy do what no child should ever have to. He had a yellow flower in his hand that he had picked as they walked. Gently, he placed it at the base of the cross. "This is for you, Mommy. You're my best friend. I love you. I hope the angels give you lots of hugs." Vera embraced him and told him he did very well, but as she hugged him tight, Connor could see it was all she could do to keep from crumbling. She held him for a long time, crying behind his back, only releasing him when she was sure she could remain steady. As she let him go, Kate came over and took Vera in her arms, giving Drew the chance to comfort the boy as much as he could.

He sucked in a breath when he realized he was crying too. He hadn't expected it. Yes, he would admit that he ached for the pain Jackson was going through, but it felt deeper than that…as if part of the loss was his as well. Perhaps he was crying for what Poe and Drew had lost too. Or maybe he was crying knowing that because of him, it could have very easily been Gabriel, Poe, or Harper in that hole, everything they had ever done and loved reduced to a cross made of sticks and twine.

Connor didn't believe in an afterlife. Of course he wanted to, especially since he was so close to his own *after*.

He looked for it inside himself, that belief. But where it should have been, that place that rested beside love and hope, there was just a hole, like a shelf that someone had taken a book from, leaving a gap in its absence. He hoped before the day came he could find it, but doubted very much that it would appear in time.

***

Several weeks later, before he locked up for the night, he saw that Kate had left the bunker. He followed her outside and found her staring up at the stars. He reached over to put his arm around her, but she pulled away. "What's wrong?" Kate had seemed distant. After she had figured out he was okay after the fire, she had started pulling away from him. He could feel it, like a piece of paper being torn apart, the ripping sensation between himself and his wife. He stared at the vacant, empty expression on her face and waited for an answer.

"We could have stopped this. I could have stopped you." She looked at him. "A girl is dead because of us. And Vera...oh Vera."

Kate couldn't mention what Vera had done for her. Vera's injuries were extensive, and he wasn't sure she would ever completely recover. She seemed to have a slight limp after what Justin had done to her, and she had said one of her eyes had become a bit blurry.

Connor noticed the devotion Kate had to the other woman during those weeks as they learned to live in the bunker: caring for her, keeping ice packs on her swollen cheeks like they were old friends. But Kate still couldn't manage to look her in the eye.

He felt as if a knife had been driven through his gut, and wondered if his heart had decided to give out right then. The way he hurt, he wouldn't have been surprised. "I didn't shoot her. They did. You can't possibly blame me." Even as he said the words, he knew they weren't true. The person whose opinion of him mattered the most was now looking at him as a stranger looks at a wanted poster, disgust emanating from every inch of her. He thought to himself, for every single desire on earth, especially revenge, there is a price to be paid. And every inch of him knew that his bill had come due.

Angry tears formed in her eyes. He'd never seen them before, not toward him, and the sight made him ill. The face of the woman who had tended the cuts on his arms after a hard day's work and put his vitamins out on the counter so he wouldn't forget to take them was gone. The tender hands that used to brush his cheek were now rigid and tense. And the eyes that were always filled with love no matter what he'd done echoed a woman who had reached her limit, now empty and cold.

"You set this whole mess in motion. It was you. You just wanted to hurt people. I understood when they all got here, I really did, but you turned into this knotted up, twisted form of the person I married. Now I see the truth. You cut us off from everyone we knew because of a few people in town. And God, before we leave, what do you do? You create a massive spectacle out of our last trip to the doctor's office when all I wanted to do was get it over with." She paused, and while he opened his mouth to speak, he thought the better of it and closed it again.

"All those people…staring at us—knowing about the most painful experience I've ever gone through. You can't blame them for that. It was all *you*." Her breath was labored, as if her anger was cutting off her oxygen. "We spent ten years here, in total isolation, and for what? You never even attempted to defend yourself, or us. You just brushed it off as you didn't want to *dignify* their accusations with a response." He saw that she was shaking. "You just kept quiet. There was no reason it should have gone as far as it did. If you had just said something, or let me say something…" She stopped and shook her head.

"No, I can't blame you for my own silence. I'm a grown woman. I could have saved us as easily as you and I didn't. I hid behind you like a scared little coward and let you use my grief over our daughter to cut us off from every neighbor, every friend…anyone! We could have *moved* for God's sake! We weren't pinned down. You just wanted what you wanted. It didn't matter who got hurt, did it? You claim everything you do is for us, but really it's been all about you this whole time. Just you."

Connor's face grew flushed. "You're really going to choose them over me? Really?"

"She was a *mother*!" Kate yelled. As she turned away from him, she said again, this time in a whisper, "she was a mother."

That was it. He'd done it. He had asked too much of her

for too long. A woman who had stood by him through everything had finally had enough. The thought made him tremble. *She* was his everything. *She* was where he started and where he ended. And now she hated him as much if not more as anyone who had ever done them wrong.

Memories flooded his mind: their wedding, walking in the meadow that swept along the road into town, late night talks that could only happen after their children went to sleep. It all seemed gone now. But maybe, just maybe, he could win her back.

If only there were still time.

But he knew there wasn't.

After Kate marched back to the bunker, Connor thought about going inside, but the idea of it made him feel crazy. The air inside felt suffocating already, before the argument, but now it would be like the atmosphere had given life to Kate's hostility and it was climbing into his lungs.

So instead, he walked into the woods and into the quiet of the night air. He pulled out his ham radio and called out for Gordon, the only person he felt like speaking to. To his relief, he picked up. The question he was about to ask had been weighing heavily on his mind, because it was both wonderful and a tragedy at the same time. "Hello, Gordon!"

"Connor! Great to hear from you!" His voice had hope permeating through it, but the sound made Connor sick. He wasn't sure what he was feeling, but it certainly wasn't hope.

"How's the vaccine coming along? Any time frame?"

"Not sure, Connor, but when I know more I'll call you, I promise."

"Fantastic, Gordon. Thanks again." He clicked it off.

In his urgency to speak to Gordon, he hadn't heard the footsteps behind him. "How long have you known?" He turned around to see Drew with an expression somewhere between horror and elation on his face.

"Two weeks."

He expected Drew to scream at him, maybe even hit him, run away and tell the others immediately. He thought for sure Drew would tell him that Blake wouldn't want them to stay trapped in that place. Drew was supposed to tell them that if she were here, she would have had a right to take her child out of the madness that the compound had become, or at least to know that was an option. But he didn't. Instead, he sat down next to him and rested his arms on his knees.

"Why didn't you say anything?"

Connor stared out into the maze of trees. "I can keep them safe here. Here, I'm in my domain. I'm not the butt of anyone's jokes. I'm not some dark misfit in people's stories. Here, I'm king." He took a deep breath. "Here, they're safe. Nothing bad can happen to them as long as they're here." Even as he said the words, he knew he didn't believe them anymore. Maybe Kate was right. Maybe it had never been about keeping them safe, but keeping them *there*.

"Well, that seems pretty far from the truth at this point, doesn't it?" Surprisingly enough, Drew and Connor looked at each other.

And laughed the dark laugh reserved for people who had been through too much.

After a silence usually reserved for lifelong friends, Drew

said, "Just tell them there's a cure. That's all. The rest can stay between us."

Connor looked at him. "Why would you do that for me?"

Drew sighed. "Because we don't know anything about it yet. There's no reason to give them false hope, just the facts. Present it as just that. Keep it mathematical, not emotional. We need to know what we're dealing with before they get too excited." He paused. "And because I know what it's like to make a mistake that you have to carry with you for the rest of your life. Because buried under that revenge fantasy you're just a scared little boy afraid of losing everyone he loves."

For some reason, Connor didn't feel insulted. Instead, he just said, "I didn't know you were that. Not that."

"What?"

"Kind."

They started to head back toward the bunker, when Drew stopped. Connor didn't realize until Drew spoke the words he said next that he had needed to hear them, desperately in fact. "And I don't blame you for Blake. Really. If you hadn't fired, I may have. You were just faster. We all thought it was a gun. I know I did."

Connor had wanted to keep believing the other group had fired first. Even after they found evidence of the explosion in the garage, he'd still attempted to convince himself that he hadn't made a mistake, that it wasn't his weapon that had sent them sailing into disaster. But the facts kept biting at him, nibbling at the back of his mind like an infestation, taking a bit more of him day by day. And he now knew that at the funeral, the pain he was feeling wasn't just for Jackson, but for himself, thinking that he was the one who had caused it.

It could have been Kate who was shot, or Harper. It just happened to be Blake instead, and because of it, a good boy was made an orphan, and some would say, a mother was made an angel. She was just standing in the wrong place at the wrong time, where his people happened to be standing in the right ones. An odd thought to realize that their lives were saved by something so trivial. After everything he had done, particular pieces of earth had protected them when he could not. And another had sent Blake to her grave. To have Drew absolve him from responsibility made the needling start to fade, and that was something for which he couldn't thank him enough.

***

Two days later, Connor busied himself taking inventory of their supplies. He looked over at Poe. She had been distant from him, same as her mother, but she didn't seem angry. She of course made sure he was all right after he had escaped their burning house, but after that, she had stayed glued to Lindsey and Darlus. As she suddenly stood up and placed herself in the middle of the bunker, her head barely not brushing the ceiling, he had a feeling he was about to find out why.

"Everyone. Darius, Lindsey, and I have an announcement." She took a deep breath. Lindsey was also standing at her side, which Connor didn't like one bit. He shivered as Poe took a deep breath. "We're leaving."

He saw Kate's face grow white and felt his own do the same. "What? No Poe that's crazy. And what about Jackson? It's still really dangerous out there. He needs all of us. We still haven't heard how long it will take to get the power back on, not to mention the cleanup. You could still get very sick! The infection from all the germs could kill you as easily as the disease itself!" Her mother had desperation bordering on lunacy dripping out of her voice.

"Jackson is part of the reason we are doing this. He will stay here with Vera and Drew. Darius can fly a plane. And Lindsey knows where some other communities are. There's still a world out there, and a future. We will come back."

"Yeah, Poe, that's crazy. You can't just leave. It will be a long time before the vaccine is ready, and even longer before everyone will have one to take. We have to stay here for at least that long. It could be a year or even more." Gabriel agreed with his mother.

She didn't respond to either of them. Instead, she asked Connor if they could talk outside for a moment.

They headed toward the pond, and sat down in the same spot where they had just before Drew and the others had arrived. The sky was clear, with stars dusting it with their otherworldly glow. Connor remembered teaching Poe the constellations when she was a little girl. Gabriel and Harper had no interest in the stars, but Poe used to sit on his lap and name them off as if she'd known them her whole life. "Dad,

I'm not happy here. I didn't realize it until recently, but now that I do, I need to go."

"It's not safe out there."

"It's not safe in here either." She paused. "Dad, I was keeping something from you."

Connor felt a tingling sensation in his head. Poe had never kept anything from him, except for whatever she had referenced at Blake's funeral, some special bond that they seemed to have that he was not a part of. "What are you talking about?"

She sighed. "I knew all along that Blake wasn't an EMT. She told me the first night."

He waited for the anger to creep in, but it didn't. Anger seemed pretty pointless. Perhaps it always had been. "Why?"

"Because she had helped me before, back when we still went into town. I wanted to return the favor. She saved me from some girls. They were going to beat me up, I'm sure." She paused. "That's not the only reason though. I didn't tell you because I wanted something that was just mine. A friend. A secret that we shared that didn't have anything to do with anyone else. I'd never had anything that belonged just to me. I don't know who I am without you, and this place."

Connor stared at her.

"Please, Dad. You know I love you. I love all of you. But I can't stay here. Not anymore." She paused for a moment, and they both looked out at the water. He tried to lose himself in the ripples, to forget for just a precious second what he was being asked, but he couldn't escape it. "You know, you're the one that made me strong, right? No matter what happened, no matter who was hurt in the process…you did right by us." She reached out and squeezed his hand. He gripped hers in return.

Connor thought about blaming Blake, or Drew for that matter. He thought about blaming anyone but Poe. But when he looked in her eyes, he realized that whoever's fault it was didn't matter. There was an emptiness there that wasn't there before. If ignorance was bliss, her bliss was gone, and there was nothing he could do to replace it. Knowing she thought he did right by his children made all the difference to him, and it would be something he would carry with him even after she was gone. He was not about to stop now. "If it's what will make you happy, then I think you should do it."

She smiled brighter than he'd ever seen. Sure he'd seen her smile, but there was something more inside it that time, something deeper. He wondered if she was wrong after all— if what he had given her all her life did not, in fact, make up for what he had taken away. As she hugged him and thanked him, sadness filled his heart as he realized that he had just done the hardest thing he would ever do. Because he knew there was a very good chance that once he saw her leave, he wouldn't live long enough to see her return.

A couple days later, all of them were working on the lower walls of the house. He and Drew were holding up the wood panels while Kate and Poe hammered until their fingers bled. There was no time for bandages; they knew they had to get the house rebuilt before the weather changed.

Kate put down her hammer briefly and came up to Connor. She had avoided him since their fight, not trying to hide it from the others and sleeping on Vera's cot with her instead of in bed with him. Though she would sit next to him at breakfast, she would never say a word, and she would keep her eyes trained on the bread and cured meat in front of her. Their children seemed to notice, but none said anything, just pretended they didn't see that what was once a team was broken in two.

She started to ask him a question about the next step. But before she had a chance, sparkling dots formed in his eyes and he slipped into blackness.

When he woke up, Drew had his hand on his wrist, and he felt the tall grass encircling him, tickling the skin on his forearms. For a brief second, he realized that the clear blue sky was beautiful, and he'd wished he'd spent more time appreciating blue, flawless days like that one. He started to sit up, and felt Drew's hands on his back. "Whoa, take it easy." He had no intention of doing that, but his body seemed to have other ideas.

He noticed Poe was also at his side. "Dad, are you okay? Please tell me you're okay." She turned from him to Drew. "Is he okay?"

Connor stared hard at Drew, willing him to realize what he was thinking, begging him with his eyes. "Yes, he just fainted. Probably didn't drink enough water this morning or something. Nothing to worry about."

Poe kissed Connor on the forehead. "That's a relief. You rest for a while, okay, Dad?"

"Yes, Connor, go rest." Kate hugged him. She started to walk back to the construction area, but hesitated. Connor couldn't help but wonder if a part of her knew, a part she wasn't conscious of...somewhere deep inside her realizing that the time she had left with her husband was becoming as fleeting as a sunrise. "I love you, Connor."

The words hit his ears like music. He *hadn't* lost her, not yet. And if he hadn't by then, he never would. Time would see to that. She may never forgive him for what he'd done, but he would always have her love. And maybe that was enough. "Okay, I love you too. As the girls walked away, he readdressed Drew. "Thank you."

"I'm not going to tell them, but you need to."

Connor nodded. "I will when it's the right time."

Drew helped him up and walked with him back to the bunker.

CHAPTER TWENTY

DREW

Drew had watched Kate work on the house for hours that morning. He had to tell her something, something that was years in the making, and he didn't have the slightest clue how to begin. So instead, he watched as she hammered one wood beam into another, sweat dripping down her forehead and hair pulled back with a scarf. Her sleeves were rolled up past her elbows, and he wondered if she had forgotten about the tank top she was wearing under her long-sleeved shirt. She seemed to be making more progress than Cassius and Gabriel put together. Perhaps it was because she loved the house in a way they never could.

She finally noticed him, and he was forced to act. He waved as if he hadn't been staring for so long and started walking toward her, hoping that the right words would come on the way there.

They didn't.

"Why don't you take a break for a couple minutes?" He said. "The rest of them can handle this for a while."

Kate let out a labored breath. "Thanks but I'm fine." She

reached into her toolbox and pulled out three nails, examining them carefully before picking which one to use.

"Actually, I was hoping I could talk to you." He hesitated. "Alone."

"Is it Vera? Is she okay? Her eye seems to be getting better."

"Vera's fine. This isn't about her."

Though her expression did nothing to hide her confusion, she consented. "All right."

They walked in silence down the hill behind the barn. From that vantage point, they could hardly see the damaged house, and if one avoided looking at it the setting was quite serene. "What's this about, Drew?"

"Where's Connor?"

Kate smiled. "Oh, he's organizing the bunker. Or talking to Gordon over that darn radio. I know he enjoys it, but really, how many updates from the east coast can there be?" She laughed awkwardly then looked at him. "Are you going to tell me what this is about?"

Unconsciously, Drew found himself sitting down in the grass, his arms resting against his knees. Kate sat down next to him. They listened to the rustling of the trees nearby, and watched as the birds flitted between them. Drew didn't speak for quite a while, and appreciated Kate's patience. Finally, he took a deep breath. "I'm sorry."

"For what?"

"Your baby. It's my fault. I know it's my fault."

Then it was Kate who initiated the silence. Drew tried to pay attention to the grass under his feet, noticing every blade as they brushed against his toes. His shoes had worn thin, and he hadn't made time to repair them. Connor had offered him a new pair, but he liked the ones he had. He'd been wearing them the day they arrived. They were worn, and familiar. He hoped after that day, the pain from what he had done would become less so. But mostly, he just wanted to do the right thing.

"Thank you for saying that. I'm sure that wasn't an easy thing."

Lovely, lovely Kate, forever a peaceful heart, despite what had been done to her. She had tasted the very worst in humanity, yet somehow was able to give him the understanding he didn't deserve. "How do you do it?"

"What?"

"Forgive."

She smiled. "Forgiveness isn't for you. It's for me. I forgave you a long time ago. Not because you particularly deserved it, but because I didn't want to carry the weight of what you did around with me. I just wanted to live my life and be a good mother to the children I had left. Those three needed me, and I had no business folding on them." She reached out and put her hand on top of Drew's. "You're a good man. You made a terrible mistake, but you're a good man. You don't need absolution from me, because I never gave you power over me to begin with."

She got up and looked at him, then gave him a small kiss on the top of his head. "You've more than proven yourself around here. You saved Poe's life. Let *that* be your absolution." As she walked back toward the house, Drew sighed, and hoped she had walked away in time to miss the tear sliding down his cheek.

Drew lingered there, staring out into the woods that had given and taken so much from all of them. It had sheltered them from disease, but it had also hidden dangers that they had barely escaped from. He realized that applied to humanity as well, and sometimes the hero and the villain were the same person. He had come up the mountain thinking that Connor was the worst kind of human being, and now he had come to think they weren't so different. Perhaps if he had been through what Connor had, he would have been the same way. Whatever kind of man he was, he knew the love of a woman like Vera, and for that, any monster that was hidden within him could stay buried there, nestled between the agony of never knowing what might have been had they had a child of their own, and the anger that he had toward himself which, despite Kate's kindness, he was sure would always remain.

***

CONNOR

The day Poe left with Darius and Lindsey was at the beginning of summer. Connor had Gabriel make a second getaway truck from his old truck, the one he had used every time he had gone into town. Despite the vaccine, he knew whoever had survived the pandemic had to do something to ensure that they lived, and many times, that meant they had to make sure someone else died. To beat a threat, sometimes you had to become one. Connor knew that better than anyone. Providing that vehicle was the last thing he could do to protect Poe from other people who had done what they needed to for survival, people who didn't know her or love her, and he intended to do it well. He trusted Gabriel to do it right. Somewhere along the line, Gabriel had turned into someone he could depend on, even if he hadn't noticed. He would regret not noticing for the rest of his life, however short it might be.

The entire group said goodbye, but only Connor and Drew stayed until the trio were so far down the road they could no longer be seen. As he stood there, gazing out at the silhouette which was all that remained of his daughter, he whispered, "Please keep her safe." His own words came from nowhere, materializing out of some unconscious place that he had just become aware of in that moment. Perhaps the empty spot on the shelf was there no longer. And that possibility gave him more peace than he could have ever imagined.

"You didn't tell her, did you?" Drew asked, although Connor knew it was more of a declaration.

"If I'd told her, she would have stayed."

Connor and Drew remained side by side for what they weren't sure were minutes or hours. But as Connor stared down the road that once held his daughter, he imagined he saw her footprints in front of him, glowing like the stars they loved so fiercely.

About the Author

Renee N. Meland is the author of The Extraction List Series, young adult science fiction novels optioned for film by 5x5 Media, INC. She lives in the Pacific Northwest with her husband and daughter,  and believes that storytelling is the best job in the world.

Follow Renee N. Meland on Twitter: @reneenmeland
Find her on Facebook:
https://www.facebook.com/reneenmelandsbooks/
Learn about her other books on her website:
https://www.reneenmeland.com/

www.ingramcontent.com/pod-product-compliance
Lightning Source LLC
Chambersburg PA
CBHW030648260626
47157CB00007B/2553